TAKE A THOUSAND CUTS

Teresa Hunter

A Message from the Author

Welcome to my novel TAKE A THOUSAND CUTS. I hope you find the story entertaining, exciting and thought-provoking. If you enjoy the plot, characters and twists, please spread the word.

Best of all, consider leaving a review at Amazon.co.uk, or .com. Please do visit my author page at www.TeresaHunter.uk for more news and offers – or to join the Teresa Hunter Readers Club.

Thank you so much for your support. You are fantastic.

FOR PAUL

Also in the Julia Lighthorn Series

DEAD MONEY

<u>What they said</u>:
Taut pacy thriller, compelling and bloody
Emma Simon
Fast-moving tale of crime and tragic romance
Terry Murden
Brimming with tension – a page-turner with a twist
Devoured at one sitting
Nic Cicutti

PROLOGUE
Cornwall

"IT'LL BE A MONSTER we can't control."

Laura Wan Sun knew she must stop them. A rumble of thunder stirred in the distance. She looked at the men seated round her at the table.

"It'll be fine, my dear." Warwick Mantel leaned forward, spreading his hands over the scarred oak wood. "If there are glitches, we can fix them. Better a diamond with a flaw than a perfect pebble."

A weak pulse of lightning threw shadows across the room. Laura shuddered. The storm was nearing.

"I'm familiar with the Chinese proverb," she said. "How well do you know your own history?" Her eyes circled the 12th century refectory, its arch-braced roof – its intricately-carved stone fireplace.

What on earth was she doing here? She wanted no part of this plan.

Peak Bank boss Warwick Mantel had gathered them here on this craggy rock jutting into the Atlantic. "Be cleverer than anyone else on the globe," he had said. "And I will make you very rich."

Madness, Laura thought, as the thunder grew louder. Lightning cracked outside the castle walls. A single skeleton danced in the painted glass.

1

She tried again. "The monks who lived here thought they were Masters of the Universe Their only talent was self-delusion – utterly unprepared for the Reformation which tore their world apart."

"They were arrogant," said Adam Lee. "And very stupid. We're none of those things. We know Peak Bank is running dry and a stagnating duck is a dead one."

Laura had known Lee, Mantel's local fixer, since she was a child. Everyone in Hong Kong knew the Lee family. Born, like Laura, on the Island, Adam had done time in all the main houses there. Never stayed long – just long enough to work out where all the bodies were buried. He was a keeper of secrets. Not a man to cross.

"I know Peak's headed for a bullet," her eyes drilled into his. "That's no excuse to blow up the global economy."

"Come, come, Laura, don't exaggerate," Mantel braced his teeth in a smile. "This is 1997. Peak is one of the strongest banks in the West. But the world is changing. It's possible the Asian bubble is about to burst. That's why I brought you here, my smart young colts. None cleverer than you my dear."

Patrick Silverman appealed to her softly across the flickering candle tips. "It's about protecting the wealth of the Island and the future for the bank's employees. These are vulnerable now the Communists have taken over. Surely you approve?"

"I understand all that," Laura wrinkled her brow. What could she say? It was a neat, even brilliant solution. "But Patrick," she stretched a hand towards him. "The potential is limitless. That's what worries me, because..."

2

She was silenced by a violent thunderclap. Mantel's goblet crashed over, spilling its red contents. The storm was breaking immediately over their heads. Shafts of gold splintered the room as high-voltage fire-bursts shot through the stained glass. In a world where few could read, these windows were their bible. To Laura they seemed cruel and sinister.

"Spooky," shrieked Stephen Chandler, before bursting into ghoulish laughter. "Those skeletons freak me out."

"Medieval morality tales. Each age has its obsessions," said Mantel, as they looked towards the glass, flashing malevolently with each blast of lightning. "Death..."

"The Day of Judgment," said Scofield Crisp, the American on the team.

"The devil and hell, *woooo*..." Chandler, always the joker, was on his feet, running round the table, arms high like a ghost.

"Money," shouted Lee, pulling a demonic face.

"Until the wheel turns." Chandler stopped dead before one of the windows, his arms dropping to his side.

"Until the wheel turns," he repeated, lowering his voice. He stepped closer to examine the luckless sinner, racked by the devil on a death wheel in hell.

From the corner of her vision, Laura watched a grin spread slowly over Mantel's face, oblivious to his toppled goblet or the inky-red stain seeping towards him across the wood.

CHAPTER ONE
Decade Later - Tuesday July 27 2007
Southwark

JULIA'S PHONE RANG HOT all morning. *The world's gone mad,* she thought, checking the time on her computer.

"Damn, five past eleven, I'm late," she spun her chair back from the desk, grabbed her coat and ran.

Bermondsey Street was crammed with pedestrians. She checked her watch.

I'd better get a cab or I'll never make it.

She ducked down Tanner Street and onto Tower Bridge Road.

Great, here's one coming.

She waved an arm at an approaching black cab. A man stepped in front of her, newspaper stretched high. The driver stopped to give him the ride.

Typical, thought Julia. *Looks a big tipper.*

The cab thief suddenly spotted her standing there. "I'm sorry," he turned towards her. "Was this your cab?"

"You know what? I've changed my mind." She spread an open hand towards the car. "You take it."

"Please, after you," he insisted.

"No, honestly. I'm late for my appointment. I've probably already missed it. Might just blow it out."

"Are you sure?"

What a nice man, Julia thought.

"Utterly," she flicked her hair back. "It's my birthday today. I'm rushing somewhere I don't want to go. You've done me a huge favour giving me the perfect excuse to duck out."

"Oh no," he grinned, throwing his hands up in mock horror. "I can't pinch your cab on your birthday."

"It would make me very happy," she laughed. "Tell you what, let's toss for it?"

"Only if I can be heads."

He flicked a coin. "Heads it is. You win. It's all yours." The man stood back.

Julia looked at her watch. *I might just make it.* "You're a star," she climbed into the cab, shut the door and sat back.

I still don't know why I'm doing this on my birthday, she shook her head, bewildered. The cab chased across Blackfriars Bridge, turned into Fleet Street, and stopped outside a private clinic. She jumped out, paid the driver, told him to keep the change, and bounded through the entrance.

"You've been here before, haven't you?" the Receptionist greeted her. "Know the way?"

Julia nodded and followed a sign pointing to the Gynaecology Department down a corridor on the left.

Another Receptionist. "Routine check?" she asked. "We're running a bit late. Take a seat."

Julia sat. *Blow me, I could've walked after all.*

"Happy Birthday," the Receptionist called across, as she looked at the notes on her computer screen. "Although not a great way to spend your big day."

5

"It's the new automated appointment system. If I'd noticed I would have cancelled."

"You came anyway. Good girl," the Receptionist smiled.

After ten minutes she was called in.

"Good morning, Ms Lighthorn," a figure in a white coat with his back to her said. "It's just morning still, I make it 11.44," he added, turning.

They stared at each other speechless, before exploding with laughter. It was the man who gave up his cab.

"I don't believe this," Julia snorted with giggles. "What are the chances?"

"I'm new here," he said. "Your last check up was two years ago I see. Even more glad now I let you win the toss. I'd have hated you to miss it. But whatever possessed you, on your birthday..."

"Automated appointment system," they said in unison and laughed.

"Maybe we should think about that, block out birthdays. Let's get this out of the way, so you can enjoy the rest of your day."

"Fat chance," Julia said softly, remembering what awaited her at the office.

BACK at her desk, the calls kept coming. Questions always the same. Why had stock markets tanked? Why were savers queuing outside a bank to get their money back? Was this the first bank run in nearly a century?

Who's this now, she thought, grabbing her phone for what felt like the hundredth time that day?

She smiled when she heard the sound of singing.

"Happy Birthday to you, Happy Birthday to you, Happy Birthday dear dum de dum."

"Chief Inspector Pitcher," she said, recognising his voice. "How wonderful to hear from you. It's been so long. And how kind of you to remember my birthday."

"No problem – July 27. Same date I won my accumulator at Kempton. No chance I'd forget that."

"So very flattering. Still I'm touched."

"You know what they say about birthdays. Forget the past, you can't change it. Forget the future, you can't predict it..."

"And forget the present, I didn't get you one," she finished for him.

They both laughed.

"How's life at the Met?"

"Not as busy as I'm guessing you are today, my little Lois Lane."

"You can say that again."

"Time to help an old friend out?" he asked. "I'm looking at a long line of people snaking round my bank. Should I take my money out?"

"So you actually rang for some free advice?"

"Not entirely. Isn't that what they pay you for, to advise your readers on their money worries?"

Julia lifted her gaze to the television fixed to the wall opposite her desk and flicked between news channels. They all told the same story. Long queues of savers outside Pendle Thrift branches asking for their money back.

He tried soft-soaping her. "Please. You know I'm one of your biggest fans."

"Really? How often do you read my columns?"

"I read them nearly every day."

"Honestly?"

"Honestly, I nearly read them on Monday, then I nearly read them on Tuesday and I nearly read them on..."

"Ha, ha. Very funny," she laughed. "So how much have you got in Pendle?"

"Like I'd tell you..."

"Not very helpful. D'you want to take your money out?"

"I will, if you tell me to."

If only life were so simple. Yes, she earned her crust as a financial journo, but that meant spinning plates heaped with maybes and second guesses. Right now, she didn't know what to make of the queues outside Pendle Thrift.

But she did live by a few golden rules, one being – *when in doubt take it out.*

"Oh, take it out then, join the queue and take it out," she said.

"Join the queue? Join the queue?" he repeated, affronted. "You must be joking."

Now Julia laughed. "I forgot. You never wait in line for anyone. Well, go in and arrest someone, and stop bothering..."

She was interrupted by the ringing of Pitcher's mobile at the other end. She zoned out of their conversation, locking onto a sea of red spreading alarmingly across her screen. The blood bath seeped further. It was a very bad day for shares.

Pitcher's words brought her back to the call.

"Right, I'm on my way. Julia, I've got to go. Body in Soho."

"Bit early for a shooting?"

"It's not a shooting. It's a – " he stopped abruptly. "Enjoy the rest of your birthday. Don't get a taste for them, though. Too many can kill."

Even on his way to a murder he can't resist a joke, she thought, turning back to stock market charts on her screen. What was going on? Prices yo-yoing for no reason. Were traders left behind for the summer by bosses soaking up sun on the Med, bored and partying? Seeing how far they could push a few prices down, before cleaning up and heading off for the wine bar?

Her gaze zoned in on one of the UK's most successful banks. Its share price had collapsed from £10.50 to £2.10.

"That can't be right," Julia said aloud, screwing up her eyes.

She opened a new document and started to type. Only a few sentences in, she glanced up again. The share price was still bombing. She finished her story and was about to send it when she checked the price once more. Mysteriously, it had recovered. Just a few pence down when the market closed at 4pm.

"As I thought," she muttered. "Summer madness." She hit send, then stood to stretch her legs. A few minutes later her phone rang.

"Nice piece on the economy, Julia, thanks," her editor Andrew Ludgate said. "What d'you make of the Beeb story?"

9

"Pendle? Hard to know..." she hesitated. "You know what Chuck's like?"

She referred to the hack who broke the story. City journalism was a village. Everyone knew everyone, and most people worked together at some stage.

"Firm denials all round. Without knowing his source..."

"He's very well connected."

She needed no reminding he went to school with the Chancellor.

"The markets don't quite know what to make of it," she replied instead. "They've had a good run of late."

This was an understatement. Anyone in shares had seen their money double over the past five years.

"The first cut is the cheapest," Ludgate chuckled at his own joke.

"Indeed. Did you see the price of S&H dropped by more than half? Not for long. Most odd."

"Savings and Homes? Strange, no I didn't. In a meeting most of the afternoon. It recovered though?"

"Yes, it did. I can't see..."

"Technical error, I guess. Keep an eye on it. Anyway, the point of this call – I'm building a new team of trouble-shooters, a kind of SAS, who can handle whatever comes up in an emergency. I'd like you to be part of it. Will you come back into head office?"

"Special attack service, eh?" she said, her heart sinking. Ludgate had begged her to join his staff, after she blew the whistle on a huge pensions scandal. Well, what passed for begging in his book. He took her out for lunch and told her she was a one-story pony, and her career was over unless she accepted his offer. His was one of dozens of lucrative overtures, and they all got the same answer. She liked her freedom.

"Andrew, we've been through this before. Thank you, but I'm happy here."

That story had cost her dear emotionally, but it had paid well, allowing her to buy a flat in Trinity Village, and rent her own offices in Bermondsey Street. She was comfortable on the South Side, with its riverside view of the casino opposite.

"I can think of a hundred other journos who would bite my hand off for this offer. I get five hundred letters a week begging for a job."

"I know, and that humbles me. Honestly I'm genuinely grateful, but – "

"You've always had a stubborn streak," she could almost hear him smiling. Then his voice came closer to the phone. "Be careful Julia. Bull-headed isn't a good look. World's changing fast. I need to hire some sharp operators. Don't get burned."

"That's a risk I'll have to take," she replied, more cheerfully than she felt.

As a freelance, Julia knew she was only as good as her last by-line. The business was full of hungry upstarts who would eat her for breakfast.

CHAPTER TWO
West End London

TRAFFIC GRIDLOCKED, so Chief Inspector Pitcher pulled his car into an alley off Leicester Square. He pushed open the driver's door, and stood to get out, catching his head on the corner of an old air-conditioning unit whirring on the wall.

Bugger, he rubbed the spot to ease the sharp pain. "Summer in the City," he sang under his breath. "Hot town – sick bloody murder."

Tourists swarmed along the pavements, spilling into the road. He fought his way across Shaftesbury Avenue to Gerrard Street. "Back of my neck getting dirty and gritty."

Funny how you can remember words to songs you haven't heard in twenty years, he thought.

At the police cordon blocking the entrance to Chinatown, he elbowed his way through a mesh of bodies. No press yet. This would be big news when it finally broke. He stepped over the barricade and left the buzz behind. Wardour Street was deserted apart from a few figures bent beneath the Friendship Gate. Red and gold Chinese banners slapped in the breeze. He walked towards the pod of Scenes of Crimes officers, who had already bagged up the body.

Thank Christ for that.

A young PC stood by watching. "So much for peace and prosperity, eh, Sir?" he mis-quoted the motto blazoned at the top of the structure, as he walked towards the Chief Inspector.

"Don't be ghoulish. If peace and prosperity are your thing officer, you've picked the wrong profession."

Pitcher lifted his eyes to survey the wider scene. It was tea-time but this gourmet paradise was deserted. Some restaurants had barred doors and security shutters. Lanterns and dragons burned brilliant at others, reminding him he hadn't eaten. Something told him, he wouldn't be eating much that evening. He turned back to the PC.

"Name?" Pitcher asked.

"PC Webb..."

"Not yours."

"Of course. Well, his wallet, and yes it was still in his pocket, has credit cards and a driving licence belonging to an Adam Lee. We're checking him out now."

"Anything else?"

"Apart from..."

"Apart from the obvious."

One of the Scenes of Crime team, clad head to toe in white protective suit, stood to stretch his legs. "Slightly strange. An orchid in his top breast pocket. Cause of death, garroting – would've been quick."

Pitcher turned back to the young officer. "Any witnesses? Do we know anything about what happened? Drugs-related? Gang feud? Mistaken identity?"

"Sorry Sir," the PC shook his head.

"What do you mean No? We're in the heart of one of the busiest districts of London. Are you telling me no one saw anything? Speak to every single one of these restaurants. Where've the customers gone? Did you move them out?"

"They moved themselves out," another Soco officer working on the ground chipped in. "Most disappeared before we arrived."

"We can talk to the restaurant staff, Sir, but whether anyone saw anything, or will tell us about it – "

"I know, I know, it's Chinatown."

"It's hard to get people to talk."

"Well, try harder," Pitcher swallowed, before crouching down to the body. "Any clues?"

"Jacket Armani. Dewitt watch. Pricey, some cost more than fifty grand," said the Soco officer.

"Nationality?"

"Chinese probably...maybe Hong Kong...South East Asian I'd say."

Pitcher stood as another uniform pushed through the cordon and came running down Wardour Street.

"PC Jed Day, Sir. This is my beat, as you liked to say in the old days. Was at a meeting with some tenants when the call came. Got here as soon as I could."

"Good to see we still have men on the beat. How are things on your beat, as we oldies like to say?"

PC Day grinned, before straightening his face. "Well, this is a busy posting, Sir. Mostly petty crime. Pick-pocketing, the odd domestic."

"And that's it?"

14

"Pretty much..."

"We have a body at our feet PC Day – brutally mutilated. A few months ago, there was a fire in that restaurant over there, the Golden Pagoda." Pitcher pointed at a building, showing no trace of a torching. "Suspected arson, wasn't it? Nothing proved. Are we looking at something more organised here? This murder looks like one hell of a calling card to me."

"It's possible," PC Day hedged, before adding, "The young Chinese are different from their parents. Skilled, sophisticated. Their talents are in high demand all over the world."

"Young man, are you trying to tell me the Triads have got an education, proper jobs and gone legit?"

"No, no, Sir," PC Day bit his lip. "They never disappear completely. It's complicated."

"Crime changes – less red in tooth and claw. I know all that," he moved closer to Day and dropped his voice to a low whisper.

"Officer we have a body at our feet with both eyes gouged out. I ask you again, could this be something more organized?"

PC Day cleared his throat.

"Since the Hong Kong handover the numbers of Chinese in this area... my guess would be – "

Pitcher looked at the Chinese flags billowing in the wind, then back to the blood-red neon restaurant signs.

"Many are right here, right now," Pitcher finished for him.

CHAPTER THREE
Evening Tuesday July 27
Southwark

"MY NAME'S CODY. I'm looking for a job." Julia looked up from her desk to see a young Denzel Washington standing in the doorway.

"How did you get in here?"

"Deli downstairs. Very nice Italian..."

"I must speak to Aldo," she laid her pen on the desk and leaned back, sizing up the intruder.

Strikingly attractive, she thought.

"No please don't. He was kind. I would never have taken "No" for an answer." He lowered his voice. "I've wanted to be a journalist since the day I was born."

"You and half the rest of the population," despite harsh words, she never forgot the bitter taste of hunger for that first break.

"The rest of the population has a fighting chance. Look at me."

Julia ran her eye over him and her heart thawed a little more. *Made a huge effort.* She guessed the smart suit was borrowed. The trousers hung above the top of his socks and the sleeves were short.

"And?"

"I'm black."

Julia trilled the names of a dozen black broadcasters, fronting the news.

"The way I speak..."

Undoubtedly, his South London accent was not currently fashionable in the nation's newsrooms. But there were plenty of offices where his face and accent would be welcomed.

"Southwark News, Lambeth Recorder. All fine places to start."

"I didn't go to college. They aren't interested without an Oxford First." He thrust a certificate on her desk. "I won the Sainsbury's writing competition at school. That proves I can write."

Julia took a deep breath. He was a likeable lad. Unless her touch for spotting talent was off beam, she sensed he could have that quirky spark, the indefinable something that separated born journalists from the rest of the population. But she travelled light, valued her space and couldn't carry another member of staff.

"I'm sorry," she softened her voice. "I wish you every success in your search for work, but I can't help you. There's no vacancy, nor likely to be one."

Cody wasn't ready to give up. "I could help you."

He's tenacious, Julia had to give him that. Another tick in his favour.

"I've been working as a City messenger," Cody continued. "Got contacts all over the Square Mile."

"What makes you think I need help?" Julia was intrigued. There were times you could learn more from the post room than the Boardroom. She scratched her temple with her pen.

"The word among the messengers says there's an almighty storm coming," Cody shifted on his feet. "Big guns will throw armies of manpower at the story. How will you compete here on your own?"

Ludgate's exact prediction. Julia stemmed an urge to wince.

"I don't expect to be writing straight away. Happy as a bag carrier."

"Bring me a story," she shot him a rapier glance. "If and when you do, I'll consider your proposition."

Julia watched Cody's face freeze, as if in shock. Then it broke into a joyous smile, stretching wide across his young face.

"You won't regret this, I promise." He beamed.

JULIA THOUGHT BACK on that promise much later, when agonising between regret and wondering what any of them could have done differently. When her phone rang that evening, as she put her key into the front door of her flat, none of them could have guessed what lay ahead.

"You're going to be very pleased with me," Cody's voice chuckled at the other end. "Big shot fund manager's gone missing. Hedge fund boss, Stephen Chandler. Tower Gate."

"Who says?"

She knew Stephen Chandler. Not well. She'd met him at various functions. His cheeky smile was topped with a wedge of unwieldy honey-coloured hair, refreshing among so much grey.

"One of my contacts. All very hush-hush. My pal had to deliver some confidential papers to the Boardroom. Caught a snatch of a conversation. Messengers are invisibles. They can't see us, so they think we can't see or hear them. Chandler had full afternoon of meetings and an important board this evening. Didn't show. No one can reach him."

"OK," Julia looked at her watch. It was 9.45pm, too late to start chasing wild geese.

"Be in the office by eight. We'll take it from there."

CHAPTER FOUR
Wednesday July 28
Southwark

JULIA LEFT her apartment at 6.30am the following morning and headed for Chandler's riverside penthouse in Butlers Wharf. She wanted to catch Stephen before he left for the office. She had always rather liked him. They first met at an industry drinks gathering in the Court Room, at Barber-Surgeons' Hall, off London Wall. Wavy unstructured hair seemed at odds with his tailored suits, as did the sassy smile. She liked the way he made time for people, not a common trait among masters of the universe, running the money machine.

Disappeared? It seems extremely unlikely, she thought, heading for his flat. She needed to speak to him to find out what was going on. They shared a love of Southwark and its history, so Julia knew exactly where he lived. Half-way there, the heavens opened. A freak summer storm drenched pedestrians making their way to work in light summer clothes. By the time she approached his building, she was saturated. Rivers of dirty London rain streamed down her face.

It was a gated block. She waited a further ten minutes in the torrential downpour for one of the residents to open the gate and leave, so she could slip inside. Progress was hindered afresh by the Concierge, who blocked her at the entrance, demanding to know who she was and why she was trespassing?

"I don't think they're here," he offered, when he heard she was looking for the Chandlers. "Didn't see Mr Chandler come in last night." He picked up a telephone receiver and dialled the number, holding on for some time.

He replaced the handset. "Nope, no reply." Julia's heart sank.

"Can I go up and try?" she asked, flashing what she hoped was a sweet smile, but doubting the jobsworth would agree.

Yet something like sympathy flickered in his eye, as the Concierge gazed at her saturated jacket dripping onto his parquet. "Go on then. Top floor. Tower Suite. Take the lift up and turn right."

"Thank you," Julia nodded, heading for the lift. *Bet he's only letting me up because he's sure there's no one there, and wants to mop the floor before anyone slips and breaks a leg,* she chuckled to herself.

HE WAS WRONG. The door was opened by a woman with rich brown shoulder-length hair. She wore a sleeveless, tailored navy dress, cut fashionably above the knees, exuding chic sophistication.

"I'm sorry, I was expecting someone else," her face fell when she saw Julia, but quickly recovered. Charm taught at the best girls' schools can usually be relied upon.

"Julia Lighthorn," she held out her hand and smiled warmly. "I'm an acquaintance of your husband. There's something I want to discuss with him."

21

"Isn't the office the place for meetings?" the wife was not going to make this easy.

"Probably. Has he already left?"

"Julia Lighthorn, you're the journalist aren't you?" *Rumbled at the first post*, Julia thought. *Nice though it is to be recognised, can be a damned nuisance.*

"You'd better come in." Mrs Chandler opened the door wider, before exclaiming, "You're soaked. Take that off. Let me get you a towel."

Julia handed over her drenched jacket. She never failed to be surprised at how kind people can be to strangers who arrive unannounced at their door. The elegant figure reappeared with a baby-soft, brilliant white towel, which she handed to Julia. Then she led her through a forty-foot reception room, past oceans of glass and out onto a terrace. Black clouds had lifted. Brilliant post-storm sun streamed in. A vast rainbow circling the Tower of London distorted the light. Tower Bridge was so close you could almost touch it.

Huckleberry Finn! The monthly repayments alone for this place, must run into tens of thousands, Julia thought as she looked down at a table set for two.

"Habit."

"Setting for two?" Julia said, noticing only one cup and plate had been used.

"It's our wedding anniversary today. Ten years. Stephen would never go off like this, disappear without saying anything. Today of all days."

Julia's pulse missed a beat.

"Mrs Chandler," Julia began.

22

"I've never been Mrs Chandler. Rebecca Withers is a good name. I didn't see any reason to change it, when I married."

"Ms Withers..."

"Rebecca."

Julia smiled at the gesture of friendship.

"D'you want to tell me what's happened?" she softened her voice.

"I don't know what's happened. That's the honest truth. My husband didn't come home last night," she started to pour coffee, but her hand shook so she put the pot back on the table. "He went for a normal early morning run along the river yesterday and I haven't seen him since."

"Have you notified the police?" Julia picked up the pot and topped up the cups.

"Stephen's PR director, Geoff Cummings, advised against it. He's worried about scaring investors. He's hoping Stevie just needs a few days away on his own to clear his mind and he'll turn up again."

"And you?"

Rebecca shook her head, her immaculately groomed brown eyebrows crumbling like splinters of rotting oak.

"Completely out of character," she said. "It doesn't make sense. His phone's dead. He doesn't have any clothes. His bank account, credit cards haven't been touched. Where is he? What's he living on?"

Her eyes followed a flock of swifts swooping down river on their way to the Kent marshes.

Cummings is an idiot, Julia couldn't help thinking. *This poor woman is beside herself with worry.*

She spoke softly. "Has he been preoccupied lately? Anything on his mind? Anything that worried him?"

"He said something strange the night before he disappeared. I didn't know what he meant. He said, if you gaze long enough into an abyss, the abyss will gaze back into you."

"Nietzsche?" Julia recognised the quote.

Rebecca nodded before completing it. "Whoever fights monsters should not himself become a monster."

"Stephen could never be a monster," Julia reassured her. "And he's a very experienced manager, isn't he?"

"Oh yes, a bit of trouble with the fund wouldn't worry him." She bit her lip. "That sounds trite. Of course it would worry him. But he would never lose his sense of perspective. There's more to life than money, he used to say. We can always start again." They sipped their coffee in silence for a few moments.

"Why did you say you came?" Rebecca returned her gaze to Julia.

"I'll put my cards on the table," Julia crossed her fingers hidden in her lap. "I picked up a whisper something was amiss. I wanted to speak to Stephen privately. Didn't want to embarrass him. Honestly? I couldn't believe it was true."

"And now I've confirmed it you'll write about it?"

"It's my job." The phone rang. Julia wasn't sure she heard her reply. Rebecca left the room to answer it.

Julia cursed under her breath. *I'd nearly won her confidence.*

Rebecca was more distant when she returned, carrying Julia's jacket. "I'm afraid you have to go. The directors are on their way up. Coming mob-handed to shut me up. They're desperate this doesn't leak."

"Could be damaging," Julia said.

"Not as damaging as doing nothing if he's lying hurt somewhere. All they're worried about is their blasted investments. I have to think of him," she paused, thinking fast and hard. "I suppose publicity might help," she said mainly to herself. Then she raised her glance and looked Julia straight in the eyes. "You decide whether to write the story. I'll leave it up to you."

"Thank you," Julia understood how much that could cost Rebecca.

"Don't turn him into a cardboard villain," Rebecca said as she showed Julia to the door. "He donated half his salary to a charitable trust."

"I won't," Julia said softly.

"And keep my name out of it. You can do that can't you?"

"Of course. Is there anyone I can call to be with you?"

Rebecca shook her head. "You must go."

The sound of lift doors warned it was time for Julia to make herself scarce, if she wanted to avoid a court injunction aimed at silencing her. She headed off down the corridor towards the back stairwell.

EARLY DEADLINES were looming, so Julia half-jogged back to the office. Mr Aldo Bardetti, the deli owner, was outside, wiping down his cafe chairs, drenched in the downpour.

"You need to slow down Julia," he said as she sped towards him. "You're working too hard."

"I've got a new assistant," she said, stopping to catch her breath. "How's business, Aldo?"

"Nice and easy," he grinned. "I never worry. That's your problem Julia. You worry too much. Take better care of yourself."

Julia laughed and ran up the stairs to her first floor office.

"How'd it go?" Cody asked as she walked in. She raised her eyebrows, discarded her damp jacket, sat at her desk and dialled her editor Andrew Ludgate.

"Cracks are starting to appear," she said. "Stephen Chandler - investment director at Tower Gate – has disappeared."

"Disappeared where?"

"If we knew that he wouldn't be missing."

"Confirmed?"

"By his wife."

"My, my, and the market smells trouble."

Julia knew Ludgate would be checking Tower Gate's share price. She got there first. It was 15 per cent down.

"She asked me to keep her name out of it."

"Be careful," Ludgate warned. "I seem to recall the beautiful Rebecca is a lawyer. Don't cross her. Get the story over as soon as you can."

Then reach for a tin hat. We shall need it to survive the fall out, Julia thought.

She began to type…

CHAPTER FIVE
3pm Wednesday July 28
HIGHGATE

PATRICK SILVERMAN stood alone at the open grave. Other mourners had peeled away. He could not bring himself to take this last farewell from the father he loved. He cared not what was happening in the world outside. He wanted this moment to last forever. Once the spell was broken, his life would change permanently. He never knew his mother. She died before his childhood memories began. So he never felt her loss. His father was mum and dad – his everything for all his life up to this point.

Now he was gone. To other eyes this might have been a moment to rejoice. Patrick was about to inherit a considerable fortune. His father was a wealthy stockbroker with a substantial portfolio of central London property. It meant nothing to his son, who had already amassed sufficient riches to last several lifetimes.

He cared nothing for the will. As executor, it would fall to him to sort it out. That could wait until later. Instead, his mind wandered over the empty, lonely days stretching ahead. He had caught sight of a few old flames on the edge of the mourners. Decent of them to come – but they meant little to him. Lucky in money, he was spectacularly unlucky in love.

He shuffled his feet. Standing still so long in the same position, his blood stopped circulating. His mind was busy, always working, never resting. As well as the will, he would have to order a gravestone. This was the first funeral he would organise. The prospect of picking a headstone and deciding on wording chilled him. Dad had always been there to advise on delicate matters.

The melody of the final hymn played hauntingly in the back of Silverman's subconscious. It continued playing as he stood there alone for three hours more. From time to time, a distant relative or friend would join him briefly, ask if he was OK, stand respectfully for a short while, then return to the wake. Mainly he waited alone.

Alone apart from a shadow he sensed watching from a gathering of trees on raised ground beyond, largely hidden by deep summer foliage. He was glad he had come.

As darkness fell, it was time to turn away. The hymn played on, Abide with me... In Life and Death Abide with me.

Only when he reached the car did he turn on his mobile and check the news. So, it had begun. The crisis Laura predicted and he anticipated.

He hit the accelerator, heading straight out the cemetery, for the A303. He was going home.

He revved the engine and picked up speed, singing, under his breath, his farewell to his father...

"Change and decay in all around I see, O Thou who changest not, abide with me."

28

CHAPTER SIX
Morning Thursday July 29
Southwark

A HERO-GRAM FROM LUDGATE was waiting for Julia in her Inbox when she arrived at her desk, the next morning, applauding her Chandler story. *Cool.* Even cooler, he called in person to reinforce his delight. *Well that's a first,* she thought.

"Well done," Andrew congratulated her. "We've caused a stink. Red tops've gone berserk. Most of the qualities followed up in later editions. A triumph."

The tabloids loved anything which smacked of money and scandal. Julia was particularly pleased to see the follow-ups in the quality titles.

"Pretty-much word for word," she couldn't resist pointing out – no higher compliment.

"Hmmm," he changed the subject. "So where is Chandler?"

"No one knows. Maybe this will flush him out."

"Anyway," he continued, "I'm calling to ask if you'd like to join me at the Chinese Embassy next week. I've been invited to some festivities celebrating the Dragon Boat Festival. Could be fun. What d'you think?"

Beware editors bearing gifts, Julia thought, but muttered something about how delighted she would be to join him.

"That's great. Know where it is?"

"Portland Place."

"Indeed. One more thing –"

Hmm, what now?

"Matthew Hopkins is joining from the Post. I've wanted to get him for some time. He'll be a great asset."

Julia's heart sank. *Andrew how could you?* she thought, but managed to bleat perkily, "Wonderful, congratulations."

"See you next week. Meanwhile, get cracking on the follow-up. Market's bound to be lively. See what Tower Gate is planning, and, well, find Chandler, if you can."

She slammed the phone onto its cradle.

"Andrew! How could you be so stupid," she shouted at the receiver. "Hopkins is the last person we need."

Matthew Hopkins enjoyed the sobriquet of Witch Finder General, partly because he shared the name of the infamous English Civil War Commander, who hunted down and hanged more than 300 so-called witches. But mainly he owed his infamy to a career dedicated to sniffing out promising subjects to satisfy a 21st century public's lust for blood.

Well, I'll never share a by-line with him, she thought. *Just about the nastiest, most poisonous journo I've ever come across.* She had dealt with Hopkins' pointed elbows and penchant for stealing other people's stories in the past.

Andrew was right about the Chandler exclusive, though. The disappearance of a star money manager, like Stephen Chandler, hit that morning's news like a jet fighter at full thrust. Repercussions trembled throughout the morning. Despite strong denials from the company, investors were panicking.

"Stephen Chandler has not disappeared," a Tower Gate spokesman emphasised. "He's working on a confidential project in the country."

Unlikely, Julia thought, as Cody walked in holding the morning's mail.

"See it worked out," he greeted her, his smile even wider than usual. "Met the postman at the door."

"It did indeed," Julia grinned back.

"Does this mean I've got a job?" he asked, placing the post on the desk in front of her.

"Undoubtedly, I owe you," she hesitated, before adding. "That was brilliant work. I'm sorry you missed a by-line. But if our relationship is to work, we need to keep you incognito, at least for the time being."

"So I've got a job?" Cody punched the air.

"Maybe," Julia took a deep breath. "Cody, as you once told me yourself, I can get into Boardrooms. Playing messenger looks a rich seam for stories. Come in here full-time and you lose that. First rule of journalism - you're only as good as your sources."

Cody was not slow following her thinking. "I could do casual evening shifts as a messenger. There's always a mad dash to get documents out late afternoon."

"Great. Come in here first thing, and we'll get you working on stories. I'll pay a trainee wage. Not much, but with what you pick up for casual work, should be enough to live on."

"Worry not," he beamed. "Casual delivery pays well."

"Let the good times roll," Julia gave him two thumbs up. "Well, let's get you started." She pulled pen paper and a

31

battered-looking laptop from the cupboard, and settled him at a spare desk.

"Second rule of journalism, always carry paper and pen," she said, handing him both, before turning back to the post. There was an intriguing brown envelope with a set of accounts, but no accompanying letter or explanation. No indication of who sent them.

"Tower Gate's put out another statement, saying anyone peddling lies will be sued," Cody was checking out the firm's website.

"One writ I'll never live to see," she replied, sliding the brown envelope across to him. "You'd better start earning your keep. Take a look at these."

Julia returned to her emails. As was often strangely the case after splashing on a big story, her Inbox was surprisingly quiet. *Uncanny,* she thought. An eerie silence descended, as if everyone was sitting back, digesting this latest news, wondering what to expect next.

Find Chandler, hmmm, Julia muttered Ludgate's final instruction. *Easily said, but where to begin?* She jotted down the possible scenarios on a pad. Accident? Lost his memory, lying in hospital somewhere, kidnapped for a ransom, run away with another woman, gone into hiding, lying dead somewhere? All seemed equally unlikely.

There has to be a rational explanation.

She randomly searched for "missing banker". A single paragraph appeared on her screen. Bank boss, Adam Lee, found dead in Wardour Street, Soho early yesterday evening. Police appealing for information and witnesses.

Pitcher's body, she racked her brains to see if she knew this Adam Lee. She quickly found him with an internet search, and was reading when her phone rang. *Talk of the Devil.* It was the Chief Inspector.

"I'm going to start charging," she joked, when she heard his voice at the other end of the line.

"No, I'm not calling about my savings, although now you mention it..."

She smiled. He was incorrigible. "What can I do for you then?"

"Surprised to see you going into the missing person's business that's all. Shouldn't you leave that sort of thing to the police? I thought money not people was your area of expertise."

"Amounts to the same thing most of the time."

"If you say so," he sounded unconvinced. "Fancy lunch? It's a long time since we got together."

"Not long enough for me," she quipped.

"Are you determined to get on the wrong side of me?"

"There isn't any other is there*?"*

He's intrigued by my story, she thought.

"Very funny. OK, I'll call Susan Ray at the Record. She's always interested in my little titbits."

"Little being the operative word. What did you want to discuss? I could manage an early supper."

"I'll see you at the Golden Pagoda at five, by the new gate. Get the drinks in, I'll have a pint. "

"Typical," Julia muttered to herself. Pitcher was quick with his invitations, but he never paid.

Time to get down to serious work. She checked her Inbox again as a final statement landed from Tower Gate. The directors had decided to close all funds until further notice. No money would be coming in or out until the fog cleared.

"They're shutting Tower Gate," Cody called across, his face puzzled.

"So I see," she hadn't intended to unleash havoc, but predicting the outcome was not hard. "Remember Cody, we didn't cause this. We reported the story. Chandler would have known the consequences of his disappearing."

"If that's what happened..."

The follow-up was effortless, and pretty much wrote itself. Closure of Tower Gate, rise and fall of superstar money house, markets tumbling on a wave of profit-taking. Investors furious at not being able to get their money out. Queues outside Pendle trebled, but panic not yet spreading. All of which said, by the time the New York stock market rang its opening bell, not long after London had closed, prices had stabilised.

Her news and features package filed, she set off to meet Pitcher in Chinatown. A young Chinese man sat opposite her on the tube. She found herself thinking again of Adam Lee. Did she know him? Had their paths crossed?

She felt a shiver down her spine as her thoughts moved next to Chandler.

Just a coincidence? Two bankers – one missing – one dead. It had to be, didn't it?

34

CHAPTER SEVEN
Thursday July 29
Hong Kong 6pm –London 11am

WARWICK MANTEL gazed out across Hong Kong Bay from his 40th floor office while he waited for his Californian marketing guru to join him. His subordinate was late. Time was money, but it made space for a rare luxury, a crack in the day to do nothing, but stare and think. A tired sun was beginning to bleed from the sky, although dusk had not yet arrived. Mantel watched the ferry crossing the bay, taking workers home to their apartment blocks on Kowloon. A few early beams dazzled from the skyscrapers crowding the shoreline. Soon the laser light shows would begin.

A Chinese junk, with red sails fully hoisted, weaved slowly across the waves, as the elegant crafts had for centuries. How he loved this spectacular harbour at dusk. Water was the city's lifeblood. Its trade winds blew ships, laden with cargoes from around the globe, in and out with the seasons. Now a new whirlwind was coming. Not all companies or cities would survive. Many would be blasted away in the wave of destruction about to be unleashed.

Then what? The seeds of world wars and the deaths of millions could be traced back to wealth destruction on the trading floors of Western capitals. Peak Bank of Hong Kong was as safe as he, its boss, could make it. He would use any means foul or fair to survive.

How easy and joyous it seemed a decade ago when they dreamed up their capital raising scheme. What a triumph it had been. That was its downfall. So sensational, everyone copied. Instead of a small scale, carefully-managed squeeze to the system, it grew to become the system itself. A nuclear option in the hands of those with no idea what they were doing.

His thoughts were cut short by a knock at the door. Scofield Crisp entered the room, looking hot, and stressed.

"Sorry I'm late. Traffic gridlocked by the pro-democracy demonstration. Chaos everywhere."

Crisp joined Mantel at the window. Tear drop neon cascaded down one of the highest Kowloon skyscrapers across the bay. Of the original five rocket scientists at that brainstorming weekend, he was the only one still with the company.

"You've seen the news?" Crisp seemed rattled.

"We don't know anything has happened to Chandler," Warwick stalled.

"They say he's disappeared and his fund's in trouble. Adam Lee is dead. We made a pact with the devil that weekend."

"Careful – your imagination's running away with you."

"Is it?"

Mantel laughed. "Adam Lee has nothing to do with Chandler's disappearance. You know his background. He was a danger junkie. Played for high stakes. I'm guessing his luck finally ran out."

"Self-destructive streak?" Crisp nodded, adjusting his gold cufflinks. "In his blood I guess – "

"Look, we created a valuable business proposition. The timing was perfect. We exploited it wisely. If others were less cautious that's not our problem."

"What happens to First State now its chief executive is dead?" Crisp said.

Mantel scanned the mountains on the horizon. He lay awake in the early hours pondering this very question.

"If First State goes down, who next?" Crisp was like a dog with a bone.

"It won't be us," came the peppery reply. Mantel walked to the cabinet and poured them both a whisky. "Hell, I've been through plenty of difficult times. So has Hong Kong. The Asian crisis of the 1990s barely touched us. We'll be fine."

"This time is different," Crisp spoke bluntly to his superior. "You need to wake up. The days of big imperial banks and investment houses are over. The Hemmings, Jardines and Matthewsons have all long gone. We no longer look over our shoulders to a distant Bank of England. China's our master now, and my guess is we can expect no quarter from the People's Republic if we screw up."

"We haven't screwed up, as you so indelicately put it," he handed Crisp a glass. "Patience – the storm will pass."

"Will it? This time? What if it doesn't? If this time the system doesn't bend and bounce, but breaks. Won't someone have to pay?"

"Yes, but I say again it won't be us. Our hands are clean."

Crisp sipped his whisky, savouring the pleasure of the burn as it scorched the back of his throat.

"We made it all possible," he pointed his glass at Mantel. "Doesn't that mean..."

"It means nothing," Mantel interjected. He walked back to the wall of glass overlooking the bay. Dusk had fallen further. Skyscraper lights transformed office towers into diamond obelisks, sparkling against the creeping dark. He turned again to Crisp.

"Make some inquiries, discreetly. See what the word on the street is about what Lee was up to. I'll press some flesh among my circle."

"What about Silverman and Laura Wan Sun? Should we warn them?"

The whirring blades of a helicopter playing cat-and-mouse around the tall buildings throbbed against the city's mountain girdle.

Mantel hesitated. Silverman was the one he feared. Suddenly he drew breath sharply.

"Yes. See if you can make contact. Silverman'll already be ahead of the curve if I know him. They should be vigilant. As a precaution, you understand."

Crisp nodded.

"I'll meet with security for the building, and click it up a notch. You may want to revisit your own personal security and surveillance at your apartment, as a precaution, you understand," he repeated.

"Of course," Crisp headed for the door, but Mantel wasn't done.

38

"While you're at it. Make sure your own money is safe. I'm rock solid. Already in gold, and I'm talking bricks. It's the only thing in times of crisis."

Crisp squeezed out a smile. He had already placed his trust in diamonds. You could carry a fortune in your pocket, if you needed to travel at short notice.

CHAPTER EIGHT
Noon Thursday July 29
Soho London's West End

SIX THOUSAND MILES AWAY an elderly man stood at his bedroom window reflecting how karma can take its time, but it catches up with you. He promised himself once he would never allow events to overpower him again. He kept that promise. Every threat neutralised. Still the dream haunted him. It always started as a happy dream. He was back in Diamond Heights, the village of his childhood. South-westerlies blew a warming wind across Hong Kong Island under a brilliant kingfisher blue sky - so welcome after the bitter cold winter. There was no school. He spent the day in grandfather's workshop, assembling toys for children far away. Father was busy sewing suits for Westerners in a textile factory nearby. Mother laboured in a big mansion, with majestic gardens stretching as far as the eye could see. From his cardboard community, the young boy could glimpse her at work, if he squinted up his eyes, serving drinks at famous parties on the pristine lawns below.

How lucky I am, he thought. In his child's eye, he had a good life - somewhere to live, enough to eat and surrounded by family and love. And when he looked out beyond the shanty village, his eyes could feast on the beauty of the mountains, the water below, and bewitching red sails of the Chinese junks gliding serenely across Victoria Harbour. *What better world could there be?*

Suddenly the scene changed with a violent jolt, as it can in dreams. It was night, and blisteringly hot. The sky ablaze like a fiery dawn. *We've only just gone to bed. It can't be morning.* He dashed out to see tongues of flames erupting all around, the air filled with screams of terror. The fragile village was ablaze.

Grandfather and father ran towards the toy factory. He was fast on their tracks until an explosion blocked his path. His face was on fire. Mother yanked him back.

"Go down to the water, Wo. Hurry. Fast as you can. Get out of here and don't look back." She pushed him into the river of people streaming down the rough track.

Then explosions began ripping through the night with ear-splitting rhythm. Adhesives, paint, petrol – innocent provisions, indeed lifesavers when providing an income – they were dynamite when stored in sweatshops buffeting family squats.

He made it to the water. It seemed to be snowing. He looked back to see an ash cloud rolling down the mountainside. The harbour sky was shot with reds and oranges, as if pumping blood into the firmament. The white storm, an ash cloud, was all that was left of 20,000 homes razed to the ground.

He heard alarm bells ringing.

No, no, you're too late. You can't save my family. You can't save the boy – he's fading, slipping way.

The boy disappeared. Wo, the man, listened as the ringing got louder, and engines hummed to a halt somewhere nearby.

"Mr Chang, wake up, wake up. We need to get you out."

He started to come to. This was not Hong Kong 1953. It was London, his home for the last half a century. He sat up in bed, and saw a man at his second-floor window wearing a brilliant yellow fire helmet and breathing apparatus.

"We need to get you out," the fireman's muffled voice came through. "Can you get out of bed and open the window?"

Wo Chang slipped open the window clasp.

"What happen?" the elderly gentleman asked.

"Nothing to worry about. A small fire downstairs in the restaurant. Our men are containing it. Can't be too careful in Chinatown. Can you manage the ladder or do you need a lift?"

"My family?" dread gripped his heart.

The fire-fighter didn't need to answer.

"Baah, Baah!" his two sons called up to their father in Cantonese. They were standing on the pavement below, safe with their wives.

"I'm coming," he said, stepping onto the ladder.

That was three months ago. A warning. Adam Lee – another. Wo Chang moved from the window to the mirror on the bedroom wall. He touched the burn scars disfiguring the left side of his face. Some wounds never heal.

CHAPTER NINE
6pm Thursday July 29
Soho

JULIA BROKE INTO A TROT as she exited Piccadilly Tube station. She was running late. She shivered as she turned up Wardour Street. *Somewhere here Adam Lee was murdered.*

Pitcher waved hello with a smile when she walked into the Golden Pagoda.

"This was the place with the fire, wasn't it?" She wriggled out of her jacket, and hung it on the back of her chair. "They've done a good job. A few months ago – no? You'd never tell."

"Three. Fire crews here in a flash. Station's round the corner in Shaftsbury Avenue. They'll never close Soho."

"You hope," she smiled, reaching for the menu. "Change is inevitable."

"Not from a vending machine," he smirked. "Don't bother with that, I've already ordered."

"Ha ha, very funny," she closed the menu and looked round the crowded dining room. "Cleared up pretty sharpish."

"That's the Chinese for you. Minimum fuss, all pull together, do as you're told."

"Much to be admired, I guess. Better than arguing endlessly about everything like we do. Hot air and no progress."

"Interesting perspective from a hot air merchant," he teased.

She pulled a rude face.

"How's your story going?"

"Which one?"

"You only write one, don't you? First as high drama, next tragedy, then satire – followed by farce."

"Oh shut up," she threw her serviette across the table at him. "So what was it? The fire. Accident? Electrical? Cigarette?"

"Accident? In Chinatown?"

Julia lowered her voice. "That body was found round here somewhere too wasn't it?"

He ignored the question, distracted by the arrival of his dinner.

"Ah, Mr Chang, you've excelled yourself. The food looks fabulous."

Julia's eye went straight to his facial disfigurement. *Poor man, I wonder what happened to him? It looks like a burn scar - surely not in the recent fire.*

"Everything has beauty," Mr Chang said, bowing his head slightly so Julia could see a tight bun on his crown. "But not everyone sees it." He smiled but not all his facial muscles responded.

Skin grafts, Julia guessed. *Not entirely successful.*

"That's what I'm always saying to my friend here. She just doesn't see it."

Pitcher winced as she kicked him under the table. Three waiters brought plates piled high. Julia was beginning to wonder how they could possibly manage such a feast, when Mr Chang pulled up a chair and joined them.

"Good to see you here, Chief Inspector," his English was near perfect but not quite. The v in everyone sounded more like a w and the s in see was hard like zee.

"Let me introduce my friend Julia." Pitcher started piling large helpings of sweet and sour pork, shrimp dumplings, dim sum, noodles on to his plate.

"Ah! A very pretty friend."

"As I'm always telling her."

Julia shot him a daggers look.

"Pleased to meet you, Julia," said Mr Chang. "Any friend of the Chief Inspector is always welcome here. Try this dish. Roast Goose, our Hong Kong speciality. Ordered in especially for you."

"You look well, Mr Chang," Pitcher continued. "Business thriving? How's the family?"

"So, so," he shrugged his shoulders. "We are so saddened by the death of that poor man. Such sorrow. So young." A veil of eastern inscrutability descended. "Any news Chief Inspector?"

"Adam Lee? We're working on it."

"I asked my grandson. He didn't know him. He joined after Anthony resigned. We are living in difficult times. Ever thus."

Pitcher turned to Julia. "Mr Chang arrived in London in the 60s with a young family."

"And now I'm a grandfather," he bowed his head slightly again.

45

"Wonderful," Julia said. "How many children and grandchildren do you have?"

"Two sons and a daughter. My sons run the restaurant. I provide, I think, you say, a little authentic colour. And I have four grandsons and two granddaughters."

"And your grandchildren? Do they work here too?" Mr Chang laughed. "Of course not, they are British. College graduates."

"Two are doctors, I think?" Pitcher chipped in. Mr Chang nodded, "Correct."

"Another a journalist like Julia," Pitcher put down his fork and stretched out an open palm towards her.

"Oh really?" Mr Chang raised his eyebrows. "Yes, my granddaughter is journalist in California for the San Francisco Bay Guardian. Choose a job you love, I always told them, and you'll never have to work a day in your life."

"One is in banking. Worked for First State Bank, in Hong Kong, before he set up on his own a few years back. Isn't that so?" Pitcher said.

"Yes. Doing well I understand. Another grandson has his own IT company, with offices here in London and in Hong Kong."

They chatted on until Mr Chang was called away to the kitchen.

Julia waited until he was out of earshot. "Where did he get that dreadful disfigurement?"

"Some childhood accident, I guess. Not the recent fire, if that's what you're thinking. No one was hurt."

"You still think it might've been started deliberately? I thought the days of protection rackets in Soho were a thing of the past."

"Tick tock – you might be right. Even a broken clock is right twice a day."

"What does that mean?"

"It means, what I said – which is more than your story did this morning. Hedge Fund Tsar Disappears. What does that mean?"

"Which words don't you get? Hedge fund, tsar or disappears?"

"Don't give me that look?"

"What look?"

"You know, that look you do. It's unnerving."

"I have no idea what you're talking about," Julia took her cue from him and tried to give him a killer stare. They both collapsed in giggles.

Pitcher straightened his face first, and spoke seriously.

"My advice is stick with what you know – money stuff. Missing people are way out of your line."

"What are the police doing about it?"

"We don't have the resources to investigate every individual who decides he doesn't much like his life."

"You've already got one dead banker, how many more d'you want?"

"Shush..." he whispered as a nearby table looked up. "I'd rather not have any."

He drained his glass then leaned across the table.

47

"How serious is all this money stuff? I don't want London swimming with white collar stiffs."

A waiter brought two hot towels to the table.

"Adam Lee. What d'you know about him?" she asked.

"He who knows all the answers has not yet asked all the questions."

"Don't you start quoting Confucius at me."

"Well?"

"Not very much. He ran a bank called First State in Hong Kong. He annoyed someone – a very great deal."

Pitcher picked up his hot towel, and wiped greasy fingers clean.

"And that's it?"

"Pretty much. I know a bit more about crime in the Chinese community in London. Or I thought I did. It's a moving feast and for once, I fear..."

"You've been left behind? Tell me about it."

"Long story. Read your history. Secret societies are part of Chinese culture. When they came to London, they formed their own associations. In time their criminals joined them."

"Triads? I thought they were eradicated at the time of the Opium Wars?"

"Their heyday was the 1920s and 30s in Shanghai, Hong Kong and Singapore. Sex, drugs, money. Like today, the rich liked to spice up their lives. Mao put a stop to their fun when he kicked the bourgeoisie out and broke Triad power in mainland China. Many upped sticks to Hong Kong and Macau... and onwards."

"London, New York, Sydney?" Julia opened her towel.

He nodded. "The Phoenix is the oldest in London, arrived here in the 1930s to escape the chaos engulfing East Asia. Started off as anti-communist. Today crime more important than politics. Remember the murder of Alex Ho-him, here in Chinatown?"

"Ho-him...vaguely."

"Chopped to death round the corner in Old Compton Street. Dozens of witnesses. No one would talk. Background said he was a regular at one of the illegal gambling dens and owed someone important a lot of money. Similar case in a cinema queue in Leicester Square. This time he lived but refused to make a complaint. Again no one saw anything."

Julia took a deep breath. "Intimidation with violence."

"Charge sheet soaked in blood. Suspicion is some kind of initiation rite. Drugs deal gone wrong. And you must know about Kevin Tang?"

"The Hong Kong journalist, who was slashed by a meat cleaver – critical of the Chinese Government."

"That was the Dragons."

"Don't tell me, more Triads?"

"They've been arriving in large numbers for the last five years. Hired thugs, not averse to working for the Chinese Government."

"So one's pro-communist and one's anti? Sounds like war."

"Which is what I've been trying to tell you. New groups have been arriving since the handover. Power bases are shifting."

"Who's behind it all? The top man?"

Pitcher threw her a caustic gaze.

Julia flicked her hair and laughed."You don't know."

"We will."

"Where does Mr Chang fit in?"

"He doesn't, I don't think. I'm fairly sure Mr Chang is what he seems to be – a restaurateur trying to stay in business. He's been skilful keeping on the right side of everyone," he paused. "Until now. Someone's unhappy."

"Was Adam Lee caught up with this?"

Pitcher sighed. "Honest truth? I don't know?"

"You still haven't told me how he died. Shooting or stabbing?"

Pitcher swallowed hard.

Julia's eyes dropped to Pitcher's thumbs, twitching nervously on the red cotton table-cloth.

"I can't tell you. It's sensitive."

Julia reached across the table and lay a hand over his fidgeting fingers. "You've always trusted me before."

He looked around to make sure no one was near enough to overhear. Then he leaned forward until their heads were almost touching. "He was garroted – eyes gouged out."

"What here, in central London?"

"Keep your voice down. Heard of Lingchi?"

"Death by a thousand cuts."

"This is the modern version. They're good at it. Razor-sharp wire and blade. He wouldn't have known a thing. And that's absolutely 100 per cent off the record."

Julia nodded. She wasn't sure, even if she wanted to write it, anyone would print the story. Not exactly news you can use over the cornflakes.

"You've got contacts in Lee's world. Can you make inquiries?"

"The grandson who worked for First State?" Julia asked. "Could that be connected?"

Pitcher's mobile rang in his pocket.

"I have to go," he stood abruptly, ramming arms into jacket as he moved for a quick exit.

On second thought, he paused. "There was a fresh orchid in his pocket. I'm having it looked at, but I'm told it could be rare."

Then he was gone.

"Nice touch," Julia muttered, as she called for the bill. After paying, she dialled a number on her mobile. She needed to find out more about Hong Kong. Much more.

CHAPTER TEN

8pm Thursday July 29
Cornhill, City of London

HUGO WAS TIRED. It had been a hard day. A pint with Julia on the way home would be a welcome release from the tortuous treadmill. Todd's Wine bar was his local, tucked away in the basement of The Jamaica Wine House, known locally as the Jampot. It started life as one of the earliest coffee shops in the City, where traders hammered out deals to fund expeditions to far off lands. Way off the tourist trail, buried down an intricate web of medieval alleyways, it had hardly budged an inch in character or purpose. The wine bar in the basement offered privacy for today's traders to hatch deals and weave secrets.

Crowds of drinkers stood outside in the courtyard enjoying the heat of the summer evening. A strong smell of ale hit Julia as she entered the dark, heavily-panelled bar, with its gold, smoke-faded ceiling. Background music throbbed unobtrusively. Blackboards behind the bar blazoned summer delights of pink gins and old mout cider. She headed down a tightly-turned staircase lined with satirical cartoons dating back to the 1700s, lampooning the madness of King George the Third, and his prime minister Pitt. Times changed but London could always laugh.

Hugo beamed when he saw Julia arrive. He was sitting at a round table hidden away in a shadowy corner. *He looks pale*, she thought, *but that could be the light.*

"Exciting times eh?" Julia greeted him with a warm smile, without sitting.

"Yeah, like driving a runaway car down Highgate Hill after the brakes have failed." He pulled a clown's grimace. Then laughed.

That's the old Hugo, she thought.

"What can I get you?" She pointed to his glass. "Maybe half to top up?"

He nodded. Julia went to the bar, and returned quickly with two glasses. The bar was rammed with traders taking stock of the days wins and losses, but she didn't have to wait long. In a world where time was money, businesses served fast.

"What d'you make of it all?" Julia picked Hugo's brains about the market turmoil, as she sat opposite him at the small round table. "Is this for real?"

"Our crazy markets?" Hugo took a sip of his beer. "Me? I'm an optimist. Markets go up and markets go down. Nature of the beast. They've been rising a very long time. Price you pay for easy profits. But you know that, and it's not why you called."

"The body in Soho," she got straight to the point.

"Adam Lee? Yes, I saw that paragraph. Met him a few times."

"Huckleberry Finn," Julia said surprised. She knew Hugo had worked in Hong Kong, which is why she asked to see him.

53

She hadn't expected to strike gold and outsmart Pitcher with her first call.

"Rather, I did know him," Hugo continued. "But not well. Strange character. Not my type. And First State..." he shook his fingers loosely, as though ridding himself of excrement.

"Shady?" Julia filled in for him.

"Rotten to the core. Open secret it was full of dodgy contracts and loans. Probably worse. No one reputable would deal with them." Hugo spoke in short, minimalist sentences, the language of the trading floor.

"How d'you know him?"

"Worked together at Tylers. He left to go to Peak. Now that is interesting. Peak is run by an old-world type, Warwick Mantel. Top man at Hemmings, before it hit the rocks in the Asian crisis."

"Scottish firm, sold to Chase," Julia filled in.

"That's right. Built on opium through its partnership with Jardine Matthewson. For three hundred years pay master of the British Empire. Mantel left long before it ran aground."

"He should know his stuff."

"Indeed. So well, he realised smaller banks, like Peak, could be blown away by the tsunami of money coming out of China. World economy rutting like a runaway train, banks around the globe running out of cash. Interest rates rock bottom, margins wiped out. You know the story. Banks can't exist without a turn. So, he put a small team together to find him a margin."

"When was this?"

"About a decade ago."

"And Lee was part of this team?"

Hugo nodded. "I never saw how he fitted into Peak Bank's top wizard team. What did they call them? The Golden Boys. Reckon they saved Peak."

"And did they? Find a turn?"

"Peak survived the Asian crisis, when banks all around were falling over. Continued to prosper. Not entirely sure how, but before long champagne corks were popping in all the major centres around the globe. It was boom, boom, boom time."

"Here in London, too?"

"Naturally."

"Bank shares went through the roof."

"And bank bosses were more famous than Hollywood stars. Governments deferred to them. They earned more than the economies of some small countries."

"Who else was on the team? Golden Boys you say?"

"They all had golden hair. Well, lightish brown. You may know some of them. Scofield Crisp. He's still with Peak I believe in Hong Kong. Patrick Silverman set up his own funds, just off Cheapside. Made a serious fortune. Bought a castle. Probably retired already. Laura Wan Sun, the only woman. Anglo-Asian. Gorgeous girl."

"So there was a woman, too?" Julia asked.

"One of the boys. You know how things were in those days. Only she wasn't, didn't fit."

"Neither a boy nor golden-haired. What happened to her?"

"Don't know," Hugo paused for breath and to sip his pint. "Parents both doctors - mother had a missionary background. Stephen Chandler – "

"Chandler!" Julia froze.

Hugo seemed not to notice and continued. "Lee was different. The others were all rocket scientists. He was more of a fixer. Local knowledge man. Knew where the bodies were buried."

"I didn't know Chandler and Lee were connected."

"I didn't say they were connected, only they worked together. That applies to most people in the Square Mile."

"True," Julia conceded. *Still one hell of a coincidence*, she thought. "Tell me about Hong Kong. I've never been there."

"Seductive. Such a wonderful city. Worked for Tylers. Ten years."

"It's a huge financial centre, isn't it?"

"Massive. Exploded with the Asian tiger. China is...what now? Second biggest economy in the world. First on some measures. Grew from nowhere. Wiped us away years ago."

"Hong Kong has always been a big banking and trading partner for the UK?"

"I don't know about always. Certainly British banks date back to the 17th century. Most were heavily engaged in opium trading. Pushed the British Government hard to go to war when the Emperor tried to stop the damage it was causing."

"Opium dens, growing addiction?"

"Exactly, though to be fair, opium wasn't illegal back then. They traded other stuff too – tea, silks. Funded by the City fathers here in London. Arrival of Japanese in World War Two put pay to all that temporarily, but most institutions got back on their feet pretty quickly."

"You liked working on the island?"

"Loved it. The harbour is ..." he shook his head. "Magical, mesmerising, hypnotic, and much more. I don't have words to describe it."

Colour returned to his cheeks, as his thoughts shifted thousands of miles away.

"Never homesick?"

"Plenty of Brits doing a stint abroad. Local Chinese population's very anglicised."

"A civilised posting?"

"Exactly, and exciting. Night markets, succulent street food, hustle and bustle. Utterly bewitching."

"You're doing a brilliant job bringing it alive for me," Julia laughed. "I must go. When all this..." she waved her hand vaguely in the air, "is over."

"Yes. And go soon."

"Before it changes? Or has it already changed?"

"Since the handover?" Hugo referred to the end of British rule after 150 years. "Not so much when I was there, although..."

"One nation two systems, isn't that how it's supposed to work? Hard call for the Chinese, I should have thought."

Hugo nodded. "It seemed plausible at the time given Hong Kong's genius for making money. Not just the money machines, but its huge port ships out China's massive manufacturing machine."

"I thought they were developing other ports in mainland China?"

"Oh they are. So Hong Kong is exposed. Money will always be its most valuable commodity."

"If markets tank?" Julia couldn't resist.

"Toast!" He blurted his brutal prophecy for the future of the island if the wheels of its money machines stopped whirring.

"Journalists are having a hard time. Censorship. Sacked or worse. People disappear overnight."

"What sort of people?"

"Sometimes, really important people. Top bosses of global companies."

"What?" Julia almost shrieked.

"Oh it's OK." Hugo reached across the table to reassure her. "These people usually turn up again."

"Do they always?" she asked softly.

He shrugged.

"What about the Golden Boys?" Julia leaned towards him, elbows on table.

"Of that team, one is missing and one is dead."

She watched as he drained his glass and placed it gently down.

"That's why I made the time to meet you," his eyes were smiling kindly, despite a worried furrow of his brow.

CHAPTER 11

9am Friday July 30
Southwark

JULIA SCANNED the morning's headlines. Serbian war criminal extradited to The Hague, US Presidential campaign plunges new depths, Chinese farmer dies from respiratory disease, no let up in the Pendle queues, savers baying for blood. Her eye lingered on the Obits page and the funeral of City luminary Jonathan Silverman; senior partner Manner & Pound, former Lord Mayor of London, Board of the London Stock Exchange. The main story and picture on the page depicted his son, Patrick Silverman, leading a procession of mourners.

"Huckleberry Finn," she muttered as Cody arrived, carrying two coffees. Her next move, after her chat with Hugo, was to hunt down each of the remaining "Golden Boys" to see what they could tell her about Lee and Chandler.

"What's with Huckleberry Finn?" Cody placed one of the cups on her desk.

"Save the other "F" word for when it counts. I need to interview someone, and it will have to wait. Loved Mark Twain as a child. How d'you get on yesterday?"

"Not sure," he replied, wrestling off his jacket.

"Try me, but be quick."

"Well," he said, opening a bacon roll. "These accounts belong to the Whittingdale Trust. Tracked it down – easy. Massive London charity with tentacles stretching across the City and beyond. Looking good, if you like social history," he made a face. "Not sure it helps unravelling these documents," he waved his hand vaguely towards the wad of papers.

"Something to do with City Hall?"

"That's the thing – the Whittingdale Trust is an independent charity. Goes back hundreds of years to Shakespeare's day. It's as old as the oldest churches in the City."

"You mean the old City of London?"

"That's right. There were hundreds of little churches. Many of the rich merchants who made fortunes in trade, shipping, insurance, left money to local churches when they died."

Cody bit into his roll, and chewed for a few seconds.

"Explains why so many of them are still in such good nick," Julia handed him a serviette as a trickle of butter oozed down his chin.

"Thanks," he nodded, wiping his chin. "Not exactly. It's easy to forget for many centuries the City of London was a normal city like any other. Full of fishmongers, bakers, ferrymen, merchants, cobblers, tailors. Before the welfare state when families fell on hard times..." he was fired up by the story.

"There was only parish poor relief. Well done, Cody, hugely interesting," she didn't have time for a long drawn out history lesson. "We'll finish this later. I'm sorry, I need to get on. Could you take a look at secret societies operating in London, particularly, any with Chinese connections."

"You mean Triads?" he raised his eyebrows.

"I mean secret societies," she repeated.

"I'm on it," Cody started tapping his keyboard.

She turned back to the Silverman funeral, this time concentrating on the deceased's non-business roles. He advised a number of London charities. Her eye jumped to the bottom of the article. Widower for 30 years. Never remarried.

She stared again at the grainy photograph of Patrick Silverman. *Who are you?* She pulled various biographies and articles onto her screen. He was a handsome devil, no denying. Most billionaires were short, fat, and bald with squidgy eyes, as though making money was the only way they could prove themselves. Silverman had a thick thatch of hair, kindly looking eyes, and a well-chiselled bone structure. Educated Winchester, Cambridge and Harvard. Aged 33, founder and Chairman of a firm called SAM, Silverman Asset Managers, with £150 billion funds under management. Without an interview with Silverman, how could she hope to find Chandler, or learn more about Adam Lee?

"Adam Lee. First State," she tapped his name into an internet search engine. First State had little on its website, other than the date of Lee's appointment as chief executive three years ago. Julia found a business magazine online, where Lee had posted a full biography himself. Studied at St Paul's School, and Chinese University of Hong Kong – joined Tylers' office as a graduate trainee, before moving to Peak.

"All interesting but this is getting me nowhere," Julia mumbled, as Cody dropped a piece of paper on her desk.

"My job application form," he said. "I sorted it last night."

Julia looked up, glancing at the piece of paper disinterestedly. Her gaze snapped back, and she began snorting with laughter.

"Rose Codrington," she collapsed into giggles. "Rose. You can't be called Rose."

He wriggled uncomfortably.

"I'm from Antigua, OK? Slaves took their names from their owners. The Codringtons were one of the founding families of the Leeward Islands, and one of their estates was called the Rose Plantation. Someone in my family must have liked that, because we have a Rose Codrington somewhere in each generation. I got lucky this time."

"No wonder you prefer Cody. So you were born on..."

"At St Thomas's." Cody cut her short.

"On Westminster Bridge Road? Have you ever lived on the island?"

"Sadly not. Beautiful place. Visited plenty for holidays and to catch up with cousins."

"So?"

"So what?"

"So how did you come to be born here?"

"Dad was a cricketer. Mum's a nurse, trained at the Antigua medical school. They visited London when he played at Lords. Fell in love with the place." He raised his eyes to heaven. "Don't ask me why. Mum found it easy to find work as a nurse. They stayed. Dad went into coaching."

"And you all lived happily ever after," Julia was still laughing, when the phone began to ring.

"Not quite. They split up when I was eight. Dad went back to Antigua. Mum stayed, said the NHS needed her."

"Well she was..." still chuckling Julia reached for the call, but killed her snigger stone dead, when she heard the voice at the other end of the line.

"Hello, my name is Patrick Silverman."

Patrick Silverman, she was stunned, momentarily lost for words.

"Hello," the voice repeated. "Is this a difficult time?" Still no reply. "Would you prefer if I call back later?"

Oh no, no, no. The reporter found her voice. "Mr Silverman, how can I help you?"

He moved straight to business. "I've been reading your columns on the current economic turmoil. Some good articles," he began.

"Thank you," she offered gingerly, wondering where this was going.

"Some absolute garbage too. Even so, you seem to be one of a tiny number of commentators ahead of the pack. Would you like to talk?"

Julia swallowed hard for a few seconds, not sure whether she had just been insulted or congratulated. Either way this was the interview she craved, and pride would not stop her grabbing it.

"I can be at your office whenever you like, in fact I can walk across now if it suits." Strike while the iron's hot – always her motto.

"I'm not in town. You're welcome to come here."

"Where are you exactly?" she hesitated.

"Cornwall. I'll get my secretary to email you details."

Of course, he retreated to the castle to nurse his grief. A vision of a long, cold train journey, without mobile signal or wifi loomed depressingly. With all that was going on, there was no way she could desert her desk. Not with competition like Matthew Hopkins breathing down her neck.

How can you turn down an interview with Patrick Silverman? a little voice inside whispered.

"I'll leave you to decide whether I'll be worth the trouble," he concluded the conversation. The line clicked dead.

"Goodbye," Julia mouthed, staring at the receiver. Almost immediately an email from his secretary pinged in.

"What a joker," she exploded to Cody. "He's offered me an interview, but I can't possibly accept."

"Why not?"

"It's in Cornwall."

"He's not exactly a mad pirate wielding a blunderbuss."

"How can I? I have to be in London on Friday to partner Andrew Ludgate at the Chinese Embassy. I haven't begun to think about that and need to prepare."

"You could fly up and down the same day. There must be a service," Cody started tapping his keyboard. "Or get the sleeper. That way you could go, say, Wednesday night, catch the next sleeper back and be at your desk Friday morning."

"I'd be throwing you in the deep end."

"You were thrown in at the deep end, weren't you? Isn't that the way in this job? Anyway, you'll be travelling at night – you won't miss any working time."

She was torn between a compulsion to go, and her duty to stay at her desk to supervise Cody.

Curiosity won the better of her. "OK, book the night train."

Travel details confirmed, she emailed Silverman's secretary, then turned to the Chinese economy. Couldn't show herself up in front of Andrew.

As she read about growth rates, earnings, imports and exports, the conversation with Silverman played at the back of her mind.

Why did he call? He doesn't know me. Is he honestly interested in my economic analysis? Or is he more intrigued by my story about the disappearance of his old sparring partner Stephen Chandler?

CHAPTER 12

Monday August 2 – early evening
Soho

CHIEF INSPECTOR PITCHER raised his eyes at the sight of the young PC dressed, not in uniform, but jeans and T-shirt, leaning against the bar of the Lyric, Great Windmill Street.

"Under what false pretences have you dragged me back to Soho, Constable?" he growled.

"You said to make inquiries. That's what I've been doing," PC Day said with a smile. "I'm the man on the beat, remember?"

"I do, and I'm the man in the office, remember?" Pitcher scowled. "The office which costs taxpayers millions of pounds a year. What's wrong with reporting back to me there, like normal constables?"

"Look," PC Day pointed at two glasses on the heavy oak bar. "I've bought you a pint."

Pitcher mellowed slightly. "Hmm, drinking on duty. Against all the rules. Maybe you do have management potential."

He sipped the head off the top of his glass. "Let's sit down, before someone sees us." Pitcher knew word of his presence in Soho spread like wildfire. "Can you order me a steak and kidney pie? I haven't eaten."

The Lyric was one of Pitcher's favourite boozers, one of the last traditional English pubs in the quarter. He retreated to a table in a corner where they could not be overheard.

"So what was so urgent I had to hotfoot it over here?" Pitcher asked as PC Day joined him.

"I've got some information I think you'll find interesting. Only picked it up this morning. I've also asked someone to meet us here."

A female bartender approached and placed a plate before the senior cop.

"Thank you," he said, squeezing lashings of brown ketchup from a bottle on the table.

"Well?" he looked up at the junior officer, mouth full of food. "Lost your tongue?"

"Actually Sir, I was lost in thought." PC Day swallowed hard as he stared at the Chief Inspector's plate.

"Unfamiliar territory is it...another country and all that?" Pitcher took a sip of his beer. "Want a bit of this pie?"

PC Day shook his head, swallowing again. "Err, no thanks Sir."

"OK, get started," Pitcher pointed his knife commandingly.

"I've managed to trace Adam Lee's movements on the day of the murder. Well most of them. I haven't quite joined all the dots."

"And?"

"We think he met someone in the British Museum."

"Cabbie?"

"A driver looked at a picture and confirmed he dropped Lee off at about 10am. We also have a receipt from the Great Court restaurant for morning coffee and pastries for two."

"Any leads on his companion?"

PC Day shook his head.

"CCTV?" Pitcher quizzed.

"We're on to it, but the museum thinks in millennia. It takes time."

"Good, keep up the pressure. Is there more?"

"Oh yes, and this is the real deal. He came to Soho for lunch."

"Do we know where?"

"Prepare for a shock."

"I doubt it. I'm unshockable these days."

"The Golden Pagoda."

"Chang's place?" Pitcher's voice softened.

"Exactly."

Pitcher picked up his glass and drew deeply. *Could I have been wrong about Chang?* He set his mouth into a firm line as he savoured the taste, a vein throbbing in his neck.

"The Chang's have no record of him being there," PC Day continued, "and no recollection – or so they claim. No plastic slip."

"You've checked with the banks?"

"Of course. Must have paid with cash. You know how busy that place can be."

"How do you place him there?"

"CCTV shows him going in at 12.30pm and coming out about an hour later."

"Was he with someone?"

"Not on the cameras. Doesn't mean he didn't meet someone there."

"Or after..." Pitcher scratched his jaw.

"The attack was a couple of hours later. No one saw a thing. Chinatown," PC Day raised his eyebrows. "It might have nothing to do with the Changs. Coincidence."

"Possible...but not likely. Then there was the fire...murky murky murky. Nothing's ever as it seems..."

"In Chinatown."

The lady bartender came to clear their plate and empty glasses. Pitcher ordered a refill for both. While they waited for her to return, the two policemen went back over the day of the murder.

An anonymous tip came into Scotland Yard sometime after 3pm. Ambulance arrived first on the scene, with Scenes of Crime Officers hard fast. Medics pronounced him dead. Given the butchery this was a formality. All the hallmarks of a professional hit. A pro could garrote a victim in a flash, slice eyes out in seconds. The assassin could have walked slowly down any of the escape routes offered by Wardour or Lisle Street, before the crime was detected. Within minutes he could have disappeared into the mobs thronging Leicester Square."

"I thought meat cleavers were the Triads' weapon of choice?" Pitcher thought aloud.

"Times change, Sir. Speaking plainly, a chopping or slashing is usually a warning, intended to maim perhaps, but not to kill."

This boy knows his stuff, Pitcher thought.

69

"This was unnecessarily brutal. Why? We have to puncture this bubble of silence."

"We will, Sir, we will."

At that moment, a well-dressed young Chinese man entered the bar and made straight for where PC Day was sitting. He addressed the young officer in Chinese.

Pitcher's eyes widened. "I didn't know you could speak Chinese." He noticed the new comer had a small tattoo on the soft inner tissue of his elbow. A magpie.

"How d'you think I get through all those tenants meetings?"

Why a magpie? Pitcher thought, as PC Day continued speaking to his Chinese friend.

Strange. Aren't they a symbol of bad luck?

CHAPTER 13
7.55am Thursday August 5
Penzance

THE TRAIN pulled into a platform siding by the sea. Julia spotted him immediately she stepped out the carriage. *Funny little man*, she thought, *like a character from a story book*. Celtic in stature for sure, with multi-toned wayward hair. He held a board with her name on it, and waved as she walked towards him.

"Call me Trigg," he beamed a likeable smile, while a bear-of-a-paw shook her hand warmly. "Good trip?" he added, reaching for her bag. "The nightsleeper's proper 'ansum, they say. Motor's outside," he jerked his head to the right. "'Fraid you'll not see much sun today."

Julia craned her head to look up as they left the station. She shuddered. The sky was black. The air tasted salty.

"That's the Castle rock slap in the middle of Sharks Bay," Trigg pointed to a craggy rock, topped by a Disneyesque fortress. "Forty-two miles from Crocodile Point to Dolphin Head. Widest bay in Britain."

He opened the door of the Land Rover, helped Julia in, and fired the engine before swinging out of the harbour car park. The coast road wound its way to the Castle in less than six minutes. Boats bobbed on the tide.

Trigg turned to her. "Mr Silverman sends his apologies. Called out last night. Be with us as soon as he can."

"Called out?"

"On a shout. Lifeboat crew."

Julia gazed up at the ominous horizon. "To a boat in trouble?" An iron claw of fear grabbed her heart. She lost someone she loved to the sea.

"Call came in about 3am. Not sure what happened. Should be back before long."

Trigg parked close to the harbour wall.

My, my, so our city slicker is a part-time RNLI volunteer.

"This is a dangerous coast isn't it?" she said. "Famous for shipwrecks."

"Not the coast that's dangerous, but the sea. Tide's in. Short boat ride OK?"

"Preferable to swimming," she laughed.

Trigg took her bag from the back, locked up, and led the way across the wide white sand to a rock, where a boat was waiting. He cast off. The boat, called Katharine, mounted the waves with a kick. Ice wind bit into her face. *Huckleberry Finn, that stings like chards of glass.*

"Good to get some fresh air into your lungs, after the city, I'll be bound?" Trigg shouted over the breeze.

Julia nodded enthusiastically, while actually thinking the opposite. She clung to the side of the boat as it crashed and reared across the top of the waves. *I'll be lucky to make it home alive,* she thought.

"Most beautiful sight in the world, I reckon," Trigg pointed to a steep rock jutting out the waves, standing legs agape, balancing perfectly into the surf's giddy dance.

Julia braced herself for a eulogy on shipwrecks, pirates, mermaids and magic – Cornwall's theme park mythology. Trigg left it at that, and concentrated on steering the craft into the Castle harbour.

Inky clouds threatened rain. Against the dark sky, the shadow of the castle towered portentously. Julia felt guilty – she had been unkind.

"A bleak beauty, I suppose," she shouted across to him.

The heavens opened as they stepped out of the boat onto stone steps, winding up the harbour wall. A flash of lightning tore across the sky.

Creepy, she shuddered. She drew her coat closer, and leaned into the wind. Gusts battered as she climbed the stone steps. *Glad that's not the only way up*, she thought noticing a rickety iron ladder pegged to the granite wall.

At the top, Trigg steered her left, towards a steep path. "This way Miss."

"Hang on a minute," Julia walked towards a bench and sat down. "If it's OK, I'd like to change into my trainers."

As she struggled to shoe-horn her foot into the tight-fitting sportswear, she heard an engine noise and looked up to see a jet ski racing across the waves. Tying her laces, with her back to the wind, she sensed a figure emerge at the top of the sea wall, not by the steps as they had, but by the rickety ladder.

"Exhausted already?" said a tall figure clad in water-proofs.

"Not at all. Just changing into suitable footwear."

"As must I. Change that is. Excuse me." He set off up the mountain path like an Olympic runner.

"All OK Mr Silverman?" Trigg called after him.

"All fine Trigg," the reply carried on the wind.

The trainers put a spring in her step. Even so, the climb to the top tested her. *This bloody rain*, she thought as it lashed her face. Once inside she faced more steps as the steep climb continued. She followed Trigg up and up and up. Finally, they arrived in a smallish book-lined room. *This must be Silverman's office.*

"Make yourself comfortable, I'm sure Mr Silverman won't be long."

Alone, Julia couldn't resist walking to the window and gawking down the rock face, battered by a turbulent sea.

Why does Silverman live in a fortress, she wondered? *What's he hiding from? Why volunteer with the lifeboats? Is he punishing himself for something or an adrenalin junkie?*

She turned on hearing the door open.

Ah! The man himself.

"Ms Lighthorn, sorry to keep you waiting." He was transformed by chinos and open-necked white shirt with an Armani flash at the cuff.

"I hope the journey was," he paused, "genial."

Broad shoulders narrowed to trim hips. Golden streaks highlighted thick fairish hair above a broad forehead and deep-set blue eyes. *Warm yet piercing*, she thought. *Arrogant for sure.* Yet she detected a fleeting unease. *Curious mixture of half panther, half panda.* He looked tired, but then he'd been up half the night. *A*

74

man not entirely comfortable in his own skin, she guessed. *Sometimes, it didn't pay to be too clever or too rich.*

He brushed past her to reach his desk. Sitting, he pointed to a chair opposite for her to do likewise.

"It was long, but the sleeper was civilized," she replied, bristling as she remembered his description of her work as garbage. *Down tiger.*

"Your night must have been considerably worse out on the high seas?" she continued with polite concern.

"You want to discuss the financial crisis?" he changed the subject.

"Partly. I also feel I should defend myself against your criticism of my work. I take anyone who damages my reputation seriously."

"As do I."

"Garbage? Surely a little over the top?" she said, with a killer stare.

"Yes, you're probably right." His face broke into a warm smile. "Fainites," he raised two crossed fingers, giving her a cute grin."Isn't that how we used to make a truce in the playground? Let's start again."

Help, he's very handsome when he smiles, Julia swallowed. *OK, I'll be big-hearted and turn the other cheek. Let's start again and do it his way.*

"The markets are extremely volatile, but they bounce at the end of the day. Are they testing floors to see how low they can go? Or is there something worse ahead, do you think?" she asked.

"You're not recording my opinions? You haven't got a notebook out."

Before she could think of a smart reply, he answered his own question. "Because you're not interested in them, are you? Not really. There are hundreds of people you could interview in London, why come all this way for more hot air?" he winked at Julia.

Startled, her face froze. Then the penny dropped. *He's got a nervous blink, a tic,* she realised. *He's not as chilled as he pretends.*

The door opened and a middle-aged woman entered pushing a trolley with coffee, croissants and one cooked breakfast.

"Good morning Margaret," Silverman said.

"Good morning to you, too, Mr Silverman, and you m'dear," she nodded to Julia. "Hear they all got off in one piece. You'll be starving," she placed a tray in front of him, with scrambled egg, bacon, sausages and toast.

"They did Margaret, thank you, but that's more than can be said for the boat."

"I took it you breakfasted on the train," she turned to Julia. "If you'd like a cooked breakfast..."

"I'm fine," Julia smiled.

"Coffee and croissant, then," she said.

"Just coffee, thank you."

Margaret finished serving, then closed the door behind her.

"Tell me about Adam Lee," Silverman began again, cutting into a sausage.

Julia exhaled slowly. *So this is the true reason for the invite.* She moved her tongue slowly around the inside of her teeth, thinking carefully.

"I don't know much," she hedged, stirring her coffee deliberately. "You probably know more than I do. He was found dead in Chinatown in London."

"You guys work closely with the police, don't you? What do they make of it?"

"I don't think they know what to make of it. Hong Kong banker murdered in London. Round up the usual suspects."

"As in?"

"Spurned lover, bitter business partner, angry debtor..."

"Are there any?"

Julia shrugged her shoulders. "You worked with him for a short while didn't you? Any theories?"

"I only know what I've read."

"What did you think of him? Did you like him? Did you trust him?"

"People have lost a great deal of money," Silverman dodged. "They're going to lose even more. Lee always flew close to the wind. People in the Far East have a different outlook on risk and reward. When they're doing well, they're happy. When things go wrong, they want someone to blame."

"So you believe his murder was in some way connected with the bank? With money?"

"As I said, I've no information. What other motive for murder is there?"

"Hundreds I should've thought."

"You must know enough about First State to appreciate that some of its clients, what should we say – well their affairs wouldn't bear much investigation. These people really don't like losing money. Explaining the vagaries of the market is probably going to be a tad," he paused, "challenging."

"Surely it could be some other entirely personal motive. An acrimonious romance? Or just bad luck. I heard on the news London's murder rate's outstripped New York. Wrong place, wrong time?"

"You said yourself those avenues of investigation were drawing blanks."

"What about Stephen Chandler?"

Silverman looked down, and slowly buttered his last piece of toast.

"Stephen is a friend." A veil had fallen.

"Do you know where he is?"

Julia waited as Silverman crunched his triangle of crisp bread. Finished, he pushed the plate away, slowly wiping his hands with a linen napkin.

I'm not going to get an answer am I? Julia watched him push his chair back and stand.

"Let me show you the Great Hall," he stretched out a hand.

They left the room together and he opened another door into the historic space.

"It's stunning," Julia said "It was a monastery originally, wasn't it?"

"Yes, for nearly 1,000 years. Eighth century to the Reformation. This hall was used as the monks' refectory, until it became the Great Hall in Georgian times. In this very room..." he stopped, as if caught short by a painful memory.

"What was in this room?"

"There were six of us."

"You all worked for Peak Bank?"

"The bank was buffeting its capital limits," Silverman's voice drifted away, lost in another world.

"Running out of money?"

"Not exactly, but there was no room left to grow. Not a great place to be with China breathing down our necks. So Warwick Mantel..."

"Your boss?"

Silverman nodded. "Brought us here to brainstorm a solution."

"Did you?""

"Let's put it this way. Eight years ago, the bank was worth £25 billion. Today its market cap is five times that."

"How d'you pull it off?"

"Why do banks need capital?"

"To cushion against risk, against Armageddon. If the economy goes into recession, and people don't repay their loans, banks will still have enough cash to keep their doors open."

Or not, as with Pendle, Julia couldn't help thinking.

He nodded. "What if you remove the risk of your loans going bad, by trading that credit risk too," he continued. "If you could sell all your risk, then capital ceases to be a problem. You no longer need to hold it. You can lend to as many people as you want."

"Who would buy your bad risks?" she asked. "Isn't that the point of dodgy loans, no one wants them."

Silverman walked towards the masterfully-carved stone fireplace, and leaned a hand on the rich oak mantel. "No one in their right mind obviously – at any price. What if you packaged your risks in mixed bags? Good risks mixed with bad."

"But the bad risk doesn't disappear does it?"

"Not exactly, but you neutralise it. That's the theory."

"And did you?"

"Look," Silverman swung round from the fireplace and pointed to the window. "The sun's come out. Do you ride?"

"Yes, I can do."

"Come on then."

CHAPTER 14

THE SUN had indeed come out – the black sky sucked far away, and replaced by a rainbow of pastel colours. Blues, pinks, turquoises. The tide had receded at an astonishing pace to reveal a vast expanse of golden beaches stretching miles in every direction. It didn't take Julia long to change into the over-trousers and polo shirt offered.

She couldn't wait to get in the saddle after seeing the magnificent steeds in the stables buried low in the island, with a clear run onto the sands.

"Where d'you learn to ride?" Silverman asked, as they led their mounts splashing through shallow water.

"Home counties girl. Nothing much else to do in the country," she grinned.

And then they were off, galloping along the sand, the sun warm on their backs. They were a match for each other as they raced across cove after cove, along deserted beaches, and shallow lapping water. A flock of birds drew letters across the sky. Cs, As, and Ds.

"Let's stop here," Silverman shouted to her, raising a hand to slow her pace. He dismounted. She followed and slipped down. They walked the horses for a bit, allowing their heart rates to slow.

"So what drives you Julia?" Silverman asked, as they ambled along the beach.

"Goodness. It's a long time since anyone's asked me that."

"It can't be the money. You're a smart girl. You could earn a fortune in the City. Is it power?"

"Curiosity, I guess. And a desire for neatness. Unless you know what's going on, you can't put it right."

"Ah, the fourth estate."

"Exactly. Sometimes the police, judiciary and church aren't enough. The media has an important job to do – investigate and expose. We're outside the establishment, yet part of it."

"Putting the world to rights," he shot her a sideways smile.

"Something like that. Making a difference."

When they reached a secluded cove, Silverman tied his reins through a brass ring buried into the rock.

"Probably smugglers," he secured her reins in another such smugglers hook. He walked towards a slit in the cliff face, just big enough to squeeze through, and turned signalling for her to follow.

Where's this going? Julia wondered as she stepped through the cave crevice. A dark narrow passageway opened up into a colossal cavern.

"One of our best kept secrets," he stood staring into a massive rock bath, cut out of the granite, and filled with shimmering water, which flickered silver, midnight blue and deep green.

"Filled by a natural spring," he flashed a torch around the chamber. "Smugglers used these caves. We think one of them carved the bath for his lover. Perhaps. We'll never know."

82

Julia shuddered. The cave was cold and damp. Light washed in and out as the sun refracted through the opening. Uncanny shadows ricocheted in every direction. Quivers of sapphire blue and sea green bounced off amethyst, glittering from the rocks.

Oh no, Julia felt a migraine stirring. Pulsing bright flashes messed with her dopamine. *If I don't get out soon, my vision will go.* Nausea started to rise. Refracting lights affected her badly.

She looked at Silverman. A strange far away expression enveloped his features. He started to speak in a low voice, almost a whisper, but his words echoed round the hollow grotto.

"There was a girl with us that weekend."

"Laura Wan Sun," Julia whispered. Her voice rang back against the rocks. She closed her eyes, as her head started to spin.

"She was the only one who spoke against the scheme. Tried to persuade us it was a genie we could never put back in the bottle."

"Was she right?" Julia opened her eyes and sought to fight the rising dizziness. The wall of the caves whirled.

I have to get out of here.

"Oh yes. When they saw how well it worked, everyone else piled in. No understanding of the risks or how to manage them. They packaged all kinds of junk and garbage together. Now they're waking up to the cesspit they're wading in..."

"That's why the markets..."

"Are on the brink of a massive collapse? The world's river of money which keeps all our wheels turning is about to dry up. Without money nothing can function. Economies suffer seismic shocks, like a heart attack or stroke. Without money no one gets paid, health care breaks down, no one can go shopping, no one can put food on the table."

"D'you blame yourself?"

"No," he answered a bit too quickly. "It wasn't our fault. There was nothing wrong with the model. We hadn't reckoned for the stupidity of others."

"What about Peak?"

"Hong Kong is not the safe haven it used to be."

"China?" Julia asked.

Silverman sighed and looked grim. "If I were in Hong Kong right now, I'd get the hell out."

"And Wan Sun?"

"Laura? I don't know," he sounded lost. "She left the bank shortly after. We kept in touch for a while. Sweet girl. Her parents were doctors. I heard she retrained, and returned to Hong Kong."

Hong Kong again. Then the crashing headache she feared, struck like an axe in the brain.

"I'd like to find Laura. Make sure she's safe. Is that something you could help me with?"

He flashed brilliant sapphire-blue eyes at her. She was utterly alone with him and suddenly frightened.

"I'm sorry, I have to go. This cave and the flashing lights are making me feel ill."

"Is that a No?"

"Let me think about it."

Once out in the fresh air she could breathe again, and the nausea subsided. The ride back along the sands eased her headache and revived her spirits. The wind in her hair blew a question.

Why did he bring me to this strange isolated location? Could it be, this cave, cut deep into the rock, is the only place he can guarantee not being watched or bugged? The only place he feels safe?

JULIA DECLINED the offer of further hospitality and headed straight back to London. Trigg drove her to the station in the Land Rover. The sun was high when they rumbled over the causeway cobbles. Julia looked back at the silver, shimmering path. As she did so, a shadow caught her eye. It disappeared in a flash. She craned her neck to see better. It was gone. And yet...

This place is driving me crazy. I must stop imagining things, she thought turning to face the road ahead, dismissing an unsettled fidgeting in the back of her mind. *That cave has befuddled me. I'll be fine when I get back to the smoke and can think clearly again.*

She took the first train to Paddington even though she had to change at Plymouth. *Six-hours, barbaric – I could get to New York faster.* Engine problem on the first lap waved goodbye to the Plymouth connection. *This journey is turning into a nightmare.*

It gave her time to think. As she swayed awkwardly in sync with the slow rolling carriage, she took stock. All roads led to Hong Kong. Her Adam Lee investigations were going nowhere. She wanted to speak to the mastermind Warwick Mantel. She would give anything to interview Laura Wan Sun, the single woman on Pluto – as Julia liked to think of that brainstorming gathering. Silverman wanted her found. Silverman was a man used to getting what he wanted.

Could it be that Laura might provide the vital clue to the recent death and disappearance?

Be honest with yourself, Julia, a little voice piped up from deep inside. *Why do you really want to go to Hong Kong? Why go half way round the world in pursuit of Silverman's old flame?*

A tough question. *I don't know the answer.* She only knew her instincts, something in her gut, told her this was where she was destined to go.

She was struggling with doubts when her phone buzzed. A text arrived. It was from the gynae clinic. "*Sorry. Your test result has been delayed. Any queries please don't hesitate to contact.*"

She smiled, thinking of the handsome consultant. "Oh well, these things happen."

By the time the train crept slowly into Paddington at gone 11.30pm, she had made a decision. *There's nothing for it. I have to go to Hong Kong. How will I get Ludgate to agree?*

She would find a suitable moment at the Chinese Embassy. *He's bound to be in a good mood. I'll slip it past him after a few glasses.*

THE HALL CLOCK chimed midnight, as she entered her flat – 7am Hong Kong time. *Give it another half-an-hour.* She fired up her laptop and Googled Richard Welbeck, a former colleague, she had an idea worked for the Economic Journal on the island. *Please still be there*, she crossed the fingers of one hand. *Yes! And a number for him. Fantastic.*

She made a reviving cup of Earl Grey tea. Bang on 7.30am Hong Kong time, she called Richard.

"Julia Lighthorn here. Not too early for you, am I?"

"This is a surprise."

She imagined him grinning, as if he were sitting opposite her, as he had for years when they both worked at the Record.

"What time is it there?" he asked.

"After midnight. I was thinking of a trip to Hong Kong."

"Fabulous. You must stay with me. Long visit or short? Have you got a Visa?"

"No."

"Short then."

"I was thinking just a few days to check out developments. Looks interesting your end."

"Not from where I'm sitting. No one queuing outside our banks last time I looked."

"Ouch. How do I get a visa?"

"It takes time. You can come for three days as a tourist. I'd apply for a visa, in case you want to come back for longer. It'll be great to see you and catch up. Right now the rest of the world is watching London and New York in total bewilderment. I could do with an inside track. Make your arrangements. I'll meet you at the airport."

Next, she searched for Peak Bank, called the head office number and asked for Warwick Mantel. She didn't expect to be put straight through, but spoke to his secretary who advised her to arrange her trip and email dates.

"I must warn you, his diary's very full."

She booked a flight for late Monday, arriving Tuesday evening, Hong Kong time, and emailed the dates to Mantel's office. Then she closed her laptop, crossed fingers, shut both eyes, and whispered over and again.

"Please let me go, Andrew."

Suddenly, she was overwhelmed with the strains of the day and collapsed exhausted into bed. She fell asleep in a wink and a nod and dreamt of castles in the sea, mystical caves and shadows.

CHAPTER 15
7pm Friday August 6
Marylebone

INCONGRUOUS choice for the London home of the People's Republic of China, Julia thought, as she stared at the elegant facade of the palace, designed in the late 1700s, by the famous British architect Robert Adams. *Equally incongruous*, she smiled watching Andrew Ludgate approach in lounge suit rather than his normal tails, standard uniform for a banquet in the city. Julia had arrived early. It didn't pay to keep your editor waiting.

Ludgate greeted her with a smile and an appreciative twinkle in his eye.

"Red suits you," he said. "Colour of good luck in China."

He made no attempt at the cursory peck on the cheek professionals sometimes exchanged. Julia was relieved. He held out his arm to propel her forward.

Once inside, Georgian splendour quickly gave way to Chinese functionality. The entrance was packed with guests thronging to the main hall. As they walked through the crush, Ludgate pointed out various figures.

"See that guy over there, the one with the checked tie? That's David Ruff. He fronts up the massive Chinese-owned electric vehicle empire in Coventry. Makes all the London cabs."

"What's Lord Parr doing here?" Julia spotted the boss of a large merchant bank.

"Chinese have the biggest stake in that too."

They arrived at the table plan. "We're on different tables," he said.

Julia nodded, another name catching her eye. Simon Chang, of Chang Technology. Could this be Wo Chang's grandson? On another table she spotted Anthony Chang from Chang Deposits. She elbowed her way through a scrum of bodies to her table.

An attractive young man greeted her with a warm smile.

"Hello, seems we're sitting together," he offered her a hand. "My name's Zhang Yong. My London friends call me Ziggy. I teach at the School of Oriental and African studies."

"You don't look like an academic," Julia smiled as she shook hands, adding, "Julia Lighthorn…I'm a journalist."

On her other side stood a giant of a man, who introduced himself as He Len, director of a Chinese-owned IT firm, operating out of Hammersmith. His bulging eyes and thin lips reminded her of a hippopotamus.

With the party assembled, they sat and the entertainment began. A troupe of dancers parading banners and flags skipped in to a robust Chinese fanfare. Musicians followed behind, marching to the top of the room, where chairs awaited them. They sat. The melodies switched to a gentler zither sound.

"That's the fisherman's song at dusk," Ziggy whispered to her.

90

"Very pretty," she smiled back.

Music subsided, and the room burst in zealous applause. It lasted several minutes. When it showed no signs of dying, the Ambassador stood, bowed, and signalled for the room to hush. Silence descended and he began his speech, first welcoming his guests, then moving onto weightier matters. It was much as Julia anticipated – the phenomenal rise in economic and technological power of the People's Republic of China, the soaring numbers of overseas students in international capitals – nearly 200,000 in London. Finally, he spoke with passion about his nation's race against America to become the world's number one superpower.

"Powerful stuff," Ziggy muttered with a touch of cynicism, as the Ambassador sat down to yet more tumultuous applause.

"Very powerful indeed," boomed He Len, rising to his feet, throwing a furious glance at the younger man. Others soon joined the ovation, including an uncomfortable-looking Ziggy.

They sat as the food arrived. A selection of dishes were placed on vast lazy susans for guests to share in the Chinese custom. Julia spooned some chicken and vegetables into her bowl and pincered them into her mouth using chop sticks.

He Len began talking to her loudly. "No question, when it comes to technology, China is light years ahead of the US. We have worked hard to become supreme. My company is now worth £200 billion. Nothing in the US is bigger," he paused to shovel food greedily into his mouth.

Julia feigned interest, as she was professionally trained to do, while thinking, *What an odious man.*

He was off again. "We know how to encourage talent. We send our cleverest students abroad to study the most advanced techniques of other economies. Then we copy them, and push further, nothing will stop us," he reached for a vegetable dish, and emptied its entire contents into his bowl.

Julia swallowed, struggling to digest his cold-blooded pride in state-sponsored intellectual property theft.

Obscene, she thought, *not to mention criminal.*

"The problem with Western democracies is all they do is talk, talk, talk," He Len continued, a sneer fixed to his ugly mouth. "In China we say, we will do this and we do it. In the UK you say we will do this, and then you all sit around talking. You can't agree on anything, so nothing happens."

Julia had sat beside some obnoxious dinner guests in her time, but this guy scraped the bottom of the barrel. Her fixed smile was starting to hurt, so when she saw Andrew rise from his table, and head presumably for the boy's room, she too made her apologies and escaped. The restrooms were off a gallery, overlooking the banqueting hall. From a bay offering a bird's-eye view of the scene below, she watched He Len rise, presumably also in search of the restrooms. He didn't get far. Another man blocked his exit. From the expression on both faces, whatever they were discussing the exchange was far from amicable. The body language was unmistakable. The newcomer was angry, and became angrier still at He Len's arrogant dismissal. Tempers rose and he shoved He Len on the shoulder, who gesticulated rudely, but turned his back and walked away.

"Simon Chang and He Len," Andrew said walking up behind her.

"No love lost there," Julia said.

"Rival IT bosses. Probably a feud over some deal. How you getting on?" he asked.

"OK, but there's only so much non-stop propaganda you can take."

"Even when delivered with a smile," Andrew nodded. "Had to cut your piece today. Sorry. Nothing wrong with it. Just tight on space. What d'you think of the Ambassador's nephew?"

"The IT plutocrat?"

"No, Zhang Yong, very useful contact. Work it."

"Ziggy? Good grief I had no idea. He Len is a pain. Creepy."

"That's what I like about you, your rational sense of objectivity."

Sensing an opportunity, Julia ignored the dig, and decided to strike while the iron was hot.

"It's all very interesting though isn't it? China? The big news story. I'd like to go to Hong Kong. See the other side for myself."

"Have you gone mad?" his tone darkened. "What on earth are you talking about? How can you even think about leaving the country with the economy imploding and gutters filling with dead and missing bankers."

"I know – but it's a big financial centre. I got a lead from Silverman. A good lead about what's going on. There're some key players in Hong Kong I need to speak to."

Ludgate shook his head furiously. "If you disappear at a time like this, there will be consequences. Careers and reputations are forged in crisis. They can be broken, too."

She knew it was a serious warning. If she left a void others would fill it. Top of that list would be the vile Matthew Hopkins. There was nothing she could do about that right now.

She opened her mouth to respond, when commotion erupted at the far end of the room below. What looked like a dozen students, armed only with banners and ribbons, ran in from a side entrance and headed straight for the Ambassador.

It was hard to see exactly what was happening, because a storm of Chinese muscle fell upon the protesters and bundled them out as quickly as they arrived. An Aide of the Ambassador rose and clapped his hands. Dancers returned in joyful colour. Musicians struck up a lively traditional Chinese melody.

Andrew and Julia's gaze met, troubled. Neither spoke, their eyes said it all.

"When are you planning to leave?" he asked her calmly.

"In a few days. There's a flight late Monday arriving Tuesday."

"OK but keep the trip short. File while you're away. I'll have a piece a day. Leave this story to me..."

CHAPTER 16
Saturday August 7
Southwark

A TIGHT STORY about a kerfuffle in the Chinese Embassy during the Dragon Boat celebrations appeared below the fold on page nine the following morning, describing the event in muted tones, and noting a couple of intruders were intercepted. It said nothing about what happened to them. Technically, an embassy was foreign soil, so not subject to British justice.

Julia waited for Sunday morning's edition for further information. Propped up in bed enjoying her first coffee of the day, her eye caught a short piece buried down-page, some way back in the book. Four students were taken to St Thomas's hospital with injuries after a fracas in Marylebone on Friday night. She didn't need any help joining the dots.

Poor kids, Julia thought, pushing the newspaper to one side and getting out of bed.

She packed a small suitcase, and began counting down the hours before her trip East on Monday evening. With the time difference, she would arrive Tuesday evening Hong Kong time.

The sun streamed in through the window so she decided to go for a walk. She hadn't gone far when a Toyota Corolla shot like a rocket out of Pilgrimage Street, followed by a black

Mercedes. Tyres screeched as they chased up the A2. Julia, trained to run towards danger, broke into a trot.

They must be doing over 80, she thought, as the two cars tore towards Bricklayers Arms roundabout.

Next, she heard a God Almighty bang. *They must have crashed*, she thought, as the blast of what sounded like gunshot blistered the air.

She ran now towards the roundabout. When she got there, the Toyota was a crumpled wreck, and smoking. The driver slumped over the wheel with a bullet in his head. From a distance, he looked Chinese. The Mercedes gone.

A police car pulled up and started to block the traffic. An ambulance followed quickly.

Julia moved to speak to the police officer, but realised she would learn little this early and could be a hindrance. She went home and tuned into the television, for news of what had happened. Nothing. An hour later she walked down to the local police station in Borough High Street and asked the Duty Officer for news of the incident.

"Looks like some sort of chase down Great Dover Street. Toyota rammed on the roundabout. Driver shot dead," he said.

"Gang related?" she asked.

"Almost certainly."

She wrote a short story of yet another young life lost to gang violence in the heart of London, which she filed for the morning's edition.

"NICE STORY," Cody said, as he arrived for work the next morning, carrying two coffees.

"Good weekend?" Julia said, head down scouring the online editions of the Hong Kong newspapers – the South China Morning News, the Standard, the Hong Kong Economic Journal.

She looked up and smiled.

"Can't complain," he placed a coffee on her desk, before putting the other down on his own. He hung his coat on the back of his chair. "How was the embassy?"

"Entertaining is probably the best way to describe the evening. Let me finish this and I'll bring you up to speed. Getting anywhere with those accounts?"

"Still struggling."

"Here," Julia threw him a business card. "Old friend of mine – forensic accountant. Get him to take a look. By the way, could you apply for a full Chinese visa for me while I'm away?"

"Tad late isn't it? You're leaving tonight."

"Apparently, you're allowed three days without Visa. If I need to go back, I'll need a full Visa. Agencies sort it for you. Here. Could you give them a call?"

She threw a second card onto his desk. He put it to one side, and dialled the number of the forensic accountant, his face brightening at a voice at the other end.

Julia turned back to the Hong Kong press. She knew some of the content would be censored, but business journalism generally managed to fly under the radar.

The Economic Journal should be reliable, she thought.

Reading between the lines, all was far from well in the People's Republic of China. A so-called anti-corruption drive was underway on the mainland. Anyone the Party leaders felt threatened by were "disappeared". The Party Discipline Commission, behind the clampdown, acted outside the law and could seize individuals and hold them in secret locations, without charge. When they were ready to confess, they were handed over to the courts where the conviction rate was 100 per cent. Human rights activists were imprisoned. There were reports of torture. The Economic Journal had a story about the disappearance of the boss of a Hong Kong cotton trading company.

Her thoughts were distracted as Cody punched the air.

"Brilliant. He said he could meet for lunch."

"OK, but don't get excited. You'll be paying – or rather I will, so go easy."

Julia's phone rang. It was Chief Inspector Pitcher. How was her trip out West, and did she fancy a whirl on the river? He was going out on patrol with the River Police; would she like to join him? Might make a colour piece for her tatty rag?

Julia froze at his words. The Metropolitan Marine Unit had many functions, but was big in fishing bodies out of the murky water of the Thames.

Dear God, surely they aren't dredging for Chandler?

"There's been some suspicious traffic on the water," he said, as if reading her mind. "I want to take a look at some warehouses down by the sewerage pumping station. See you at the London Bridge jetty in fifteen minutes."

I can make it in ten, she thought, grabbing her coat.

A speed boat was waiting at the jetty. Pitcher greeted her with a wave, but kept his distance. She recognised most of the crew from Wapping Marine Station. They had helped her before with colour backgrounders.

A young officer she had never met walked towards her and handed her a life jacket. "You'll need this. You're the journalist aren't you? I'm PC Day from Soho."

Long way off your patch, Julia thought as she wriggled into a life vest. When it came to stepping into the high speed police craft, her legs froze. It was only a year since she had lost her lover Sandy to a tragedy on the seas. His body had been brought home in just such a police boat. Memories of what happened that dreadful night paralysed her.

"Come on, step lively," Pitcher grabbed her arm and propelled her into the vessel. As they both landed with a jump, he gave her an understanding smile, before resuming his normal devil-may-care persona. She knew he understood. He was with her, when she lost the man she loved to a watery grave.

The launch took off with a kick. Silverman's face rose before her – risking his life to save those in peril on the sea. *What a mystery that man is,* she thought as the wind lashed her face. Its icy bite dulled the pain of memory. They moved fast, the fastest shark on the river, whipping along the tide, dodging pleasure boats, and other traffic. They slowed as they approached the Night Rider steps leading to China Wharf, creating a powerful wash lashing the ancient stone walls. A crumpled skeleton of a once magnificent pier poked out of the water by the steps, which though narrow, steep, and open on one side, looked sturdy enough.

Pitcher was first to the top, his team hard on his heels. Julia followed, determined not to be left behind. Their target was a large Victorian warehouse, built like a prison in London brick. It stood proud and magnificent, four storeys high – five barred, braced, windows wide. It was a building she knew.

"It's the old print works, isn't it? Visited it years ago," Julia said to PC Day. For most of the last century it was owned by a consortium of newspapers and printed most of London's daily titles. When the industry modernised, and it was surplus to requirement, no one knew who owned it. A battle dragged on for years in the courts. With property prices along the river on a steep upward trajectory, no one was in any hurry to resolve the matter.

"If you say so," PC Day charged ahead.

Two officers carried bolt clippers. They snapped the lock and pulled the giant double-doors open wide, exposing a massive loading void, leading through to derelict machinery. A pack of rats scuttled in the dark. Julia choked on the stench of decay as she watched officers ducking and diving between the redundant printing presses, a sense of loss overwhelming her.

How I loved the thunderous rumble of those old presses, she thought.

"Nothing 'ere Gov," shouted one of the officers. Shrugs of shoulders and shakes of heads confirmed there was nothing significant to report.

"OK, you guys better get back." Pitcher disguised his disappointment. "Send someone down to make good the lock."

"Hang on," shouted PC Day. He raced up dilapidated rat-eaten stairs, shoes clattering on each step. "Mezzanine floor up here. Nothing though."

He waved down to them, then ran on. More echoing steps.

"You be careful up there," Pitcher bellowed.

"No, not here either," clatter clatter clatter. "No," he shouted again, his steps rattling around the derelict void as he race upwards. "Wait a minute there are boxes up here."

A pause. "Yep, it's all up here. Quite an arsenal. Two cases of machetes. Another of meat cleavers and a couple dozen hand guns."

"Good work PC Day," Pitcher shouted up to the top of the building, before turning to one of the senior officers. "Get forensics down here."

"What d'you know about the building?" Julia asked Pitcher, as she headed for the stairs

"No, you don't. It's not safe." He pulled her back. "And this is a scene of crime – out of bounds."

He looked at his watch. "Fancy a quick bite in the Mayflower? I missed breakfast."

"Don't you have things to do here?"

Pitcher shook his head. "Not right now. All as expected. Plans in place before we left." He spoke loudly for his men to hear. "My crack team will be able to manage fine."

"Will the Mayflower be open?" It was hardly gone 10am.

Pitcher threw her a quizzical look.

"I know, don't tell me," she said. "Everywhere in London is open to cook breakfast for the Metropolitan Police. Well, bully for you."

It turned out he was right. The landlord of the Mayflower was delighted to serve him. They chatted at the bar about coppers they both knew, now long retired, and crimes in which the river had played a central and dramatic role.

101

"What a chase your guys gave the IRA after they tried to bomb Battersea Bridge..." said the landlord.

"Remember when we caught the Romanians people-trafficking three wharfs up." Pitcher winked at Julia.

The landlord pulled a half and took a sip.

"Wouldn't it be lovely to go back to the quiet old days of the Krays? At least you knew where you were with them."

"And they were very good to their mothers," Julia couldn't resist. This was as much as she could bear, so she took her coffee to a table overlooking the river.

What's happening in London? she thought looking out across the water. She bit her lip. She was still shaken by the horrendous scene she had witnessed less than 24 hours ago. The landlord's voice dropped. She could no longer hear what they were discussing.

"What was that all about?" she asked, when Pitcher finally joined her, carrying his breakfast.

"Don't you worry your pretty little head."

"God you can be so patronising."

"Sun too strong? You must be burning here in the window, because you're so hot today."

"And you're so not," she slapped him down. "I hate you when you're like this."

He looked up and grinned. "You make a magnificent job of hiding it. Come on, cut me some slack. We've scored this morning."

He dipped white bread into his runny egg yolk. "Why didn't you call me yesterday?" he said, putting it into his mouth.

"Honestly? I think I was in a state of shock."

"You witnessed a murder."

"Pains me to say it though it does, gang violence and murder is something we have to live with in that post code. I left a full statement at Borough Station."

"Have it your own way. So tell me what you know about that warehouse?"

"Not too much. It was the old printing works for most of London. I used to be sent down here to deliver pages and changes as a rookie. That's over a decade ago now. Very valuable piece of land. The newspaper barons can't agree on how much their companies each invested back in the 1930s, so have argued in court for years. That's why it's one of the few warehouses not converted into flats."

"It's rented out today for storage."

"Sensible while they're trying to resolve the issue. Who's the tenant?"

"We've got the name of a company, but we can't get behind it."

"I can take a look if you like, but I'm guessing you have more powers of discovery than me."

Pitcher shrugged. "Powers yes. But resources?"

"Where did you get your tip? By the way, who was that young PC Day. He's not part of the usual Marine crew, is he?"

"Works in Soho. He's been helping me out with some inquiries."

"Is this to do with Adam Lee? I think the victim yesterday was Chinese. Where are you getting with Lee – and Chandler?"

He ignored her and concentrated on his breakfast.

"Isn't it time you started sharing?" she asked softly.

"What d' you think this is all about, if not sharing? If it's sharing you want, you go first. Adam Lee was a banker. You're the banking expert. What have you found out about his customers and clients?"

"I'm going to Hong Kong."

Pitcher dropped his knife and fork. They clattered on the white plate. He looked up. His face deadly serious.

"When?"

"Later tonight. Flying Heathrow at 10pm. Cathay Pacific."

"You be careful out there. It's a dangerous world, I can't protect you."

"Protect me? When have I ever needed your protection?"

"I'll remember that the next time you..."

"OK, OK." She raised both hands in surrender. He had a fair point. More than once he had saved her from mistakes.

"So you want to know what I know," he was serious now. "I know he came to London for some meetings in the City."

"Looking for money?"

"If you say so. He had other meetings and lunched in Soho, where sometime later he was brutally murdered."

"Do we know where he lunched or who with?"

"Not quite, or rather not entirely. We're working on it."

"We?"

"Like you, I have my contacts."

"Snouts, don't you call them?"

"I usually call them Sir or Madam and say please and thank you."

"Came across one of Chang's grandsons the other evening at the Chinese Embassy."

"Which one?"

"The IT one. The other's in banking, isn't he?"

"What was he like?"

"Didn't meet him. Looked OK. He had a blazing row with another character. Looked ugly."

"What are you doing in Hong Kong?"

"Tying up some loose ends. It's a big financial centre."

They both knew neither was being entirely honest with the other.

"I repeat. Be careful. These people are dangerous. Remember what they did to Lee."

"The people I'll be interviewing are respectable bankers, not criminals. Certainly not violent thugs."

"Come on Julia, wake up. Why d'you think Lee was murdered? Where's the easy money made these days? The big easy money? You of all people should know."

"Financial crime," she said, the awkward truth dawning.

"Money laundering, VAT fraud, internet, banking, benefit fraud. It's a multi-billion business. These are clever skilled operators."

"In London, or in Hong Kong?"

"Take your pick, but London's my only concern. Something big's stirring. Someone's angry."

"You think Lee was somehow involved in this?"

"His murder was more than a ritual killing. It was a warning."

"To a rival gang?"

"Perhaps. And now we have another Chinese body. We need to stop this before a wholescale war breaks out on the streets of London."

"Yesterday? You think that was connected?"

"Tit for tat," he tapped his nose.

"Revenge for Lee. I still don't see how reputable bankers can be involved with criminal thugs."

Pitcher raised his eyebrows.

"Maybe they're not. Maybe Lee just invested a lot of money on someone's behalf, who's down in the mouth about where the markets moved. Some of these guys are seriously wealthy. A 30 or 40 per cent hit on their portfolios will amount to the loss of a great deal of money. Someone might be taking this all very personally."

"Scary stuff."

"And right out of your league. Have a good trip. By all means nose round. But for once listen to your friendly Inspector. Be careful."

CHAPTER 17

A year earlier - August 6 2006
Hong Kong

LAURA WAN SUN scrubbed and scrubbed her hands with anti-bacterial hand wash and water for a full four minutes, rubbing palm against palm, left palm against the back of her right hand and vice versa. She interlaced her fingers and kept on rubbing. When there was nothing left to rub, she rinsed and dried using a paper towel.

Textbook method for killing germs. Yet the textbooks couldn't help when it came to watching five-year-old Ai choke to death. Laura moved from the sink in the corner of her small office to the fridge and took out an ice-cold bottle of water. She leant against the wall and glugged with the thirst of the parched. The whirring of the air conditioning unit drummed a background score to the painful scene she reran in her mind's eye.

"If only we hadn't gone to visit my sister over the border," Ai's mother had wailed. "If only she didn't live in a remote village. If only we hadn't visited the wet markets."

Laura's life was full of "if onlys". *If only people didn't get sick. If only Governments didn't lie. If only medicine could cure all diseases. If only everyone could afford the best medical care. If only sweet five-year-old girls like Ai didn't die. Ai meant love. Love shouldn't die.*

She gazed at the letter propped up on her desk. It would have to be opened. She stretched forward, and reached for it, twisting it in her fingers. She slit the seal as the door pushed ajar and her friend and fellow children's doctor, Kathy, entered.

"Are you OK?" Kathy asked. "I'm sorry it was so brutal. Vicious way to die."

"She couldn't breathe, Kathy. I've always hated that sound of someone in the last throws, desperately gasping for breath. She was such a pretty little thing."

"She'd not long returned from Guangdong? We'll never contain this dreadful illness unless the Government comes clean."

"The Government says it urgently needs doctors." Laura waved the letter at her friend.

"Oh no Laura, you must be joking," Kathy stepped towards her and snatched the letter from her hand. "You can't believe a word the officials say."

"They say it's a small outbreak," Laura shrugged.

"A handful of cases? Then why do they need doctors? What when you get there? You're Anglo-Chinese, from Hong Kong. Two things Beijing hates."

"The Chinese people don't hate us. They are kind and patient. I don't recall the Hippocratic oath pledging to only treat people who like us."

"When did you apply?" Kathy furiously dead-headed the orchid on Laura's desk.

"Kathy," her friend put out a calming hand to stop her. "A week ago, when the cases started coming in. We need to get to the source of the outbreak. Unless we deal with the source, we're only treating the symptoms."

"Don't be foolish Laura. Think they'll let you anywhere near the truth?"

Laura smiled kindly. "What I know is, I can't stay here and watch more innocent children like Ai die such a disgusting death. We need proper data and information. That's the only way we'll win."

"That may be so," Kathy slammed her hand against the wall. "But the risks are high. You could catch the disease yourself with no one to look after you. The local community could be hostile. You could end up quarantined for months. Maybe years. If you find the root, do you honestly believe you'll be allowed to come back to Hong Kong and tell the world about it? More likely, you'll be thrown into jail. You think the Communists will want news like that broadcast to the world? To even think about going is reckless, when doctors like you are in such short supply."

Laura shook her head. "Surely, you know me better than that," her voice softened. "I never take risks."

"Oh yes you do. What about your days in high finance?"

"Ouch, below the belt. I left that world a long time ago, precisely because my colleagues planned a gamble too far. Sometimes there's no alternative. You have to take a calculated risk. This letter's asking me to travel to Guangzhou next week."

"We can't afford to lose you," Kathy repeated, frustration furrowing her brow. "The hospital won't release you. They won't let you go."

"They will, if the Party asks them," Laura stretched to the calendar on the wall, and tore out the next few pages. "It's true, I hadn't expected to go so quickly. But the sooner I go the speedier my return."

"No, no, no, no, no," Kathy banged the desk with feeling. "I don't trust them. You're risking your future on what? People disappear Laura. You must be crazy."

There was an awkward silence.

When it broke, Laura said, "You've been such a good friend to me. Think how happy we'll all be when I return, with lots more information and experience about fighting this dreadful killer."

"There must be another way," Kathy stared at her friend, eyes brimming with anguish.

"Give me your blessing. Let me do it for Ai?"

CHAPTER 18
5pm Tuesday August 10
Hong Kong

EVENING WAS BREWING a dank mist as Julia drifted across the water from Hong Kong Island to Kowloon. Lights from mega towers were already glistening against the dusk. *What a strange mysterious world I'm entering*, she thought, as she looked back at her friend and former colleague. He hadn't changed – still the same cheeky smile hiding a razor-sharp mind.

"Is it what you expected?" Richard grinned.

"I don't know what I expected. This is breath-taking, dreamy," she paced back and forth across the deck of the Star Ferry, drinking in the beauty of Victoria Harbour. "It's magnificent."

"Not even a dot on a map three hundred years ago," Richard said, his brown hair rippling in a warm breeze. "Look at it now. One of the richest metropolises in the world."

"Despite the ravages of war."

"Phenomenal ability to bounce back. I'll take you out to the port before you go. You'll never see more shipping in your life. The trade coming in and out of China will blow your mind."

She leant against the wooden bow. "Right now, I'd settle for some hot strong coffee."

"Tired?

"Not too bad."

The flight was a manageable twelve hours, but the seven-hour time difference was taking its toll.

"Any plans for tomorrow?" Richard turned his face into the warm wind.

"Lots. D'you have any contacts in the medical world? Any hospitals or charities?" She noticed a couple of fellow passengers wearing white masks, which she always associated with Asian travellers. Inscrutable.

He raised questioning eyebrows. "I thought you were here to write about the markets?"

"I am, and to dig around Adam Lee."

"The banker found dead in Soho?"

"What's the word here about Lee and his sudden death?"

"Uncomfortable, that's the only word that springs to mind. With everything else going on…"

When the Star Ferry docked, they joined the crush spilling off, then pushed their way through the crowds on Kowloon harbour, gathering on the Tsim Sha Tsui waterfront for the lightshows and other evening entertainments. Richard led the way down an arrow straight road, lined with glitzy high-end retail palaces.

"Who needs so many vast stores? Can they all survive?"

"Oh yes," Richard nodded. "Shopping's a national sport in this part of Asia."

Beyond and behind the shopping spreads were ugly towers where ordinary families lived. They reached Richard's flat on the 25th floor of a soviet-style block after about twenty minutes. It was small, but comfortable.

Julia collapsed on a sofa. "I'm trying to track down a woman called Laura Wan Sun. She works as a doctor here. I've no idea where."

"I could call a couple of people for you," Richard handed her a mug of hot jasmine tea.

"Thanks, that would be great. Meanwhile, I need to talk to the people at First State Bank. I also have an interview with Warwick Mantel."

"At Peak?"

She nodded. "What d'you know about First State Bank?"

"Nothing I could put into print," he said, sitting opposite her. "Everyone knows First State. Remember BCCI that went bust?"

"Bank of crooks and cocaine, we used to call them."

"Exactly, but the Bank of England happily gave it a thumbs up for years."

"It was a different world back then," Julia narrowed her eyes, remembering past battles.

"First State operates much the same way. Deals with poor Chinese customers, from areas where they struggle to get a bank account."

"That's the front?"

"In the background, powerful customers call the shots."

"Money-laundering?"

"Almost certainly," he nodded again. "Dodgy developments."

"Bankrolling criminals?"

"Wouldn't be surprised. You need money to buy people, premises, stock and equipment, whatever kind of business you're in."

"Watchdogs?"

"That's the strange thing. They gave First State a wide berth."

"Could someone be protecting the bank?"

"It's possible."

"Or afraid?"

"That too."

"Could the Chinese Government be involved at some level?"

"Seems unlikely. Remember First State is a Hong Kong Bank. Special Administrational Region."

"Local gangsters then?"

Richard bit his lip.

"There are rumours of Triad involvement, but don't get too excited. Everything in Hong Kong has rumour of Triad connection," he said, standing.

"Triads? Not nice people?"

"Nice? Oh I think they're nice enough…" Richard smiled at her, "…if you stay out of their way. Cross them and they are violent and vicious, with a particularly mean streak in revenge."

"Crime of choice?"

"Well, they ran the heroin trade, and pretty much all the gambling joints on Macau. More than that..." he shrugged his shoulders. "I'd better get us something to eat, before we give ourselves nightmares."

Julia laughed. "Don't worry I'll sleep soundly tonight."

RICHARD returned with some noodles, but Julia found she was past eating. Conversation became hard work as weariness overwhelmed her.

"Can't think straight."

"You need to sleep." He took the half-empty bowl from her. "Take my bed. I'll sleep on the bed settee."

Before she hit the sack, Richard gave her a map of the city, and pointed out her way back to Star Ferry. Then he showed her how to get to the Foreign Correspondents' Club, in Lower Albert Road.

"This'll be a useful base for you to work out of while in town. You'll always find someone to help you if I'm not around. Strictly members only, but I'll arrange temporary membership for you."

They agreed, unless events intervened, to meet there for a late supper the following evening.

As she nodded off, Julia found herself thinking of her meeting with Warwick Mantel the next day. She had emailed his office details of her trip and suggested a time, which had not yet been confirmed. What would she ask him? What did he know about Adam Lee and First State? Had she heard from Stephen Chandler? What was his view of the meltdown in the markets? Was Peak robust and would contagion spread to Hong Kong?

RICHARD had already left when Julia woke the next morning. She opened her eyes to see a note on the table by her bedside. Four words *turn on the news.*

She fired up her VPN link to circumvent Chinese internet walls. For a moment, she couldn't take in what she was reading. While she was sleeping, Pendle Thrift, was rescued by the Government. Founded by anti-slavery Quakers, it was now owned by the British taxpayer. A number of white knights had attempted takeover during recent troubled weeks. All bids collapsed, once the books were opened. Toxic. Politicians barely caught their breath, when Martin's Bank, one of the big four, announced it would be merging with S&H, Britain's giant lender. Another rescue. Markets were in spasms of paralysis, but this time no dead cats bounced. This was Armageddon. The Chancellor and the Bank of England made bold statements aimed at calming worried investors. No one believed them anymore. Share prices continued burning.

Chaos leaked morbidly from the US. Fannie Mae and Freddie Mac, government-backed agencies guaranteeing the US mortgage market, announced they were bust. Federal Reserve pledged to pump more than $100 million into the broken system.

"Fuck, Fuck, Fuck!" Julia cursed. The biggest story of her career had just broken, and she was on the wrong side of the world.

116

CHAPTER 19
6am Wednesday August 11
Hong Kong Island

SCOFIELD CRISP was the first customer of the day, when he entered Cafe Gray Deluxe at the Upper House Hotel – a prominent haunt for business executives. He ordered coffee, and sipped it slowly as he waited for Warwick Mantel.

Certain conversations are more comfortable outside the office, Crisp thought.

This Californian son of Silicon Valley was the oldest of those who had gathered at that fateful meeting at Sharks Bay. Then 30, he could have been a father figure – a role he was singularly unsuited for. A steadying pair of hands, he was not. He started out in foreign exchange, a high-voltage jungle of fortunes made or lost in a day. At Peak, he moved into marketing. His job was to sell. He loved new products and did everything he could to encourage the young whiz kids to design ever more fanciful tricks and tools. Did he understand what they were doing? Hell no. It wasn't his job to.

Finance was a young man's game. Rightly so. Catch them early before they understand the danger or risk, or lived to see its consequences. He only advised caution, when he knew it wouldn't sell. Memories were short. A half-life in this business might stretch to three years, if you were lucky.

Had they been lucky? Silverman? Lee? Chandler? Laura? Oh yes. Incredibly lucky. They were well-paid for their work at Peak. More than the average Joe would earn in a life-time. As far as he could see, they got out with their hands clean. Silverman made a fortune with his fund company. Then Silverman was always going to make the Fortune 500. Formidably bright, with a pristine pedigree. Old man in money – the business in his DNA. Laura Wan Sun had an attack of conscience. Dropped out. Moved into fixing bodies instead of fixing futures. He bumped into her occasionally in town. Chandler was more of a mystery. Clever by God. The creative genius of the team, for sure. The man from Pluto. But he didn't understand the psychology of markets, nor how humans interact. Why should he? He was just a kid. They all were. You can't learn these things living through rising bull markets. Only those who survive catastrophic crashes learn the lessons and bear the scars. Then there was Lee, the true child of this high-octane pleasure island – a place to make as much money as quickly as possible, while keeping a keen eye on an escape route. Lee's destiny lay in a bullet in the back from the time he began trading football cards in the playground of St Paul's, one of the oldest schools in Hong Kong. He came from a long line of wheeler dealers. His family not only survived the Japanese invasion and occupation, but thrived. No one knew when the Lees first arrived in Hong Kong. Probably part of the mass migration during the Taiping Rebellion. Like all great entrepreneurs they grew until they had a finger in almost every pie from shipbuilding to plastics. The Lee empire built the first gambling Mecca in Macau. Rumour had it they were first into opium too, but then who with money and sense wasn't back in the day? Suffice to say, Adam was not the first Lee found dead in a back street.

Scofield's thoughts were interrupted by the arrival of Warwick Mantel, a tall man, with a thick crown of dark hair, peppered with silver. He looked like a surgeon, a man you could trust. Never had appearance and reality been at such odds.

"Good to see you, Scofield," Mantel sat, oozing charm and charisma. He had been off island for a few days. It was more than a week since they last met.

Scofield nodded and smiled a weak welcome. His eye went straight to the orchid the older man always wore in his breast pocket. A different species each day. Today he wore pink – the symbol of joy.

"Good to be back in the office?" Crisp asked. A waiter brought coffee, orange juice and croissants to the table.

"What's so important you wanted to meet me here for breakfast, with chaos breaking out at home?" Mantel poured himself a black coffee.

"UK still home?" Scofield raised a cynical eyebrow, before continuing, "I wanted to see you before the interview with the journalist. I need to know how far you plan to go with her."

"You're my marketing guy. That's what I pay you for. We don't yet know what exactly she's interested in. She implied..."

"Come all this way at a time like this, just for a chat about the markets? Surely you don't buy that?"

"Why not? Biggest crisis in a life-time."

"Not here there isn't. Lee was found dead on her patch. Someone's pushing her to get to the bottom of what happened."

"How can we help with that?" Mantel paused as the waiter came to take their order. Crisp declined to eat. Mantel chose smoked salmon and scrambled egg.

"If you remember, I asked you to..." Mantel stopped as the waiter returned with plates. He glanced at Crisp from the side of his eyes. "Any progress?"

"Beyond the obvious you mean? Gossip is growing daily. First State was a dung heap. Money-laundering, dodgy loans. Word is — it goes way beyond that."

"Tell me something I don't know." Mantel gave a strange laugh.

Crisp hesitated. He thought he saw a glint flick across his boss's eyes. It disappeared in an instance.

"Two stories doing the rounds. One – it's a Triad front, a money printing machine to fund their businesses." Crisp looked around to make sure he was not overheard. "Lee's family were always..."

Mantel reached for his napkin and wiped his mouth.

"I know all about that," he waved his hand dismissively. "First State had some rich investors from mainland China, too. Very powerful shareholders. The Communist Party wouldn't tolerate any dealings with Triads."

"You're living in the past. Times change. And look at State's share price. A lot of people will lose a great deal of money before this fiasco is over."

"Aren't we jumping guns here?" Mantel leant back in his chair and spread powerful palms across the table. "Would anyone kill over a share price collapse?"

"They kill over loss of face. If someone looks at them in a way they don't like. Warwick we're talking about murderous thugs who call in Red Pole and his vicious fighters over nothing. Not to mention a ruthless regime at the top of the Communist Party."

Mantel was silent for a few moments. He stretched slowly across the table and calmly reached for some toast, which he buttered deliberately.

"Lee, State..." he flicked a hand as if swatting a fly. "None of this is our problem. Lee died on the streets of London."

"But his murder must have been planned here on Hong Kong Island. You must agree?" Crisp involuntarily clenched a fist.

Mantel ignored him. "You see this journalist, make up some excuse for me. Redirect all her questions back home. Steer her away from Hong Kong, and kill any connection with Peak. Tell her Lee only worked here in a minor capacity years ago. We've enough problems to concentrate on."

121

CHAPTER 20
7.30am Wednesday August 11
Kowloon

JULIA SAT WITH her head in her hands, trying to imagine the scenes at home, as banks and share prices tumbled. *So much for an end to boom and bust*, she cursed. She felt sick – until her inner dynamo kicked in. *Come on, move forward, what's done is done,* a little voice whispered. She turned to her emails. One from Ludgate screamed from the top of her Inbox, ordering her home immediately. It came as no surprise. Smacked between the eyes by the morning's news, Julia was under no illusions – her trip would be cut short. Another email jumped out confirming an interview with Warwick Mantel at 9am at Peak's offices on Hong Kong Island. She decided to ignore the first and get ready for the second. Now she was here, she would stay a day or two whatever happened and face Ludgate's fire on her return – but she would have to work fast.

The sun burnt down with a terrifying heat from a cloudless blue sky as she left the comfort of Richard's air-conditioned flat and headed for the ferry.

Huckleberry Finn, she thought, *it's like stepping fully-clothed into a sauna. Where are my sun-glasses?* She found them at the bottom of her bag and put them on. Searing heat sucked oxygen from the atmosphere. Julia's chest tightened, a trickle of sweat slithering down her back. Her eye was drawn to locals sheltering from the bleaching sun under umbrellas.

Missed a trick there, she thought.

She queued at the Star Ferry terminus for a crossing, and before long was sailing towards her interview with Mantel. She picked a seat in the shade with a 360-degree view. Mountains ringed the harbour, bursting with geological arrogance, surely the inspiration for the city's architecture, which sweated hubris. Nerves may have been jittery in the run up to the handover, but its towers of glass and steel boasted of great wealth and confidence.

Julia spotted Peak Bank's offices, standing proud in its showcase position, as the ferry glided effortlessly towards the shore opposite. She had done her homework and knew, though Peak was one of the island's original founder banks, today's modern building, was the work of British architect Norman Foster. Many of its components were forged half-a-world away by UK companies, then shipped thousands of miles across treacherous seas.

Five minutes later she was stepping inside, refreshed by an icy blast. Her rib-cage swelled. *Great I can breathe again*, she thought, wiping sticky goo from the back of her neck.

"Take a seat please," a Receptionist pointed to a waiting area. "I'll let his Secretary know you're here."

Julia sank deep into a soft leather sofa, happy for a chance to cool before the interview. She took a notebook and pen from her bag in readiness. A Hong Kong Economic Journal faced her on a glass and chrome table. She smiled to see

Richard's by-line blazed across the front page. Relaxed as he appeared at the airport last night, earlier he was busy. She turned from the headlines and peered out the glass frontage, watching boats, and river traffic flowing past. She noticed a few individuals wearing the white half-face masks.

Next she reached for the Financial Times' Hong Kong edition, to catch up with developments at home. Political rows had erupted in parliament over the scale of support the banks would require. Jobs were beginning to shake out. It all looked ugly.

A shadow fell across the pink page. She looked up to see a tall figure looming over her.

"Ms Lighthorn, I'm Scofield Crisp. I'm afraid Mr Mantel's been called away to a meeting with Mr Yang, our Chief Regulator. Difficult time." He raised his eyebrows, inviting her to agree. "He asked me to handle your interview on his behalf."

Julia took a deep breath. *I've come half-way round the world for this interview. How dare Mantel off-load me onto this minion with a Californian accent?*

She seethed inwardly at the insult, but had little option than to follow the American to the elevator, as he called it. Only when she sat opposite him at his desk on the 44th floor, did she let rip.

"I've travelled a very long way for this interview. I wish no disrespect, but your views, on anything very much, do not interest me, I'm afraid. Not one iota."

"Never talk to the monkey when you can..."

"Your words not mine," she interrupted. "When I arrange an interview I expect the other party to do me and my newspaper the courtesy of showing."

"Hardly a binding contract," he grinned a mock apology, adding, "I believe you were warned he would be busy."

"For pity sake, the world's going to hell in a hand cart," she threw her notebook down with a thud on his desk. "We're all busy."

"I get it," he reached across the desk and pushed the notebook back towards her. "But situations change. Let's be sensible. You can speak to me, or you can fly home again without an interview. Then your journey, well, a complete waste of time."

He's right. Julia thought. *Ambushed, hook, line and sinker. No time to reschedule with Ludgate breathing down my neck. I'll have to salvage something. If I remember, wasn't Crisp one of the original Golden Boys? Where to begin?*

Crisp pre-empted her, with a warm smile. "Let's try and start again. You're interested in markets. We don't believe Peak's in any way exposed to the toxic investments corroding so many other balance sheets. Have you truly come so far for me to tell you that?"

"You mean toxic instruments you invented which poisoned the entire global financial system," she went straight for the jugular.

"I invented toxic instruments did I?" he laughed. "Goodness me, I must have missed that."

125

"I've spoken to Patrick Silverman," she continued. "I know what went on at that fateful weekend in the West Country all those years ago."

"Ah, how is Patrick?"

"Faring better than most of the participants at that brainstorming event."

"Perhaps," he said, quietly.

"Have you heard from Stephen Chandler?"

"Ah, Stevie, good bloke, I think you Brits say. Look, I'm sorry to disappoint, but I honestly don't remember much about that weekend. It was freezing cold, an almighty storm crashing overhead most of the time. I seem to recall we learnt afterwards, a couple of boats were lost."

She flinched at these words. "So you weren't part of the brainstorming sessions?"

"I'm the marketing guy. I was there to advise on the saleability of whatever the rocket scientists came up with."

"And you could sell it?"

"Read your history."

"Are you ever afraid, Mr Crisp?"

"Afraid, of what?"

"Ominous clouds. Hong Kong isn't quite the safe comfortable home it once was."

"Tell that to the prisoners of Stanley Jail, or the victims of cholera. You've been reading too many historical romances. The colonies were never safe, comfortable places. They were amoral, brutal, corrupt and at times extremely dangerous. Count the grave stones. Death rates from tropical diseases were high, rebellion and invasion constant threats."

"And yet they came. Why do you wonder?"

"Because the alternative was that cold, wet, grey, class-ridden place you Brits call home. Even after the hardships of the war, many opted to stay here, rather than return to a bombed out Britain, with its dreary rations."

He leaned forward on his elbows, stretching towards her across the desk. "But it was even more than that. Hong Kong has always promised a life of ..."

"Adventure?"

"Opportunity. To live free of boundaries, in the fast lane – a life full of colour. To pursue the dream of wealth...to be different."

"Is that what keeps you here?"

"Me? No. California's neither grey nor cold and the dream of wealth can be pursued in my own back yard. Some of the greatest fortunes have been spun there in the sand."

"Is that where you're headed next?"

"I'm not here for good necessarily. For the time being, it suits me to stay. I'm not blind. The Chinese behemoth is stirring. Things could go either way. For the time being, they need us to create wealth."

"Money moves in cycles. Cycles are something the Communists have difficulties with. What happens when it next turns to destruction?"

"I'm guessing it already has," he gazed directly into Julia's eyes. "Aren't you? It's more complicated than that. Don't forget the trade winds. From April to October the South-Westerlies make easy passage through the South China Sea for ships coming from the West. From November the reciprocal North-Easterlies blow them home again."

"The winds must be less important now we have satellite navigation?"

The more they talked the more she liked Crisp, just as she had liked Chandler and Silverman.

"China's building huge new mega ports elsewhere on the mainland. Once these flourish, won't Hong Kong's day in the sun be over."

Scofield shrugged.

"What d'you know about Adam Lee?" Julia twisted the knife.

"I can't help you with Lee. I can tell you our banks are built on rock, apart from the odd suspect operation. Hong Kong's a survivor. It will adapt and flourish. This storm will not destroy us."

"Suspect operation? You mean First State?"

"I'm saying nothing. Hey, I like you. I'd like us to be friends. Take this," he handed her a card. "I'd hate you to go home empty-handed. It's my contact at the city's fraud squad. Mention my name. He'll be happy to help a prestigious London journalist."

"You worked with Adam Lee?"

Scofield shook his head.

"Not me. Not in any meaningful way. The truth is I don't know the man. The only time I met him was at that jolly in Cornwall. Not that it was all that jolly. It says much for the Brits that their idea of a sun-kissed vacation is a craggy windswept outpost jutting into the Atlantic."

128

"You know he's dead?"

"Of course. Surely the answer to that must lie in London. That's where the crime occurred."

"What d'you know of his family...his background?"

"I'll not speak ill of those who've passed. Ask your colleagues in the local press – or maybe look through their archives."

"I see. Famous – good or ill?"

"It's complicated. Large family. Won't be hard to track down."

"What about Laura Wan Sun?"

He reached for a paper clip and twisted it between his index and second finger.

"Dear Laura. Sweet kid. Didn't have the balls for this business. Came back to Hong Kong you know? Works in a hospital somewhere on the island. Her family were doctors, but they died young. Not sure what happened. Her grandparents brought her up. Grandfather was an English missionary and her grandmother a Chinese doctor. They ran a mission amid the Godowns after the war. Hong Kong has a great system of health care now, but not always so. Took time to eradicate poverty and disease, particularly in the slums by the water."

"Is she still at the hospital?"

"I used to run into her from time to time," he shrugged. "Haven't seen her for while."

"You didn't answer my question."

"Which one?"

"About being afraid. Businessmen are disappearing in strange circumstances every week."

"Not really. It's all largely exaggerated. They turn up again. The Chinese do things differently that's all."

"Not all of them. They don't all come back."

He looked away, playing with his solid gold cufflinks.

"As I say, I'm not necessarily here forever."

CHAPTER 21
Wednesday August 11
Hong Kong Island

SMOOTH OPERATOR, Julia thought, settling back in the taxi. The clock was ticking fast. S*o much to do – so little time.* The air-con blasting full tilt was fighting a losing battle against the Hong Kong heat. The taxi twisted through the helter-skelter streets up the mountainous metropolis, where life was lived on so many different levels. Her shirt stuck to her back. She sat forward, tugging the cotton free. Out the window was a sign for Lower Albert Street. Buildings flashed past, testament to the former Empire and her Colonies.

It must be like this in cities all over the world, Julia thought. *Vestiges of a past regime - the things we left behind.* Prisons, law courts, police headquarters, customs offices and barracks. All now controlled by new masters. She passed the Department for Sewerage, once a magnificent classical facade.

The Chinese had to go one step further and rub our noses in it. Who can blame them?

One building evaded their clutches - the Foreign Correspondents' Club. The taxi pulled up outside the Edwardian colonial frontage. The bar, a stage post for journos from all over the old Empire and East Asia, doing what they always did, right under Beijing's nose. She paid the cabbie and stepped out into the Hong Kong heat.

Not my true style, she thought, *I'm not the clubbable type, but this far from base I couldn't ask for a better support network.*

Security staff on the door directed her to the Reception. "This is amazing," she said as she stepped inside, grinning from ear to ear.

"We like to think so," a woman behind the Reception desk smiled warmly. "Welcome. Are you a member?"

Oh yes, I belong here, Julia thought, as she explained she was a visiting London journalist, and believed a colleague had arranged temporary membership for her. Richard had been as good as his word.

"The bar is through there, and off at a side, a room you can work in – telephone lines, check emails and so forth," the Receptionist pointed the way through.

"This is remarkable," Julia said as she entered the bar, and found herself in a slightly less smoky version of the Jamaica wine bar, in St Michaels Alley, off Cornhill. The likeness was uncanny. The bar lined with heavy wood – same tables and bar stools, even the same ceiling fans, though these whirred energetically.

Built by the same people that built the City of London, Julia mused.

Same cartoons, same caricatures gawped from frames on the walls, front covers of the same magazines - the Economist, Spectator and Times.

Different subjects though. This satire twisted knives and drew blood over the betrayal of Hong Kong.

How I've dreamed of this place. The Hong Kong Foreign Correspondents' Club had filled Julia's imagination since she was young and read about turmoil in Asia and human rights abuses. She was humbled by those heroes, who daily risked their lives to record the Japanese invasion, rise of Mao Zedong, and the Vietnam War. They shone powerful spotlights through chaos and suffering.

She walked through the bar to the working area, found a seat, fired up her laptop and checked email, bracing herself for another deluge from Ludgate. *Nothing. Of course it's the middle of the night back in London.* Richard had emailed with a potential name and number for tracking down Laura Wan Sun.

What a star. A pal on the health desk called round his contacts and came up with this suggestion.

"Brilliant!" Typing fast she emailed back. "One more favour? Do you have a crime correspondent? If so, can you ask about the Lee family?"

Crime correspondent! O*n the Economic Journal – I don't think so.*

She twisted between her index and second finger the card Crisp had given her for Hong Kong's top fraud man.

"Tick-tock, the clock is ticking," she muttered, dialling the number for Michael Chen, Chief Fraud Investigator. It clicked through to an answer machine. She left a message.

Switching back to Richard's email, she began to dial the number for a doctor named Tsim Koon Lan. Half-way through dialling, she stopped.

An uneasy misgiving checked her.

What has this Chinese doctor Laura got to do with me?

Chasing her, as Silverman wanted, could be harassment.

133

I simply don't have time for this. If he's pursuing an old flame, he can get a private detective to do his dirty work.

She sat motionless for a few moments, torn by what to do next. Against her better judgment, she began to dial the number again.

A pleasant voice answered at the other end. "Hello, Dr Kathy here."

"Dr Kathy? I'm looking for Dr Tssss..." she stumbled over the Chinese name.

"That's me, please call me Kathy."

"Hello, you won't know me, I'm a London journalist, Julia Lighthorn, visiting Hong Kong. A friend asked me to look up a doctor, Laura Wan Sun, while I'm here. A colleague suggested I give you a ring. Can you help me to track Laura down?"

There was a pause at the other end of the line.

"Laura's a great friend of mine," came a cautious reply. "We work together at the Duchess of Kent Children's Hospital in Sandy Bay."

"Fantastic. D'you have a number for her?"

The voice hesitated again. Julia waited.

"I'm off duty until this evening. I was planning to take a walk in the Botanical Gardens. Would you care to join me? You should see them while you're here. Where are you staying?"

"I'm at the Foreign Correspondents' Club right now."

"The gardens are nearby – a short walk. Shall we say 11am, by the King George the Sixth statue? You'll find it easily."

Julia collected her things and set off. The gardens may be a short walk, indeed she could see them towering above from the door of the club, but the climb up, in the humid, blistering heat,

134

was exhausting. She reached the outer rim soon enough, but this jungle in the sky just kept soaring.

What a crazy weird city, she thought as a heady aroma of exotic plants, palms and shrubs burst all around. Then a screwball cacophony of chattering, laughing and screaming tumbled down towards her. *Huckleberry Finn, what in heaven's name is that noise?* she wondered. *Gorillas in a city centre garden?*

She passed a map which highlighted directions to King George.

"And there he is," she spoke out loud. "Bizarre." She gazed mystified at this quintessentially English King, complete with crown, dressed in all his coronation regalia, amid a jungle of exotic Asian foliage. *In all this tropical heat too.*

"At least it isn't Queen Victoria," she said to herself, swallowing a chuckle.

"Oh, we have one of those too."

Julia jumped slightly and turned to see a beautiful Chinese woman, probably in her 30s. "Hello, I'm Kathy. Hope I didn't startle you," she held out a friendly hand. Julia noticed how delicate it looked, and perfectly manicured.

"No, no, absolutely not. I'm so pleased to meet you Dr..."

"Call me Kathy." She was tall by Chinese standards, slim, and extremely elegant, with startling dark eyes. A warm smile lit up her face. "Shall we walk for a while? Did you know Laura in London?"

They headed in the direction of the chattering gorillas.

"No, I didn't. I'm writing about the financial crisis in general. Some of the people I'm interested in worked with her."

"Ah – her time at Peak."

135

Julia nodded. "Maybe I'm barking up the wrong tree, but I've been told she could be a useful source. Maybe she has nothing to tell me. If I could just locate her I could extinguish her from my research."

They had reached the zoological section of the park. Julia was able to admire what turned out not to be gorillas, but De Brazza's monkeys. Up close, they were noisy, mischievous devils, swinging powerfully around large cages like athletes or male dancers. Their random dynamic moves created a breathtaking ballet – a joy to watch.

"Just like the alpha beasts of the financial jungle," Julia couldn't resist.

"If you say so." Kathy smiled.

They stood watching, then walked on, past long-tailed lemurs, sloths with hideous faces, meercats. They exchanged smiles as a toddler tried to squeeze her hand, unsuccessfully, through a cage to pat a turtle.

Eventually they came to an elegant fountain, spraying cooling jets. "Let's sit for a bit," Kathy said.

"I needed this," Julia tilted her face into the chilling mist.

"It's a long way to come for a chat about finance."

"You're not the first person to say that."

Kathy twisted nervously scouring the other visitors. No one was close – too early in the day. A mother with two small children paddled in the fountain. An elderly woman several benches away fed some birds. A park keeper was clearing leaves. Julia thought of Silverman, and the cave. *What is everyone so afraid of?*

Happy no one was close enough to hear, Kathy continued, "Julia I am so sorry to have to tell you, I've no idea where Laura is. Some of us are very worried about her."

This is not what I want to hear, Julia swallowed.

"What do you know about bird flu?" Kathy asked.

"There are reports from time to time. We live in terror of a killer epidemic for a couple of weeks, but nothing happens, so we move on."

"We're not so lucky here. In poor rural communities on the mainland, they are very unlucky. Regular outbreaks. Children account for about half of all reported cases and a third of deaths. They often care for their families' domestic animals – feeding them, cleaning pens, gathering eggs. That's their role in life."

"And Laura?"

"Word came of a particularly nasty outbreak, in the countryside around Guangzhou, not far from here. Health care is not so freely available to the rural poor as it is in Hong Kong, or the wealthy in the Chinese cities. We started to see cases. Laura volunteered to cross the border to help out for a while. She wanted to gather data to help us better understand the disease. The Government..."

"Covers up outbreaks?"

"We don't know. It's possible. So she offered her services to the local Communists."

"How long's she been gone? Guangzhou, as you say, is not so far," Julia mimicked Kathy's pronunciation of Guangzhou, saying "gwanjo".

"She left a year ago. Nothing's been heard since. We don't know if she's dead or alive."

"Surely if she's working for the Communists there must be some record."

"You'd think so, wouldn't you? We have tried. They say they have no knowledge of any such individual. You see..."

Kathy bit her lip.

"Yes," Julia willed her to continue.

"It's easy to fall foul of the Authorities. Laura's not always circumspect. I don't know what I'm afraid of.

"But I am afraid —"

CHAPTER 22

JULIA CLASPED her hands in her lap and squeezed until her fingers hurt. *This is shocking news,* she thought. *What can I say? This poor woman looks distraught.* She thought back to the look on Rebecca Withers' face when she confided her husband had disappeared.

They lingered a while longer, exchanging pleasantries, before Kathy stood and said goodbye. Julia watched her walk away but remained sitting, soaking up the cool spray from the fountain, while contemplating the very dead end frustrating her. Her thoughts were interrupted by the buzzing of her phone in her pocket.

It was Ludgate. "What the hell are you playing at?" The line crackled but she could still hear he was shouting at her.

"London's burning while you sun yourself on a holiday island."

"I realise things have moved quickly back home," she said calmly, trying to placate him.

"Not as fast as you're going to move. Get the next plane home, hear me? And straight into the office, I've had enough of your lone-ranger shenanigans." He sounded like he was hyperventilating at the other end of the line.

Phew, fur flying back at the ranch. She agreed to fly back immediately. Ignoring him would be the kiss of death to their relationship not to mention her career, so with a slightly heavy heart, she decided to return to the Foreign Correspondents' Club – the nearest place she could access the internet, and book a flight.

Still it hurt. *I've come so far, discovered so little, and am returning before I've begun.* She stood to make a move when the phone rang again.

It was Pitcher. *What on earth's he calling for?*

"Why didn't you tell me to take my money out, Lightweight?" He might be at the opposite end of the world, but his voice could still pack a punch. "Am I going to lose all my savings?"

The question millions would be asking this morning, Julia thought.

"I very much doubt that," she said. "Anyway, what are you worried about with your fat inspector's pension?"

"That's years away."

"It may be closer than you think, given your recent record of solving crimes."

"Excuse me, I must have misheard. Is the line poor your end? Or has your story just fallen through?"

Ouch, closer than you know.

"My job's in no danger," he continued. "It's your job I'd worry about. I see your friend Matthew Hopkins has his name all over the front page this morning. How's the holiday?"

That hurt. Julia could feel her blood pressure rising.

"And if your friends in the City have fouled up," he was in full swing. "The party's over. You'll all be out of a job. There'll be riots."

"Well, go home and dream about all that overtime. I'm busy and you're wasting my time," she cut the call dead.

Julia left the park and descended to Albany in the direction of the Foreign Correspondents' Club. Her phone rang for the third time – a number she didn't recognise.

"Chen, here," came an unfamiliar voice. Then a light switched on. Chen was Crisp's contact at the fraud squad.

"Mr Chen, my name's Julia Lighthorn. I'm a London journalist. I was hoping we could perhaps meet up. Sadly, I've to cut my trip short. I'm leaving later today."

"Anything in particular?"

"I'm interested in First State Bank."

"Ah! So is everyone," he sighed gently. "If you can get here now, I'm free for the next hour. After that my day's committed. We're in the International Finance Building by the harbour. Know the Maritime Museum?"

"I'll find it," Julia responded, pulling Richard's map from her pocket.

Traffic was gridlocked, the atmosphere stifling, as the midday sun baked down from an unforgiving sky. She pushed her way through crowds, then climbed several flights of stairs leading to a web of walkways. These straddled city centre highways, vibrating under the force of fast-moving traffic below.

Once across, a maze of further steel skyways stretched ahead. Pedestrians raced along, like worker ants, eyes pinned to the ground.

Creepy, she thought, walking swiftly past tacky shop fronts. *I'll be glad to get out of here.*

141

She froze at a crash of glass shattering, which sounded as though it was coming from round the corner. She took a left and the first thing she saw was a policeman standing guard outside a shop. Three yobs with baseball bats were smashing up the display windows. All other pedestrians had disappeared. Seeing her, the policeman blew his whistle and waved her on. Eyes fixed to the steel walkway, she scuttled past as fast as she could. A quick glance from the side of her eyes told her all she needed to know. It was a bookshop.

She was shaking by the time she reached Chen's office, where she was shown in straight away.

"Sit down, Ms Lighthorn," Michael Chen pointed to a seat opposite his at the desk. "I trust you're having a good trip. How do you find our magnificent city?"

For a moment she was tongue-tied. "Actually, I've just seen something very strange."

"Don't worry," he said in perfect English. "We are a city of surprises. Enjoy those you can."

And turn a blind eye to the rest, she thought, deciding against confiding in him further.

"So you're interested in First State," he said.

"Partly," *come on Julia focus*, a voice inside said. "Its boss Adam Lee was murdered recently in Soho's Chinatown in London. Our police've hit a brick wall. I'm trying to find out anything I can, while I'm here."

"I'm not sure how I can help."

"Scofield Crisp suggested I should have a word with you."

"Ah! Mr Crisp," said Chen.

Obviously a name, which unlocks doors.

142

"Yes, we have the bank on our radar. Off the record – not for publication, we're only days from arrests."

"Thank you Mr Chen, for the tip. I confess I wasn't expecting such frankness."

That said, Julia thought, *this is hardly the "hold the front page" story it once was. With almost every major institution in the West rocked or crumbling, will anyone care about an obscure Hong Kong bank?*

"We're examining the books now," Chen continued. "It's likely some executives will be taken into protective custody."

"Protective custody?" Julia raised questioning eyebrows.

"Mr Lee might have been glad of some."

"What are you suggesting?"

"Accidents can happen anywhere, especially if your customers are gangsters."

"What makes you think..."

His face darkened. "Money laundering, loans to terrorists, drug cartels, arms dealing, and that's all before simply atrocious management."

"You can see all this in the accounts?"

"We're working on it," he ticked a page lying on his desk. "First State won't be in business much longer."

Chen got to his feet, indicating the interview was over.

"When I have something more, you'll be the first to know," he promised.

"You have my details. Please let me know when the story's about to break. Anything early, ahead of the game's always extremely useful."

"I'll see what I can do," Chen nodded.

CHAPTER 23

WHEN SHE LEFT Chen, Julia was still shaken by the attack on the bookshop. It looked like a crime, but a policeman was standing watching. She shuddered. *What a strange land*, she thought. She took a different route back to the Foreign Correspondents' Club, crossing three inter-connected shopping malls, then descending to ground level. She wended her way past traditional workshops. Tailors were lighting up their windows ready for afternoon and evening business. Made-to-measure could be bought for a fraction of the price in London. Brilliant greens flashed from jewellers' windows crammed full of jade.

Everywhere clamour and hubbub. Bustling back-streets a universe away from the modern high-rise city - a world of their own. Smells of street food marinated nostrils. Julia swallowed deeply as she passed Dai Pai Dongs, traditional fast-food hawkers. The noise was deafening, orders shrieked above clattering plates. Exotic shell fish, live eels, ugly swimming sea food, grisly crabs and lobsters, bright red, unlike anything she had seen before.

Fascinating but definitely alien. She picked up her pace to the Foreign Correspondents' Club, went straight to the workroom, logged onto her laptop and booked a flight home that evening. Next, she ordered two large cool drinks.

"Boy, do I need this," she said to the barman who laughed. She retreated to an armchair in a corner and called Richard about her change of plans.

"Hardly a surprise," he said. "I'll finish up and join you shortly."

Flight booked, she had to face the reality of her return. Ludgate would vent his anger by relegating her to the most demeaning stories. *Hopkins will love it*, she thought. She could fight back. A woman in a man's world, she had been forced to learn early how to battle her corner and when necessary draw blood. She could destroy competitors – but mainly she chose not to.

Pointless destructive games, she sighed. They never interested her. They sucked energy and oxygen, leaving the players too exhausted to pursue the most crucial job in hand – collecting facts and presenting them accurately. Imaginations become distorted, if the main task each day is grabbing headlines and top slots. She hated all that, but it went with the territory. Sadly, there was little point being sweet and kind, if few with ethics sat at the table when big decisions were made.

She turned her mind back to the disturbing scene at the bookshop. Police openly hand-in-glove with bully-boy thugs. Cast it any way you wanted, something had to be wrong. If this was an unsolicited attack, who could you report it to with the police involved?

Her eyes scanned the walls hung with framed newspaper pages. Nothing excited her like spectacularly-constructed newsprint, and these were all award-winners, forged in blood, sweat and tears. For her, they symbolised humanity at its finest.

145

She understood, as few do, the enormous achievement of taking something as ordinary as a blank piece of fairly cheap, scrappy paper, and transforming it into the first, often bloody draft of history.

Academics could debate for years, indeed centuries, what particular calamities meant. But there would be nothing to discuss without that first draft, created by teams of dedicated wordsmiths, with the power to change the very path of events. Their words could protect the vulnerable, check the powerful and punish.

She liked to think she followed in their footsteps, but self-deception was not one of her short-comings. Sufficiently rehydrated, she stood to read them. They told a similar story of war, violence, oppressive regimes and corruption. The earliest dated from the Japanese occupation when the club was set up in Chongqing, a city controlled by nationalist leader, Chiang Kai-shek. After Hiroshima, the club moved with the action first to Nanjing and then Shanghai as the struggle between the Nationalists and Mao Zedong's Communists intensified. It finally retreated to Hong Kong in 1949 when Mao's victory was complete.

The bulk of the framed pages related to the Vietnamese War, in which the club played a vital role as a haven of R&R for the often exhausted international press corp. Pictures and stories relating to Charlie Company and its role in the My Lai massacre, which the US army tried to cover up, took centre stage.

146

The death of dissident and Nobel peace prizewinner Liu Xiaobo, the rights campaigner, imprisoned several times by the People's Republic of China, was among the roll call of honour.

There were other stories. She blushed with shame when she reached the five booksellers abducted when crossing into mainland China. They sold books in Hong Kong critical of the Communist regime.

A very frightening world, she thought, and one far from the security of her desk in Southwark. *Is this why I write about money, because I'm too big a coward to take the risks these front-line journalists take?* She usually answered her life wasn't a cop out, because in the end everything was about money.

Who're you kidding? Nothing's more terrifying than raw violence. The scenes she witnessed that afternoon spoke volumes about her courage, or rather lack of it.

She returned to the armchair and fired her laptop to catch up with the latest headlines. No reprieve. The financial storm raged on.

Richard arrived a bit after three, with two fellow hacks in tow.

"Mark Holloway, a colleague from the Journal," he said introducing one of them. *Hmm, he reminds me of a handsome greyhound*, Julia thought.

"And Ken Woo. He looks after crime for the South Morning China Post."

He was smaller, with big bright eyes, *like the lemurs in the Botanical Gardens this morning.*

"I thought English tea time would be appropriate and should cut you enough slack to get back to the airport,"

Richard said, as they walked to a table. "How d'you get on this morning?"

She smiled as she sat, giving him only the barest update. He knew better than to ask for more with others present. Their eyes locked knowingly. She would keep her secrets until later.

"What brings you to Hong Kong?" Mark Holloway asked.

"With London ablaze?" she smiled. "Where to begin," she flicked her hair. "All sorts of things. If I had to pinpoint one story, it would be the murder of Adam Lee."

"Ah, Lee," Ken Woo said, knowingly.

"D'you know anything about the Lees? Someone led me to believe –"

Ken Woo burst out laughing and Mark Holloway began banging the table.

"Everyone knows the Lees," said Mark.

"Actually to be fair, I didn't," said Richard.

"All you care about is markets," Mark Holloway teased his colleague.

"Tell me," Julia asked.

"Your area old man," Mark signalled for Ken Woo to take up the tale.

"Difficult," he began gingerly. "They're a very old family in Hong Kong, and very big, so you have to be careful. Certainly many are respectable businessmen. Probably arrived from Guangzhou –"

"Canton," Richard translated.

"...during one of the mass migrations." Ken Woo nodded. "Like many, they followed traditional raffia trade, then moved

148

into textiles. They diversified and grew. Lee interests are pretty ubiquitous."

"All legit?" Julia asked.

"Ah!" Ken Woo stalled. "As I say, it's a big family. Some branches run legit corporations. Others' interests here in Hong Kong include gambling, maybe drugs and prostitution. The younger generation's more interested in hi-tech crime."

"So they're criminals?"

"Tad hysterical, I'd say. Is the British Government criminal? It dealt in drugs."

"Connections with Triads?"

Ken Woo smiled. "What does Triad mean? In Hong Kong everything is smoothed by personal relationships."

"And Adam Lee?"

"Lee was no saint. More than that I couldn't say."

"You've probably said enough," said Mark Holloway. "You'll give Julia nightmares."

"Actually, it's not my imagination that's overheated. I saw a rather nasty scene at Connaught Road near the International Finance Centre. A bookshop was being smashed up, and a policeman was standing by watching."

"Must've upset someone," said Mark Holloway. "It'll have come down from Beijing."

"What can you do?" Julia asked. "It was a bookshop."

"Nothing. If the police are there. Bookshops are particularly vulnerable. Beijing can't stand criticism."

"Other businesses too. Last week a company chief exec disappeared," Richard straightened his chopsticks, as if trying to exert control over chaos.

Mark nodded. "Can you imagine Warren Buffett, or Bill Gates, disappearing without explanation? That's what's been happening to their counterparts in China. Social media said he was spotted being taken away by police at Shanghai's Pudong airport."

"This guy's huge," Richard stretched his palms wide for emphasis. "You'd think untouchable. He would be anywhere else. Owns fund houses, hotels, some of the richest in New York, holiday clubs in the Med, online retail networks, high class stores in Bond Street. This is not a provincial Chinese company without influence."

"It doesn't mean he's guilty of anything," Ken Woo said as the food arrived. "I'm sorry you were upset Julia. Remember this is no longer part of a British empire. China does things differently. Crimes are swiftly punished. Witnesses can be "taken away" to help police and investigators build cases."

"China is obsessed by corruption," Richard snapped.

"Be fair now – with good reason," Ken Woo spooned noodles into his bowl. "For all its many faults, the UK economy is one of the least corrupt. So many out here and indeed in the Middle East and Africa have been ruined by corruption. It was endemic in old China – a way of life in Hong Kong."

"Not anymore?" Julia asked sceptically.

Her three companions laughed.

"Like beauty, corruption is in the eye of the beholder," Ken Woo sniggered.

"We have the best Government money can buy," Julia laughed, shaking her head.

"Steinbeck," Richard spat. "No, wait a minute," he corrected himself. "Mark Twain."

"It's not power which corrupts but fear," Mark Holloway offered.

"Steinbeck," all three shouted in one.

.

CHAPTER 24
Late Wednesday August 11

JULIA HATED take-offs. The Cathay Pacific jet hit seven miles high in just a few minutes, setting a Westward course at 11.10pm Hong Kong time.

In London the Ritz is serving afternoon tea, she thought, wriggling down in her seat, ready to sleep. She was drained by her whirlwind of encounters, and sank quickly into a restless slumber. Cabin lights switched on two hours before landing when she was offered a breakfast of noodles or rice.

How did I guess? she swallowed a chuckle, reaching for the airline's business magazine in the pocket in front of her. She flicked through its pages, picking at her vegetable noodle dish. Suddenly she dropped the fork as though it were red hot.

"Bastard," she cursed under her breath. "Too busy for interviews with journalists, are you?" She stared at a profile interview with Warwick Mantel, smirking repugnantly from a full-page glossy picture. She was so cross she couldn't read it, but rolled it up and stuffed it in her bag.

The plane landed in a rainy London just before 5am Thursday British Summer Time.

Usual chaos at passport, Julia frowned as she looked at the queues. It took more than an hour to get through, and run for the Heathrow Express. She emerged from Bank tube at 7am, and as per Ludgate's instruction, walked quickly to Square Mile's offices.

The streets of the City were hushed; eerily quiet, as though the inhabitants had suffered a collective shock. Even more than usual, people avoided each other's gaze, and hurried along eyes pinned to the pavement.

"I had not thought death had undone so many," Julia shuddered, as the line from TS Eliot's Wasteland popped into her mind.

The office was already full – not a time for late excuses. Yet a creepy silence reigned. Reporters kept their heads down, staying below radar.

Ludgate saw her the minute she walked in and called her into his glass bubble. He wasn't smiling.

"So you're back," he said grimly. "Markets have steadied after yesterday's shock. Shame you weren't here, but Matthew did a stunning job. Good we had him."

Julia smiled weakly. She expected to have her nose rubbed in her failure to cut mustard when it counted.

"No one knows where the next crack will appear," he continued. "My guess is it won't take long. So all hands to the pump."

"Now I'm back, you can count on me," Julia beamed a bright enthusiastic smile. "Shall I make some calls and get a heads up?"

Ludgate avoided her gaze. "No, that won't be necessary. Matthew has everything under control. I'd like you to look at these stories. File as quickly as you can, and get your brain into gear. You're back in London now."

She felt sick, running an eye down the list of stories, as she walked to an empty desk. They were all subjects he knew she detested, and well-below her pay grade. Long-dated gilt movements, copper prices, business rate relief. These were stories for worker ants, not star writers. She had little option but to swallow her punishment and put nose to grindstone.

Petty games, *games, games*, she whispered to herself, head bowed low over her desk. *How soon can I dig an escape tunnel*, she wondered, *and go back to my office in Southwark*.

Ludgate gesticulated to Hopkins to join him in the bubble. For half an hour, they laughed and plotted together like best buddies. When Hopkins exited the editor's office, he beamed with evident self-satisfaction.

Smug bastard, Julia clenched her jaw.

Her heart started to pound as he walked in her direction.

He paused at her desk and smiled down – an ugly leer.

"We're back are we? Shame you missed the fun and games yesterday," he patted her hair. "Top team was here. Don't worry your pretty little head."

I don't believe this. She wanted to punch him in the face, but her mobile started to ring.

"Sorry I need to take this," she said turning from him. It was Cody, wondering if she was back and when he could expect to see her in the office.

"I'm here for the time being. You keep cracking on with your investigations into that Trust, and get me anything you can about Triads operating in London. It's becoming more important."

"Sure," he said, hanging up.

She churned out the dreariest stories to the best of her ability. When it was time to pack up, one of the reporters asked if she fancied a drink. She declined, and watched as a pack of hacks left for the pub. Matthew Hopkins went with them, spreading an odious grin in her direction as he passed her desk.

When she was sure they had gone, she put on her jacket, and headed for the door. She stopped when her mobile phone rang. Michael Chen's name flashed up.

"I promised a heads up. We're moving against First State Bank within the next six hours. Closing them down."

"And the executives?" she said, walking back to her desk.

"Can I suggest you contact their PR agency? They have an office in London."

Julia searched online for First State's London office, and found the name of its PR. *Great,* it was an agency she knew well, and which owed her a few favours. *Time to call them in.*

"Let's be honest Julia," her contact Sophia said. "This bank is rotten, and I say that as its PR." She confirmed everything. First State already had the fraud squad on its premises, and several executives were "helping with inquiries."

"What does that mean?"

"Come on Julia. This is China. They've gone. Disappeared. To be honest, I'm glad it's you that called. This is one occasion where publicity, or rather accurate coverage, may be more help than hindrance."

"Phew," Julia let out a sigh. "More bizarre by the minute."

She put the phone down and walked calmly towards Ludgate, who was checking final pages at the other end of the office. He did not look at her when she spoke.

"That was the Hong Kong fraud office. I've a contact there now. He's tipped me off they're freezing First State Bank within hours. Car-wreck."

"Criminality?"

"Oh yes. Crooked loans, dodgy developments, tax avoidance. Running funds for drugs and arms dealers, and just sheer incompetence."

"OK." It sounded like he was only half-listening, but she knew he was already rethinking the front page.

"Three of its executives have disappeared," she landed her killer blow.

"What?" he turned to her now, but there was no friendly light in his eyes.

"Dragged across the border to China is best guess."

"What d'you have confirmed?" he asked.

"All of it. We'll be first. It isn't going on general release until tomorrow. The executive stuff I've just confirmed with the agency in London, and my fraud squad contact is the real deal. If he says they're closing it down, they're closing it down."

"OK, I'll clear some space. Keep it tight... don't forget to mention Adam Lee." She headed for her desk to start writing.

He called after her. "Don't think you're out of the dog house yet."

SHE FILED HER story, and got ready to leave. She was slightly miffed at Andrew's silence. No usual "well done," or "good work".

He must have missed me, she smiled to herself, skipping down the stairs. She stopped abruptly on the last step, as Matthew Hopkins re-entered the building.

Off to brown-nose with the editor, she thought.

"Sucking up to the boss are we?" he slurred, the worse from drink. "Good little workhorse. Next time try flashing your tits. Not up to much, but might work."

"Fuck you," Julia lashed viciously with her tongue, as she brushed past him.

"Stay out of my stories or you'll be the one who gets fucked," he shouted after her – an unmistakable threat in his voice.

CHAPTER 25

Midnight Thursday August 12
Epping Forest

JULIA COLLAPSED exhausted into bed, oblivious to a sinister scene unfolding a dozen miles East at a Girl Guide camp on the edge of the Epping Forest. A group of young girls were stirring. Outside their tent all was deathly still – apart from an owl, eyes like staring moons, who swivelled his head full circle and back again.

Troubled.

"You awake? Must be midnight," said Grace. Like the first beat of a symphony, six torches switched on. The Panda Patrol sat up in sleeping bags.

"Who's got the crisps?" said Lily. Beams of torches danced a merry jig around the tent, as each Girl Guide rustled with her rucksack.

"Why they have to take our mobile phones," moaned Issie.

"So mean!" Brittany echoed.

"I've got the drumsticks," hissed Minnie.

"I'm the chocolates!" squealed Coco in anticipation.

158

"SSShhhhh," came the chorus back. "We'll wake Old Chocolate-face. Then we'll be for it."

The girls unzipped their sleeping bags. They had been at camp for a week and were going home tomorrow. A midnight feast was their rite of passage.

"This can be our table," Issie spread the rug her mother had carefully packed to protect her from the damp night air.

"What would Leo, Josh and Ryan say if they could see us now?" Minnie giggled. "Wish they were here."

"We don't need boys to have a good time, hey Coco, don't hog the chocolate spread," Lily slapped her fellow patrol member on the arm.

Grace was busy spreading Nutella nut chocolate thickly on sour cream Pringles crisps.

"Yummy," she licked fingers coated in sticky brown goo.

"Anyone got any new jokes?" Minnie hollered.

"Shush," hushed her five companions.

"You'll wake the leaders up," added Lily.

"How about..." said Coco, chocolate smudged around her lips, "a man entered a local paper's pun contest. He sent in 10 different puns, hoping one of the puns would win."

Coco waited for someone to say something. When no one did, she delivered the punch line. "Unfortunately, no pun in 10 did...dada!"

The others groaned.

"Me next," wriggled Issie. "Why can't a nose be 12 inches long?"

"It would be a foot," they hissed in unison.

159

"I've got one," Minnie took her turn. "Police arrested two kids yesterday, one was drinking battery acid, the other was eating fireworks."

"Yuck!" the Pandas made vomiting noise.

"They charged one – and let the other one off." They burst into giggles.

"Not bad," Issie said, adding. "Grace – you've gone a funny colour. You OK?"

"No, I'm suddenly not feeling at all well."

"Nutella and Pringles never a good idea," said Brittany, who always knew best.

"I think I'm going to be sick." Grace's stomach started to make heaving motions.

"Errrrrr," the girls moved as one to escape what was coming next.

"I need some fresh air..." Grace, stumbled towards the tent opening.

"I'll come with you," said sensible Lily, who began fiddling with the tent ties to let her out.

"Keep the noise down," said Issie.

"I'm being as quiet as I can," Lily spat back.

The owl hooted, as the cold night air hit Grace full in the face.

"I can't hold it in anymore..." she bent double, holding her stomach.

"Not here – it'll alert the grown-ups."

They lumbered in the half-light towards a wooded area – torches switched off. The night was clear under a full moon. The owl hooted again.

160

When they reached trees, Grace stood to her full height and steadied.

"Are you OK?" Lily stroked her hand gently.

"Just needed some fresh air, I think." The nausea seemed to be subsiding, when suddenly, with a vengeance, her insides retched and heaved. She vomited violently.

"This is so embarrassing," she started to cry softly.

"Don't be silly – you're supposed to get sick at a midnight feast," Lily squeezed her friend's arm.

"I need a drink, some water," said Grace. "There's a tap over there."

The girls crept as carefully and quietly as they could to the tap outside the shower station. Grace washed her hands, before wiping cool water around her face. She cupped her palms, filled them, and sipped.

"Ready to go back?" Lily asked, when she finished.

Grace shook her head. She felt queasy at the thought of returning to a clammy tent smelling of sweaty bodies and the debris of the midnight feast.

"I need more air. I might walk for a bit, clear my head. You go back."

"No, no, I'll come with you." They walked gingerly through the coppice down to a little stream, where they had washed their lunch kit earlier in the week, earning a telling off from Chocolate-face, aka Mrs Cadbury.

The owl watched their progress, turning his head full circle again, his body motionless on his perch. The water shone silver in the moonlight. They were about to hop over some stepping-

161

stones, when the owl hooted again. Lily turned back towards him, and realised the early dawn was stirring.

"We'd better go back," she said. "Feeling better now?"

Grace nodded, adding, "I'll race you to the tent."

It was dark back in the coppice, but the girls sped on. Lily had pulled ahead, so Grace decided on a shortcut to head her off. She took a diverted path, which crumbled under foot, and sent her skidding forward, twisting an ankle. She bent to rub the injury, but looked up when she felt something dripping down her back.

At that moment the early dawn broke, shafting a bright light through the trees.

"What the ..." Grace gasped, too stunned to scream. The owl hooted in a continuous pulse, ringing alarm.

When the scream finally came, it woke everyone – except the dead.

"IT CAN'T BE MORNING," Chief Inspector Pitcher stretched to stop the piercing ring of his phone. It was nearly 4am.

"This had better be good," he shouted down the receiver. He listened to the station officer recounting details of a call from a Mrs Cadbury at the Chigwell Girl Guides camp.

"Pull the other one," Pitcher scoffed.

"No Sir, it's for real. Body hanging among the trees. Looks like the victim was hacked to death. Meat cleaver buried in his back."

"Found by two little girls?"

"Only what we've been told, Sir. Scenes of crime are on their way."

Pitcher dragged himself out of bed, dressed, splashed some water on his face and without stopping to eat or drink, drove East. He hated the Epping Forest. Sure, it was pretty and treasured by millions of East Enders. It was also London gangland's favourite burial ground. As a young copper, he spent half his life traipsing through the woods looking for bodies.

A corner of paradise? I don't think so. No one will ever know how many corpses are buried beneath its soil.

This was his first call to the Girl Guides camping site on the boundary between Hainault and Epping – landing it firmly in the Met's district. As London expanded, so did the reach of its police.

A few yards East and the Essex squad could be singing the dawn chorus, he grumbled to himself.

Chief Guider Mrs Cadbury waited for him at reception, along with a WPC from the local station.

"I hope this isn't a Friday 13th practical joke," he said to the WPC.

"It's for real I'm afraid, Chief Inspector."

The three of them walked down a narrow path, which opened into a huge field, sloping towards a coppice. Pitcher eyed various cabins and huts called things like St Pancras and Charing Cross.

"So the girls feel at home," Mrs Cadbury explained. Other long timber blocks – washhouses he guessed – bordered the opposite end of the field with names like Trafalgar Square and

163

Piccadilly. Canvas tents clustered in various corners of the vast meadow, deserted now the girls were bussed home to safety.

They trudged down the field until they reached the coppice. Scenes of crime officers were already there working on the body.

"Blood everywhere," Pitcher swallowed hard, as bile pumped into his throat.

"I can't tell you how distressing for the two girls," said Mrs Cadbury. "One actually slid in the disgusting gunge – covered in it. She'll need help coming to terms with all this."

That's an understatement, Pitcher thought moving towards the team on the ground.

"What can you tell me officers?"

"Looks like a savage machete attack."

"Here?"

"Probably not. Guides here all day – would have seen something. Possibly nearby."

"How long's he been dead?"

"Not long. Blood still dripping."

"This is the tree he was hanging from?" Pitcher pointed up.

The officer stood.

"That's right." He moved his arms to show where the rope would have hung. "He was hoisted under his shoulders. Already fatally wounded. Haven't counted the slashes in his back. Left to bleed dry."

"Death by a thousand cuts," Pitcher muttered under his breath.

"If you say so, Sir."

Pitcher shifted towards a bagged item on the floor.

"This the weapon?" he stared at the blooded meat cleaver. "Find anything else?"

"No sir."

Pitcher strained his neck to look up again at the tree.

"One thing," the Soco officer added, almost as an afterthought. "There was an orchid in his breast pocket."

CHAPTER 26
Tuesday August 17

JULIA SAT UP WITH A jerk – woken by an ear-splitting ringing. She grabbed her phone. *Have you gone mad Cody? It's 5.30am*, she cursed, when she saw the number.

"Yes," she barked down the line.

"Good morning Julia, great to hear your voice," he sounded maddeningly perky. "Couple of things we need to talk about."

"Not at this time we don't. Call me later in the office."

"I've been trying to call you for two days. I can't get through."

"Look, I'll be back in our office soon, I promise."

"I need to speak to you urgently. Can I come round now? It's about the Trust."

"No Cody. Absolutely not. This is a ridiculous time. I need my sleep. Then I'm going for a quick swim."

She rubbed her shoulders, and winced as a sharp pain stabbed. *Huckleberry Finn, I need to get some oxygen into these muscles. Factory journalism's killing me.* She had worked fourteen hours a day since returning on Thursday.

"Then I'm heading straight to Square Mile," she was firm. "You'll have to wait." She clicked off the phone, snuggled back down in the bed, but sleep had fled. She tried her mindfulness exercises, but wakeful thoughts refused to co-operate. She tossed, she turned, she wriggled.

No! It's no good. I'll never get back to sleep, she thought, swinging her legs out of bed. She pulled on her swimsuit, tracksuit on top, put work clothes in a holdall, poured coffee into a portable cup and headed out to Southwark Leisure Centre.

The water felt cool and releasing as she swam her first couple of lengths. She was not alone – 6am swims were popular. She rolled on her back. *Sheer heaven, suspended in nothingness.*

A whooshing sound disturbed her peace, as someone splashed into the pool beside her. It was Cody. *This can't be real.*

"No, don't stop swimming. I could do with a splash myself. We can synchronise side by side. I'll talk while you listen."

Despite herself, Julia laughed. *He's certainly got what it takes when it comes to tenacity,* she thought.

She let her feet drop to the bottom of the pool. "Cody you can be a real pain in the butt, but you'll go far one day. I give up, shoot."

She lay back in the water. Cody reeled over and paced his strokes to match her.

"Your friend, the forensic accountant, thought there were a few anomalies in those accounts. He kept digging and now says a million pounds is missing. Numbers don't add up."

"The accounts have been audited, they must add up," said Julia. "Have you spoken to the Chairman of the trust?"

"Literally the numbers add up – but they don't make any sense. I'll come back to the auditors. I called the Chairman, without giving too much away and he said to speak to the Treasurer."

"And?" They reached the pool's edge, spun for the return lap, back-stroke arms swinging in sync.

"No one knows where he is. They can't find him. Coming into the office less and less, sending apologies to meetings etc. Apparently, no one's seen him for a couple of months."

"Are you telling me he's disappeared?" Julia swivelled onto her front, picking up speed.

"Here comes the clincher," said Cody mirroring her manoeuvre. "The auditors don't exist. They did, old family firm etc. They audited the accounts free for years, because it was a charity. Anyway that firm closed a bit over a year ago."

"Who's been signing off the accounts?" they reached the shallow end. Julia stood to face him.

"Without jumping to any conclusions, I'd say someone's been pretending to be the auditor and signing them off fraudulently. With the Treasurer gone, it's not hard to wonder who?"

"That's quite an allegation."

"Not really. Treasurer's role, like the auditors, was voluntary. When people do good deeds for nothing no one looks too closely. Too noble to come under suspicion. I've got some pals in the post room of the accountancy firm where he worked. Apparently, he'd started splashing money around – said he'd come into an inheritance."

"Which is why someone sent us those documents – smelt a rat. Come on, let's get out of here. You need to tell me everything you know." Julia hauled herself out of the pool.

They regrouped by the coffee vending machine – the cafe wasn't opened yet – then sat at a round table by the huge glass frontage. A tide of people flooded along the pavement, walking to work, or the tube. Buses were packed like sardines.

"Now tell me everything you know about this trust. It's run by City Hall?"

"No, No, I've already told you all this. If I go through it again, will you listen?"

"Sure," Julia looked apologetic.

"The Whittingdale Trust is an independent charity going back hundreds of years – to Shakespeare's day. The City was always a centre of money and wealth, and many people, not just Dick Whittington, enjoyed massive – what we today would call – social mobility."

"Rags to riches?"

"Indeed. Once they made it, many saw it as a duty to take care of the less fortunate. So, they left money to the church for the poor. Of course some may have wanted to wipe the slate clean before arriving at the pearly gates – after a lifetime of supping with the devil."

"Buying their way into heaven eh?" Julia patted her hair dry with a towel.

"Feared the final reckoning? Quite possibly."

"I'm guessing, being the City, the money was wisely invested," Julia shook her hair free.

169

"Absolutely, pretty soon these churches were sitting on piles of gold, while at the same time, the poor had disappeared."

"I'm sorry?" Julia raised eyebrows.

"Of course, the poor are always with us," Cody continued. "But they weren't living in the Square Mile any more. They were in the East End and well let's face it, right here in Southwark. They moved with the jobs industrialisation brought."

"So the churches were left with vast wealth but no congregations and no one to give it too?"

"Pretty much. In 1878 Parliament stepped in and merged all these small parish legacies, and gave them a new purpose. Instead of feeding stomachs, it ordained the money should be used to feed minds and promote good health."

Julia made a wheel-winding motion with her right hand to speed Cody along.

"Their new role was to promote education, libraries, art galleries etc and also to encourage public health by buying up open spaces."

"I've never heard of all this."

"For a reason. It always guarded its privacy. Kept a low profile while doing good. Discreet."

"Sounds like another secret society."

"In some ways it was, and still is. Today it has an income of about £49 million annually – largely from rents and endowments. It gives all this away in grants and more."

"And the income comes from?"

"It owns oceans of the Square Mile, plus huge tracks of Essex, Kent and down as far as Sussex and Hampshire. It's one of the biggest property owners in the South East."

"A fortune. Have we got a list of these assets?"

"No, that's another weird thing. There doesn't seem to be one, not publicly available. As I said, the trust is very secretive. The Guildhall archivist implied there may be no definitive list. To find out what properties are involved, you might have to go back to the original wills and trust deeds held by the individual churches."

"So we think there's a million missing?" Julia looked at her watch.

"Something of this order," Cody confirmed.

"And no one knows where the Treasurer is?"

He nodded.

"Walk with me for a bit will you?"

"Sure."

They pushed through the swing doors, out onto Elephant and Castle and made for the Tube.

"Good work Cody."

"There's something else. I've been looking into a secret society like you asked. Rather, I've been staking out the newish Chinese Cultural Association in West London – Hammersmith way. Its membership has grown rapidly, and word is it could be a front for various Triads. Remember Triads are often little more than trade associations, like the old guilds here in London."

"Not a comparison I would make publicly."

"Maybe. The biggest operates like a well-oiled corporate machine, supports the Arts and show business. Main backer behind the West End's latest hit musical. On the face of it a pillar of respectability."

"How touching."

"Anyway, I've got some pictures here. People coming and going. Thought you might like to look at them," he handed her an envelope.

They had reached the tube. Julia stopped to flick through the pictures quickly.

"Know anyone?"

She froze.

"Oh yes." He Len's face stared out of three of them.

I would recognise you anywhere.

"He seems involved with one called the De Brazzas. It's a kind of gorilla – also known as swamp monkeys."

Julia burst out laughing.

How apt, she thought, remembering the Alpha beasts in the Hong Kong Zoological gardens and their boisterous ballet.

"Can you leave all this with me for a few hours? I need to think about our next move."

"OK."

"Great work, Cody. Keep digging, but carefully."

CHAPTER 27

JULIA left Cody and took the tube to work. As soon as she stepped into the office, Ludgate signalled for her to join him in his bubble. His face looked grim. He asked her to close the door behind her, but did not invite her to sit.

Door closed, he pointed to his computer screen and asked what the email displayed on it meant. She moved behind his desk to read it.

This is awkward, she thought, feeling flustered invading his space. He stepped closer to her, arms folded tightly, a deep scowl furrowing his brow.

He's furious. The vibes were unmistakable. She leant over his desk to read the email, sent from her email address – a long rant of poison, criticising the newspaper, his leadership in particular and tendering her resignation.

"I didn't write this," she said. "It's a prank. Someone's hacked my email account." She paused before adding, "It's malicious."

He took his phone from his pocket and began dialling a number.

Oh no, he's lost interest already, she thought.

Deciding better of it, he threw the phone on the desk. "I realise you didn't write it." Journalists knew each others' writing style as intimately as lovers their sexual partners. "You've never

173

been able to spell anathema correctly." His foot strummed impatiently.

"Too many a's and e's," she joked, trying to lighten things up. He ignored her, waving his hand for her to move to the other side of the desk.

He rubbed his jaw, as if carefully weighing his next words. "I also realise you're not happy here. We're in the middle of the biggest financial story of our lives, but you seem entirely pre-occupied elsewhere. Lesser journos are running rings round you. You're at odds with senior colleagues you're supposed to be working closely with..."

Is it any wonder with spiteful pranks like this? she wanted to say, but bit her tongue. She needed to salvage something of her relationship with her editor, or her career would go up in flames, the moment she stepped out of his bubble.

"I need team players Julia, and let's face it, you can't run with the pack. You never have."

I'm about to get the sack, she thought, swallowing hard.

He took a deep breath. "So where do we go from here? Do you want me to make a huge fuss about this email, find and discipline the culprit and potentially unsettle the entire office, when I need everyone focussed on the big story?"

Julia stared down at her feet, nausea mounting in the pit of her stomach. She didn't know how to respond.

Finally, she looked up and said gently, "You're right. I'm not happy here. Maybe you're also right, I've lost focus. I can't move for loose ends and I can't tie any of them up."

For the first time in the interview, he looked her straight in the face, his voice softening. "All I need you to do is concentrate day-by-day. Take each step at a time. You of all people know that's the way to build the picture and nail the story."

She shook her head.

"Not this time. It's no good chasing stories day-by-day. What's coming will be bigger than anything any of us have lived through. I need time and space to join the dots. I'm almost there, I promise you."

He looked at her intensely, as if trying to read her mind. She knew he wanted to help.

"I'll give you a month to come up with something good."

"Can I go back to my office?" she asked.

He sighed, but nodded reluctantly.

"Now get out of here, and stop wasting my time," he sat and reached for his phone. Interview over.

Julia didn't hang around, but hit the floor running.

"Leaving so soon?" Matthew Hopkins walked towards her. He couldn't resist gloating. Whether he wrote that email or not, she knew without a shadow of doubt he was behind the assassination attempt.

"It's been a blast," he said, shoulders bouncing with stage laughter.

She ignored him. *I'm not rising to your bait.*

Smiling, as she waited for the lift, she whispered her favourite Chinese proverb. *If you sit by the river long enough, the bodies of your enemies come floating past.*

She exited the main door without a look behind her, walked through St Paul's gardens, then took the Millennium Bridge back to the Southside. It was already crowded with tourists heading for Tate Modern. A few business people flowed against the tide.

She picked up her pace to stem the tears pricking the back of her eyes. Tears of anger, frustration and hurt. The row with Ludgate had upset her. *I'll get over it*, she tossed her head defiantly.

Hopkins I'll never forgive, she swore under her breath. *But, hey, tempus fugit, all things are passing, I can do without the Square Mile.*

Exhilaration soared. She suddenly felt free, as free as if she had escaped from prison. *I'll never have to go back into that crummy office again.* She looked up at the sky. It was a cloudless blue. In rhythm to her steps she started singing the Cream song, *I feel free, boom boom boom baboom boom, I feel free boom boom boom baboom boom.* Light sparkled on the water below. New and old beckoned on the other side. Southwark Cathedral's spire nestled beside glass towers. Cardinal's Wharf waited in her path – Shakespeare's globe beside it.

A woman passed with a baby in a sling. Runners jogged by, wearing shorts of every colour – pink, orange and violet. She smiled to herself. How she loved this ridiculous young city, full of zest and energy. She envied their fixed path, settled destination.

Where to go, what to do now? With no deadlines looming, she felt lost, adrift. On impulse, she slipped down a stone stairway onto the muddy foreshore below, a private world, secluded alone. She could see mudlarks scouring the bank opposite for trinkets and treasures.

I need time and space to think. She propped her back against the sea wall, stretched out her legs dead straight and closed her eyes. Instantaneously, a vision of the repugnant Hopkins floated into her mind. She didn't banish him immediately, but concentrated on her intense loathing, then breathed long and deep.

So he's gone, she clicked her fingers.

The warmth of the sun revived her, as she reran the scene with Ludgate. It was true she didn't need the Square Mile, she could find work elsewhere. But the media was full of charlatans and dictators. She would be foolish to burn her bridges with Andrew. He was straight and he was fair – a good friend to her on numerous occasions.

We'll patch it up, we always have, she thought. *He'll be under pressure to produce the best coverage. I probably pushed him too far.*

She took out the pictures Cody gave her. No doubt at all. The broad sneering face was He Len. What was he up to? She replaced the photographs in the envelope.

Leaning back against the wall, her thoughts drifted to Cody and his discoveries about the Trust. This could be the story to win back Ludgate's confidence. It was the sort he liked. So far they had it to themselves, but it would need tricky handling. The authorities should be informed. Julia needed to think carefully about who to report their discoveries to. Ultimately the Charities Commission, but if it was straightforward theft, it was a police matter. Or should she and Cody continue their own digging until they had the whole story complete?

She would call Pitcher. Annoying though he could be, she would trust him any day over the Charities Commission. She could speak to one of her tame lawyers, but they were all so straight, they would insist on reporting it immediately.

That'll blow the whole thing, she thought. In a strange way, she and Pitcher saw eye to eye. He respected the fact she had a job to do, a living to earn. He was often only too happy to let her do the spade work, when it came to white collar crime.

Suddenly, the air chilled and she shivered. She opened one eye gingerly to see why the sun had gone in. It hadn't. A dark silhouette was standing blocking its fiery beams.

"Thought you looked lonely down here," said a voice she vaguely recognised but couldn't quite place. "And in need of refreshment."

As both eyes focused she realised it was Ziggy, the Ambassador's nephew, holding two ice-creams.

"PEACEFUL DOWN there?" he said, handing her a cornet. "One of my favourite places to escape. Can I join you?"

She licked the melting ice cream. She liked Ziggy, but as the Ambassador's nephew, he couldn't be taken at face value.

"Did you enjoy the entertainment the other evening?" he sat beside her on the sand.

"The music and dancing were wonderful."

"I meant the finale. The students storming the barricades, priceless."

Julia gave him a sideward's glance. *Can he be for real,* she wondered.

"To be brutally honest, I couldn't see what was going on. The whole thing was over in a minute." There was something

178

about him she didn't quite trust. "Was the muscle the Embassy's security? They seemed pretty efficient."

"What can I say?" he evaded her question. "China's hierarchy is multifarious and its practices complex."

"So I'm learning – the inscrutability of the East."

"All societies have their secrets and..." he hesitated, "discombobulations."

"I'm not sure what that means."

"I thought you were the journalist."

Julia laughed. "Secret societies eh? Does that mean Triads? Are they discombobulating in London?"

"These are interesting questions," Ziggy licked his fingers, ice cream melting down the cone.

"Are they of interest to the Embassy?" Julia persisted. "Were those security men connected to a Triad?"

"Do you expect me to answer that question, even if I could?"

She shrugged, her mouth full of wafer.

"It takes a lifetime for a European to understand the Chinese perspective."

"Try me," she said, wiping her sticky fingers on her trousers.

"China is a very ancient civilisation, and our history flows with rivers of blood. Dynasties which survived endless civil wars and rebellions did so by force. Order, civilisation if you like, could only be maintained through violence. Crime was brutally punished. The smallest crime attracted barbaric retribution, not just against the perpetrator, but his family and

179

even his whole village or town. This is our way. Our people know this."

"Poor excuse. We were monsters in the middle ages. This is the 21st century."

"And now you are all heavenly choirs of angels."

"Hardly. You haven't answered my question about the Triads. I thought they'd been stamped out."

He laughed, eyes dancing. "This is heavy stuff before lunch. All I wanted was a peaceful break from the class room in the sun, not an interrogation about the crimes of my predecessors."

"The Triads. You must know," she pressed.

"As do you or you wouldn't be asking."

"They're alive and well in London?"

"If you say so."

"Any guests at the embassy Triad members?"

"What do you think?"

"What about that chap I was sitting next too...He Len wasn't it?"

His playful expression vanished, and his eyes darkened. "Let me give you a friendly warning. I'd stay well away from him if I were you. Not a man to menace with. I think we should change the subject."

"You can trust me. I've never disclosed a confidence or let a contact down."

"Silence of the confessional eh?"

"Something like that."

Ziggy hesitated, then lowered his voice. "You can find speculation in some press, that the Chinese Government uses friendly Triads to do its dirty work."

"I thought the People's Republic hated the Triads."

"Times are changing. China's breakneck economic growth has brought forgiveness to some hearts. Criminals have malleable loyalties – allegiances are shifting."

"Hong Kong?"

"There's a feeling – since the British left – Triads have not been as toughly controlled."

"Maybe the People's Republic of China wants a private army on the ground?"

Ziggy stretched his lips into a thin smile.

"And you, Ziggy, what brought you to London?"

"I thought you knew. I came as a child. My family traces its history through the diplomatic corp."

"You went to school in the UK?"

"In Marylebone, yes."

"So you're very pro British."

Ziggy climbed to his feet.

"I wouldn't jump to too many conclusions if I were you."

Julia also stood and they both walked towards the steps.

"Thing I can't work out is, where you sit with all this?"

Ziggy laughed that warm, infectious laugh.

"Why, I'm the Ambassador's nephew and China is my home."

CHAPTER 28

AT THE TOP of the river steps, they said goodbye, exchanging a vague promise to meet for lunch when a gap appeared in the diary. *Another empty promise*, Julia thought, as she walked along the South Bank back to the office, puzzling over Ziggy's surprise appearance. *Was it really a coincidence?*

Cody's face lit up when she entered the office. "Didn't think you'd be back so soon."

"I got the sack," she pulled a face, sitting behind her desk. "Could murder a coffee."

To his credit he stood ready for the coffee run. "Black as usual?" he asked, heading down to Mr Bardetti's.

"Yes please."

"Anything to eat?"

"Maybe a wrap." At the thought of food, she realised the ice-cream was all she had eaten that day.

She watched him go, then sat with her head in her hands. *What a mess,* she thought. *Total financial fiasco, a charity scandal, and now Triads in London involving brutes like He Len.*

"Better get cracking," she tapped the desk with her index finger.

She reached for her phone to call Pitcher, when it began to ring. She answered.

"Julia, it's Alek Yazov here," said a voice at the other end. "We've met a couple of times. Do you remember me?"

Oh yes, I remember you. "How can I help Alek?"

"I've got a cracking story for you."

Pull the other one, she thought. "OK let's hear it."

She knew the Russian earned a crust from his Embassy touting stories damaging to the UK.

"Gold reserves in the Bank of England. Gone. Empty tomb. Government's sold them to China to fund the banking bailout. Britain's bankrupt," he began.

"That's 400,000 bars, worth £200 billion?"

"Brilliant, isn't it?"

"How d'you know this?"

"Saw the army moving it out at 1am this morning. Tip from one of my deep contacts. Turned up to see what was going on."

"Well, it's very kind of you to think of me, but I'm not sure it's one for us. Crime's not really our thing. Thank you anyway. Feel free to try elsewhere."

She replaced the receiver as Cody entered with two coffees and wraps. He raised questioning eyebrows.

"Russian nutter. Master of Soviet misinformation," Julia shook her head. "Claims we're bankrupt – all the gold in the vault at the Bank of England gone. We've sold it to the Chinese."

"Wow, that's a big story," Cody leaned across to hand her a coffee.

"It would be if there was a shred of truth. Alek is always ringing with barking leads. Likes to hint he has contacts with

183

the KGB – or whatever they're called these days. Decent broker, until he was sacked for manipulating prices by Goldmans. Found guilty at Southwark Crown Court and served a couple of years. Now dabbles in Kremlin black arts."

"Nice chap. So we're not bankrupt?"

"Oh yes, we're bust – or we will be when all this is over. They'll shake the magic money tree, push our debts from one Government spreadsheet to another –but we'll still have gold in the Bank."

"Shouldn't I call the Bank of England?"

"By all means check if you're worried. Here, call Sue Evans. Mention my name." She threw a card across the table. "I must call Pitcher." She dialled his number.

"I need to see you," she said.

"Ah, it's Lois Lane. You seem to forget, my little noodle, I work for Our Majesty's Government. Not only is my time not my own, it sure as hell, ain't yours."

"What if I ask nicely? Darling, handsome, clever, dapper, intelligent Inspector –"

"Better. Keep going."

This was too much for Julia.

"Oh shut up," she said. "You're infuriating. When can we meet?"

"Tut-tut. We're tetchy today. Pressure getting to you, Lights-out? Little birdy told me you've been having troubles with the boss. One problem I don't have."

"I know. Being the boss. Lucky you. And stop teasing me about my name."

184

His voice turned serious. "Truth is I'm incredibly busy. Ever heard of the River Ching?"

"Can't say I have. Where is it? China? Vietnam? Thailand?"

"No, but I've got a call to make this afternoon. Want to come? You can run whatever's bothering you by me on the journey."

"Can I bring Cody? It's time you two met properly."

"Sure. It'll be great to have someone intelligent to talk to."

Julia stuck her tongue out at the phone and replaced the receiver. Cody was also hanging up.

"Spoke to your pal – she nearly died laughing," he grinned across at Julia.

"Nothing in it?"

"Nothing in it."

"Good, but journalism rule...what are we up to now?"

"Honestly I've lost count. Maybe four."

"OK Rule Number Four – check out every lead, no matter how bonkers. Fancy a ride with Chief Inspector Pitcher?"

Cody's face lit up. "When?"

"About 20 minutes."

THEY WERE WAITING outside the Deli when Pitcher pulled up in an unmarked car, driving himself. Julia got in beside him, Cody climbed in the back.

"Pleased to meet you Cody," Chief Inspector Pitcher said, putting the car into gear. He pulled away smoothly, turning towards Rotherhithe tunnel.

"Bridge due up," Pitcher said. Tower Bridge was raised half-a-dozen or so times a day to let tall ships through.

"What's it like working for Lois Lane here?"

"Don't answer that," Julia said. Cody sniggered. Once through the tunnel, Pitcher steered onto the East India Dock Road. Before long they were cruising past Canary Wharf.

Rear view of our financial metropolis – considerably less impressive than the magnificent water approach, Julia thought.

"So you fancy a future in the media?" Pitcher asked Cody over his shoulder.

"It's all I've ever dreamed of."

"Where are we going?" Julia asked.

"Magical mystery tour," Pitcher turned to her, grinning.

"Spare me please. Not a tour of all your old Essex haunts, I hope?"

"My scenes of romantic conquests?"

"What conquests? Your love life is like a diary with all the pages torn out."

"No dates, ha ha. Cody if you ever tire of working for this comedian, we're always looking for bright young Londoners at the Met."

Pitcher picked up speed as they raced down the dual carriageway for about 20 minutes. Julia fiddled with the radio to tune into the midday news. Nothing new, just a rehash of earlier bulletins. Pitcher switched it off, and took an exit. Soon they were driving through suburbia.

"We're heading for Chigwell – a Girl Guide camp. I was called to a murder there a few nights ago. I should warn you, this is gruesome stuff. It'll be a big story when it breaks though."

186

He swung off the road, and steered down a lane, until they arrived at the campsite. He pulled into a long drive, careered a bit further, took the car out of gear, and silenced the engine.

"Everything you'll see today is..."

"Off the record?" Julia nodded.

"Absolutely."

They got out the car. Pitcher waved at a middle-aged woman in Guiding uniform walking in their direction.

"Hello Mrs Cadbury," he greeted her. "Thanks for allowing me back to inspect the site. This is a colleague from the press and her assistant. Is it convenient for us to walk down to the woods again?"

"We're not keen on publicity." Mrs Cadbury's forehead wrinkled into a worried brow. "Must think of the safety of the girls."

Julia stretched her lips into what she hoped was a winning smile. "Good to meet you Mrs Cadbury. Please rest assured, we'd never do anything to jeopardise their safety. In fact, this is way outside our remit. I write about economics. I needed to speak with the Chief Inspector about another matter, and he asked us to accompany him."

"If the Chief Inspector is happy..." Mrs Cadbury relaxed her frown. "Come on then."

They set off down the drive, shoes crunching the gravel. Mrs Cadbury asked Julia if she had ever been a Girl Guide. She responded in the negative.

"Shame," said Pitcher, grinning. "She might've learnt something useful."

Julia pulled a face.

"And she would've looked so cute in uniform."

"Chief Inspector, I think that is quite enough."

Julia was beginning to like Mrs Cadbury, even if the whole scene smacked of Enid Blyton.

"You're right, and I apologise, Mrs Cadbury," he straightened his face. "You've all suffered a terrible shock. Can you bear to go through it with me again?"

Mrs Cadbury took a deep breath and, as they emerged from the path into the huge camping field, she began. "It was the last night of camp, and the Panda Patrol, who largely come from Stratford, were celebrating with a midnight feast," she raised her eyes to heaven. "Innocent enough. They got over-excited. One of them, Grace, felt sick. She left the tent with her friend Lily, for some fresh air."

"They didn't go far?" Pitcher asked.

"Not at first. Grace was very sick, and couldn't face getting back into the tent. They should've called us, but they didn't."

"Mrs Cadbury, had you or any of the staff or campers noticed anything out of the ordinary during the day?"

"Nothing."

"That night, did you hear anything?"

"Again nothing I'm afraid. Grace and Lily wandered down to the trees," she pointed ahead of them. "Then on to a stream. The girls knew this was out of bounds. One of them could've fallen, then heaven knows what might have happened."

"Full moon that night," Pitcher reminded her. "Very bright, so the girls could see relatively clearly?"

"Yes. That's correct, Chief Inspector. But it was dark in the copse. They decided to race back to the tent, and ended up on different paths."

"The sun started to come up," Pitcher helped her.

"Grace fell. She slipped on some sticky gunge. She looked up and..."

"Saw a man hanging," Pitcher finished for her.

"Dear God, those poor girls," Julia said.

"Indeed."

Mrs Cadbury stopped walking when they reached the trees.

"I'll stay here if you don't mind Chief Inspector."

Pitcher led Julia and Cody down to the spot where the body was found.

"He was hanging," Pitcher pointed up to a tree. "But that's not how he died."

"You say murder, could it have been suicide?" Julia asked.

"I don't think so."

"Hell of a lot of blood here judging by the staining," Cody pointed to dark stains drained deep into the undergrowth.

"Yes there was. Walk with me down to the stream," Pitcher led the way. It was little more than a trickle of water. He stared into the shallow current then spoke softly.

"He was hacked to death. A meat cleaver still rammed in his back."

"Triads," Cody said. "Lingchi – death by a thousand cuts." He sneezed.

Julia clenched her jaw.

"OK, let's go."

189

Mrs Cadbury waited for them by the trees, and walked back with them through the field.

"Gruesome business," she said.

"Thanks for letting me have another look," Pitcher nodded.

"Always a pleasure Inspector," the Guider gave a little giggle.

Julia cringed. *Don't tell me even the sensible Mrs Cadbury with her brown lace-ups has fallen for his charms. He's a handsome devil. Trouble is he knows it.*

"Does that little stream have a name?" Pitcher asked.

"I don't think so, but it drains into the River Ching."

They were back at the car. Pitcher turned to shake hands with Mrs Cadbury and say goodbye.

"One last question," he said. "Who owns this land? Is it the Guiding Association? This camp's been here since I was a kid."

"Oh no no. The Girl Guides don't own anything Chief Inspector. It's a big trust. Now let me think. The Wallace, no, that's a gallery. The White, White, no, I'm thinking of the cube. Wait a moment, it'll come. That's it, I've got it. The Whittingdale Trust. Our landlord is the Whittingdale Trust."

"Oh yes, we know all about the WhittingdaleTrust," Julia said looking at Cody.

"Do we?" the Chief Inspector asked.

"Oh yes we do," Cody replied.

They said their farewells and got back in the car.

190

PITCHER SWUNG the car out of the lane, turned left, and pulled up a few minutes later outside the Two Brewers pub.

"I need something to eat," he said, switching off the engine and getting out. They followed him inside. A log fire burned for atmosphere in "ye oldie English inglenook".

Weird, Julia thought, *in the middle of summer.*

Pitcher went straight to the bar. "Serving food?" he asked the landlady, who handed him a menu.

"I'll have a braised shoulder of lamb, dauphinoise potatoes, tenderstem broccoli, rosemary gravy – and a pint."

Julia couldn't help noticing it was the most expensive item on the menu.

"Just a coffee for me," she said, passing the menu to Cody, who ordered burger, chips and a coke. Julia paid for them all. They took their drinks to a table in the corner.

"What's with this Whittingdale Trust then?" Pitcher began. "How come it's on your radar?"

Julia scratched her ear. "You could call it a coincidence. I'd go further. I'd say it's uncanny – downright creepy. It's why we wanted to see you. A few months ago, a set of accounts arrived anonymously in the post. It was just after Adam Lee was found. I was up to my eyes with the financial crisis. So I asked Cody to take a look. Anonymous packages are ten-a-penny in our line. If people suspect something but don't know what to do, they send stuff to us. It usually turns out to be nothing. So with everything collapsing around us – " she looked at Cody. "Why don't you take it from here?"

"I found it hard to get anywhere at first. After hours in the Guildhall Library, I discovered the documents related to the

191

Whittingdale Trust. I was still struggling to work out what they meant when Julia put me in touch with a forensic accountant. He spent days pouring over the accounts and reckons not only don't they add up – they're £1 million out."

"Fraud?" Pitcher sucked the froth off his pint.

"Certainly looks that way."

"Some £2 billion goes missing each year from charities doesn't it?"

"My, my, Chief Inspector. You surprise me," Julia raised her eyebrows.

"Crime is my speciality. Little's ever recovered. Go on Cody."

"We needed more. So, I kept digging. Next thing, the Treasurer's gone missing."

"Not another disappearance," Pitcher banged his forehead with the stub of his right palm.

"Fraid so. Have you identified this body?"

"No, but I wouldn't jump to any conclusions. My guess is your Treasurer hot-tailed it to Panama, and is necking glasses of Martini in the sun. What is this trust anyway, this Whittingdale Trust?"

"Very old City of London charity. Set up in Shakespeare's day to..."

"The Chief Inspector doesn't need a history lesson, Cody," Julia interrupted.

"Sorry," he grinned sheepishly. "Well, today it owns most of London's green belt, plus huge chunks of Epping forest and other land around the capital."

"Ripe for the pickings. A lost million sounds like small change."

"And small time crook," Julia agreed. "Still theft from a charity – stealing from society's most vulnerable. What d'you want us to do?"

"Keep digging for the time being. I've got this murder, plus Lee."

"Spectacularly brutal, wasn't it?" Julia said.

"Yes but I've got a feeling..." he paused, as if he thought better of sharing his suspicions. "How d'you get on in Hong Kong?"

"Learnt a lot about the People's Republic of China, the Lee family, First State, and a bit about Triads."

"See any orchids?"

"Lots, they're everywhere. National flower, I believe. Why ask?"

Pitcher stretched for a toothpick in a box on the table and began poking his teeth.

"Getting anywhere with Lee and Chandler?" Julia continued.

"I've never been convinced by Chandler. Doesn't smell right." Pitcher looked at Julia, his eyes narrowing. "Have you spoken to his wife recently?"

"No I haven't. Haven't had time."

"Might I suggest you're spreading yourself too thin? You're hunting for bogeymen over half the globe, when the answer's most likely right in front of your eyes. No Julia. The River Ching isn't in China or Vietnam. It's right here in London. The

193

simplest explanation is usually the right one. I'd bet my shirt Chandler's laying low."

Julia made a face. Pitcher could be so annoying, but he was echoing Ludgate's warning earlier in the day. Two men who knew her so well. Perhaps they had a point. She was a money hack. What was she doing wading in blood?

CHAPTER 29
Wednesday August 18
London

PITCHER MUST have second sight, Julia thought as she woke the next morning to a story so big, she had no idea how they would ever manage to cover it. And it was breaking right here on her doorstep. The UK's biggest global bank, Gold & National, had run out of money and been taken over by the Government in the middle of the night.

"Fuck, fuck fuck!" Julia sat bolt upright in bed, listening with horror to the 6am radio bulletin. "If GNB is bust, the UK economy's about to be flushed down the drain."

Still listening, she swung her legs out of bed and went into the kitchen to make coffee. *Never in my wildest nightmare could I have imagined such a seismic shock.*

Government pledged to inject £500 million into the UK banking system to shore up confidence.

Where will this money come from?

Ludgate called at 6.30am. "I've spoken to the Chancellor. He took a call late last night from GNB's James Ackroyd. Said the bank was bust."

"Nice they gave plenty of warning."

"Can you get into your office pronto and start digging? Unlikely any of the other banks will be able to open first thing.

We need to get to the bottom of what caused this almighty..." he didn't finish the sentence.

She dressed, emailed Cody, drained her mug and headed into the office. *This is the collapse Silverman warned me of in that cave*, she thought as she jogged to the office.

The Chancellor appeared on television throughout the day reassuring the public British banks were sound, but needed support because of what was happening in the US. By 11am, as a result of behind-the-scenes alchemy, all the main UK banks were able to reopen their doors. Analysts expressed doubts about how many of them were any more secure than GNB.

Julia spent the day on the phone.

"This £500 million's just the start," carped one of her contacts. "Mark my words, it'll end up costing upwards of £30 billion to bail the lot of them out."

"What? Who's going to pay?"

"Our children and their children. This total fuck up will have a very long tail for us all."

Many she spoke to were furious at the banks' wrecking orgy, and the damage to their own businesses.

"If I could get my hands on Ackroyd I would string him up," said one.

"Hope someone goes to jail for this," vented another.

She worked efficiently back in her own office. Pitcher's number popped up on her mobile several times. She was too busy to take his calls.

As her main deadlines approached, she surveyed the material of the morning. It was all good and worthy – a sound account of the crisis of the day.

Not enough, Julia drummed her fingers on her desk. *A crunch on this scale needs more. Why's this happening? What's caused it? Who's to blame? That's what readers want to know.*

Politicians, bankers, economists and historians would argue about these questions for decades. But she had a head start. Silverman had given her an inside track.

Why? she asked herself, thinking of Silverman standing in that cave, haunted by – what? She didn't know.

"He wants it all to come out – that's why," she answered her question aloud.

"What's why?" Cody stopped typing and looked up at the sound of her voice.

"Nothing. Just thinking aloud." A light had switched on. "Silverman wants it all to come out. Only once the authorities understand what's happened, can they fix things."

"You really think they can fix this?" Cody asked.

"They always do. The question is who pays? How you getting on?"

"Fine. I'll be ready to file my City reaction in about five minutes."

"That's great. I'd better get on."

She started to write probably the biggest scoop of her career. She told the story of how sliced-and-diced debt packages infiltrated the entire global financial system to create a shadow banking monster. No one knew what they were worth or where they were. Only that they fuelled a boom built on worthless promises. The wealth of the world was primed with deadly incendiaries, and the touch paper was burning.

Ludgate called a few moments after she filed. "Where d'you get all this?" he asked.

"Deep source..."

He didn't need to ask if it could be trusted.

He paused for a moment, thinking. When he spoke again, she could hear the weariness in his voice.

"OK, let's get this out and see what response we get. Good work. Seems you haven't been wasting your time. I owe you a drink."

"Thanks."

"I'm going to New York later this evening on the Chancellor's plane. He's addressing the IMF. Just keep doing what you're doing."

"Will do," she cleared her throat. "Andrew, they must've known, mustn't they? They must all have known what they were doing."

"They didn't have a fucking clue," he was angry. "None of them. Not the traders, not executives, not the agencies, not the Treasury, the Fed or the European Central Bank. They should all be lined up against a wall and shot."

"What about us, we should've known?"

He sighed.

"These shadow banks are all off balance sheet. We can only report what we can see – but you're right. We could have tried harder. Some of us tried."

She was glad he included her in the "us".

CHAPTER 30

Thursday August 19

PATRICK SILVERMAN called the next morning. "So you decided to run with the story?"

"D'you mind?" she took a sip of her coffee. "It's nothing like the whole story, but it's time. Time to begin the drip...drip...drip to see where it leads."

"No, I didn't mind. As you say, it's time. The faster they understand what's happened, the quicker they can put it right."

"In your dreams, don't you think?"

He smothered a deep chortle. "Maybe."

"I'm sorry I've not been in touch." Julia felt guilty at not making contact since returning from Hong Kong.

"How long've you been back?"

"Around a week, but it's been crazy."

Cody arrived and gave her a thumbs-up good-morning. She smiled at him despite a sinking feeling. She would have to come clean and her news wouldn't be welcome.

"Truth is, I didn't call, because I didn't have anything to tell you."

"About Laura? You drew a blank?"

"No, not entirely. I discovered something, but it doesn't take us much further. You were right she's been working as a doctor in Hong Kong. I met one of her colleagues."

"So you found her...that's brilliant."

"No, the thing is..." Julia breathed deeply. "Have you seen the stories about a new virus outbreak in Southern China?"

"You mean Avian flu?" he stretched the words, as if apprehensive about what might follow.

"I tracked down a friend of Laura's. Another doctor – Kathy – lovely lady. They worked together at the children's hospital in Sandy Bay. Kathy told me the Republic of China appealed for doctors to go and help with a new outbreak of the virus. Laura went. I didn't have the correct visa, so I couldn't go – and my paper called me home urgently."

"Sounds just like Laura. How long's she been there? When's she coming back?"

"That's the thing Patrick. No one knows. She's been out of touch."

"How long?"

"A year..."

Silence. Julia waited for him to react. Cody's phone started to ring. Silverman said nothing.

Where do we go with this now? she thought. She could hear deep breathing at the other end. Finally he spoke.

"Did I say I'm in London. Can we meet up? I won't take much of your time."

"Sure, earlier – rather than later – better for me. You in the office?"

"Yeah."

"OK, how about I see you in the Jampot in an hour. Few things to sort out here first."

"Let's say 11 o'clock," he put the phone down. Julia looked across at Cody and pulled a face.

"What?" he said.

"I've got a feeling I've just walked into a trap."

"Don't worry, be happy. I've got some good news for you. Chief Inspector Pitcher called and said the British Museum's finally got its act together and I can go and look at the CCTV for the morning Adam Lee died. OK, if I shoot across there now?"

"Absolutely, but why isn't he sending one of his officers?"

"Something about couldn't spare anyone for a wild goose chase."

"And he thinks we can? Thanks Pitch!" she raised her eyes to heaven. "Try not to be too long. Deadlines, copy etc. OK, and remember the fifth rule of journalism – use your eyes. Seeing is believing."

"He probably wants us to take the first look. See if we recognise anyone. Honestly I don't mind going."

Cody left, and Julia wrote a short piece looking at what the crash could mean for ordinary borrowers and savers. It didn't work well, so she cut it, reinstated it, chopped it again, then hit send.

That'll fill a hole, she thought, grabbing her coat and heading for the door. She crossed London Bridge, and made her way to the Jampot.

I didn't imagine it, she thought, stepping inside. Echoes of the Foreign Correspondents' Club in Hong Kong reverberated all around. *Same bar, same furniture, same satirical cartoons.*

She skipped down the stairs, her eyes feeding on a Georgian skit on bankers, in their top hats and expensive suits, betting who would win the war with Napoleon. Ruin for all – if Britain lost. *They got lucky*, she thought. *Maybe we will too.*

Silverman was sitting at the same table she sat at with Hugo. The bar was empty. He had already ordered coffee. She took off her jacket, sat down and reached for her cup.

"Busy morning?" he greeted her.

"Busy for us all. Is that what's brought you up to town?"

"Partly. I was due a trip. It's good to catch up with friends and colleagues. Good to see you, too."

She nodded. "Let me apologise again, for not getting back about Laura. I didn't know..."

"So she's disappeared?" he raised eyebrows.

"We don't know she's disappeared. There could be a number of explanations. Without more information it's impossible to say where she is or what's happened. Her friends keep trying to get information – only to hit brick walls. They're worried about her."

Julia thought Silverman winked at her, then she remembered his nervous twitch. She looked down and saw his index finger tapping under the table.

He seems very stressed.

"What do we know about this virus?" he continued, the left eye winking again.

"Nothing or not very much. That's partly why Laura volunteered. The medics in Hong Kong were worried the Chinese Government wasn't telling the truth."

"A cover-up? And you didn't have the appropriate visa?"

Julia nodded.

"D'you have a visa now?"

"Yes, I do. It came through a couple of days ago."

"Good, that's the reason I wanted to see you – to ask you to go back and try again."

Julia belched out a belly laugh, stunned. "Don't be ridiculous. I've a job to do here. We're in the middle of a meltdown. This is where I belong."

He took a telescope of papers from his pocket and unrolled them before her on the table.

He hasn't heard me, she thought. *Or doesn't want to.*

"I ran off a few internal reports on that region," he continued. "We too have our contacts. If Laura's still in China, she's at grave risk. The numbers are far higher than the Government acknowledges, trebling each day. She needs to get out."

"If she can."

"Exactly. China's becoming more draconian as it attempts to silence critics and stories about its mishandling of the crisis."

"With all due respect Mr Silverman, we know all this. It just doesn't have anything to do with me. Honestly, I wish you luck with your search. You could go yourself, or you can afford to pay people, professional rescue teams who extract expats from dangerous areas. It's not my problem."

Out of the corner of her eye she saw Hopkins enter the bar and sit at a table at the other end. He waved an acknowledgement in her direction. She ignored him.

Silverman was speaking again. "I'm afraid it's about to become your problem. You've been too busy to keep an eye on stock exchange share transaction notices. My fund made a large purchase at 9am. Technically, I'm now controlling director of the Square Mile – the title you mainly write for. We had a small stake. When prices plunged, it was too juicy a prospect not to buy more."

Julia's jaw dropped so far and so fast, she thought it might smash the table.

"Don't worry, I've no intention of interfering editorially – unless I have to –"

His meaning was clear.

"I'm a freelance."

"Yes I know that. I also know you care very much about children. Find Laura, and I'll give you £10 million to donate to any children's charity of your choice. "

"This is blackmail," she blinked rapidly. "Twice over."

He smiled, and this time a kindly glint twinkled in his eyes.

"I just want you to understand I'm serious. You asked why I can't go or send someone else. I honestly don't believe she would come. You're like her in some ways. You remind me of her. You already have good contacts in Hong Kong. You'll be fleet of foot and move under the radar. Most important of all, I think you might be able to persuade her to leave."

You must love her very much.

Julia watched Alek Jakov join Hopkins at the table. She laughed. *Good luck punting that story again,* she thought.

"You find me amusing?" Silverman looked puzzled.

"No, not at all, I'm sorry, something else caught my eye."

"So will you go?"

She evaded his question.

204

"Have you heard anything from Chandler?"

"I'm really sorry. I haven't seen him for it must be..." he paused, thinking before adding "...well over a year."

"Have you spoken to Rebecca?"

"We were never close."

"If you're so worried about Laura, why are you so unconcerned about Stephen?" He didn't respond. "I knew him you know. Liked him. Why haven't you hired a private eye to look for him – for old time's sake?"

She noticed Hopkins go to the bar.

"Will you excuse me please?" she said to Silverman. Getting up, she headed in Hopkins' direction.

Beside him at the bar, she said, "Look, I know we've not been mates, but I should warn you about Alek. He's a bullshitter. Don't touch any of his stuff."

"He's just given me a fantastic story."

"Not this Bank of England garbage."

She saw a flash of recognition in his eye.

So it is the Bank of England tip? Surely even Hopkins can't be stupid enough to fall for that?

"Honestly, for once I'm trying to be a friend. At least wait until Ludgate gets back."

"I think I know how to judge a story. Keep your nose out of my business."

He turned in a huff and headed back to Alek – carrying two glasses.

Julia leaned on her elbows across the bar for a moment. *Why is the world suddenly so crazy*, she thought.

She returned to Silverman, and sat bolt upright in her chair.

"OK I'll do it. I'll need a few days to get things sorted this end."

He released a long slow breath.

"Thank you. I'm sorry I had to come on heavy like this. But Laura is special."

Oh yes, that's one message I got loud and clear.

CODY BOUNCED up wide steps at the colonnaded main entrance to the British Museum.

"Map Sir?" an attendant approached, offering him one.

Cody grinned. "Thank you, but I don't need a map to find my way round here."

School in Southwark meant termly trips. His heart leapt as he stepped inside the cathedral-like arena – the closest he would ever get to the inside of a church. He loved its very smell. Moving briskly past retail outlets selling mummy pencil cases, Lewis chessmen, Viking rubber ducks and Trojan war shields, he walked to the rear of the gallery and the security office.

He waited a few moments to be admitted by a techy-type who introduced himself as Will, and led Cody through to the office.

"I think this is what you're looking for." Will handed him a still shot from the CCTV of Lee having a coffee with another man.

"The time of this one is 10.45am."

He pushed a second still across the desk.

"As you see, his companion stayed on for lunch, when he was joined by a second man. Does this help?"

Cody took a deep qi gong breath to calm his excitement. He exhaled slowly as he had learned in his Tai Chi classes.

"Can I look at the tape?" he asked.

"Of course, it might make things clearer."

It didn't take long to pull up the relevant sections. "Crystal clear and no mistake," he said, mainly to himself.

CHAPTER 31

JULIA'S HEAD spun as she trotted back to the office, down Cornhill, over London Bridge, across Tooley Street. *I'm absolutely trapped*, she thought, a knot forming hard in her stomach. *How could he? What an absolute bastard!*

The first thing she did once back at her desk was check the Square Mile's share price. "Huckleberry Finn!" she exclaimed to an empty room. At one point that morning, the paper's share price had literally touched 1p. "That's when he struck. Any of us could have bought the damn thing. Look how it bounced!"

She wanted to speak urgently to Ludgate, but he was on his way to New York. So she settled for an email. She hit send as her line rang.

"That was quick," she said. But it wasn't Ludgate. She immediately recognised Rebecca Withers, Chandler's wife.

"I've made a discovery. I don't know what to do about it. I need advice." She sounded anxious. "Could we meet?"

"Sure. Shall I come to you?"

"The Fashion and Textile Museum is across the road from you, isn't it? How about there at 2pm?"

Julia checked the clock on her screen. It was 1.25pm. Enough time to gather her thoughts and maybe grab a bite.

"I'll be there."

She skipped downstairs to the deli to buy a sandwich, but Mr Bardetti insisted he put together a healthy salad for her. He had a rare talent for stirring the stomach juices with exquisite cheese, parma ham, herring flakes, artichokes, black olives and dried tomatoes.

"You gotta start eating right – or you'll be old before your time. Which dressing you want? Tuscany, Modena, Napolitana, Venetian?"

"You choose!" Julia was bemused at the proliferation of bottles for salad dressing on the counter – all home made. He handed over the lunch.

"Thank you Mr Bardetti – you're good to me."

"I'm good to all my customers, but some are more special than others. What I do if you move out? You're my best, most considerate tenant."

"Don't worry we're not going anywhere."

"Good and tell your young man, I've something special for him, when he gets back for lunch too."

"I will," she said, heading back upstairs.

He's right, Julia thought. *I need to take better care of myself.*

She switched off her screen, removed all distractions, sat back in her chair and calmly enjoyed his delicious salad. When she finished, she scrawled a note for Cody, and headed out across the road. Office workers and mums with pushchairs dotted the grass in Tanner Street Gardens opposite. Toddlers ran crazily in the sunshine. *How I love this scene*, she thought.

She found Rebecca at the exhibition of Designs from the Swinging Sixties, staring at a mannequin modelling a Mary Quant orange mini-dress.

She looks lost, Julia thought. "These prints are so familiar aren't they?" she said, shuffling alongside Rebecca.

"Familiar. Yet not of our age," Rebecca nodded. "Backcloth to our childhoods – Mum's dresses and pinafores."

She moved to the next stand and pointed at a textile display.

"This fabric is still on sale at John Lewis – amazing."

"So new and so timeless."

"They wanted a fresh start after the war," Rebecca bit her lip. "Sweep away the past. Think we'll manage it so easily?"

A video montage of newsreel replayed scenes from the swinging 60s – Profumo scandal, Bay of Pigs, Martin Luther King, Vietnam war. These were interspersed with showbiz clips of the Beatles, the Stones, Jim Morrison. Julia looked round. They were alone. No one else cared about fashions of the past or this gem of a museum, tucked away off the beaten track.

A bench was positioned in front of the video. "Shall we sit?" Julia suggested.

They sat in silence watching the Sixties video and its walk down memory lane.

When Rebecca spoke, her tone was dead and lifeless. "I wanted to see you..." flickering shadows from the moving pictures flashed across her face.

"There's no news about Stephen, I take it?"

"No Julia. With everything that's going on, he's become old news."

"I'm sorry. I've neglected you."

Julia's eye fell on Rebecca's manicured fingers. Two of the nails were broken.

"I found something," Rebecca started scrabbling in her bag. "I tore the place apart looking for a clue. Then I found this."

She held up a cheap-looking phone.

"It's a burner. Pushed right to the back of a drawer under our bed. I thought it was an old phone discarded ages ago. When I looked closer, I realised Stephen was running a second phone, that couldn't be traced back to him."

Julia narrowed her eyes. *I have a bad feeling about this*, she thought.

As if reading her mind, Rebecca said, "No, it's not another woman. My first thought too, although I couldn't believe it."

"You found the pass code?"

"Not too difficult. We've been together a long time."

Julia waited for her to continue.

"He started using it a few days before his disappearance. Only a few calls, and the numbers don't mean anything to me. But the texts tell a different story. He arranged to meet Adam Lee at the British Museum for coffee the day he disappeared."

Julia blinked in surprise. "I see. Can I take a look?"

Rebecca handed her the phone and Julia switched through the text trail. No mistake. They made a firm arrangement to meet at the museum.

"Now I think about it, I remembered he mentioned Adam Lee out of the blue the week he disappeared. I wasn't really listening. He muttered something at breakfast about that crackpot Adam Lee."

"Doesn't sound as though he liked him, I wonder why he agreed to meet up."

"The last day I saw Stephen," Rebecca's lip trembled. "And the day Lee died."

"It must be a coincidence mustn't it? How could they be connected?"

"Let's walk a bit," Julia said. The screen flashed scenes of screaming Beatles fans as the pop icons arrived at J F K Airport.

On the left they passed a collection of Mary Quant's plastic alligator and banana split mini-dresses.

On the right Terence Conran's iconic cone chair, along with sundry other Chelsea-set furniture.

"Why meet up? Were they friends?" Julia asked.

"No. I'm sure they weren't. Must've been business."

"Stephen did business with First State?"

Rebecca shook her head. "I doubt it. From what I've read it's not the sort of outfit Stephen would touch. Hong Kong, yes of course. They ran one of the biggest book of Asian Tiger funds. I know he spoke to his old boss Warwick Mantel regularly. I'm pretty sure they had dealings. Perhaps he met Lee to catch up on Asia?"

Julia stopped before a space-age silver dress and a bond-girl mini with pull-string zipper running from top to bottom.

What I'd give to rip down the zipper on this whole mess, and see what's going on underneath, Julia thought.

Instead she said, "After this meeting one of them is dead. And the other..."

"Vanished." Rebecca's eyes moistened with tears.

"You're tired," Julia said. "Are you sleeping?" Rebecca shook her head.

212

"We'll have to tell the police."

"Could you see to that for me? It's embarrassing, humiliating, me being a lawyer."

Julia nodded. "I'll call them as soon as I get back to the office. You may not hear from me for a few days. I'm going to Hong Kong. If you need anything while I'm away call the office. My assistant Cody is a good lad. He'll help you."

"Hong Kong?"

"Know Patrick Silverman?" Julia changed the subject.

"A bit. He and Stephen were close when they were younger. Less so once I came on the scene. I was never very keen on him. Had a friend who..." she stopped herself. "That doesn't matter now."

"Once a heel always a heel," Julia raised her eyebrows. "I'm beginning to see."

"Why are you going?"

"Various reasons. Silverman wants me to track down another former colleague, Laura Wan Sun. Thinks she might be able to shed light on what happened to Lee and your husband."

Rebecca's face brightened. "Ah, Laura," she said. "Truly special person. One of nature's magic people. Pure saint."

Julia's brow darkened. *If one more person tells me how wonderful Laura is, I'll start to hate her.*

"Look Rebecca, I need to get back and call the police. Are you OK?"

Rebecca nodded. "I think I'll stay a while longer. It's peaceful here. There's nothing to rush home for."

"OK, if you're sure," Julia smiled, adding, "You take care of yourself. If you need anything call me or Cody. The police will be in contact to help very soon I'm sure."

Julia turned back to look at Rebecca as she reached the door.

A lost soul, she repeated to herself, *hiding in a world that's gone.*

AN EMAIL FROM Ludgate was waiting for her when she returned to the office.

Should have told you. Heard the news about the buyout on the trip over. He's a fund manager. He buys and sells all the time. Our price crashed and he got lucky. We'll bounce, he'll take his profit and get straight out. Don't sweat it, but yes, for the time being he's our boss. It's OK with me if you want to go back to Hong Kong for a few days, but we need stories every day.

Julia made a noise like a strangled cat, after reading the message. She reached across the desk, grabbed her phone and started dialling Chief Inspector Pitcher.

"Ah, it's Lois Lane. How are we today?"

"Puzzled, but I have some information I think you'll want."

"How did young Cody get on at the British Museum?"

"I don't know, he's not back yet. While we're on that subject, can you please not use my staff as errand boys."

"Sorry, he's a bright boy. I'm not sure you're making the most of his talents."

"Like you do your PCs?"

"That's not fair. We're the police force. They're not allowed to have fun. Serious business. Why d'you call?"

"I don't need to see the CCTV, I know who Lee met that fateful morning."

"Go on."

"I've just been with Rebecca. She found a burner phone hidden at home. The text trail points to Stephen Chandler meeting Lee at 10.30am at the British Museum."

"Why? They aren't connected?"

"It seems they are. The connection lies in Hong Kong. I'm heading back there in a day or so."

"I've warned you already. Hong Kong's a dangerous place."

"Isn't London?"

"In London I can protect you."

"Your new best friend Cody will hold the fort. Look after him for me will you?"

"It'll be a pleasure."

Julia replaced the receiver as Cody burst puffing into the office. His jaw line was set hard, but his eyes burned bright.

"You'll never believe who's captured on the British Museum's CCTV?"

"Stephen Chandler. I've just left Rebecca."

"Well done, you got there first. But there's more."

"Go on –"

"Who did Chandler have lunch with after Lee had gone?"

Julia had no idea.

"It could be anyone. His partners, lawyers, anyone."

"Take a deep breath," Cody said, putting a copy of a still of the CCTV on her desk.

She stared at it for a few seconds, unbelieving, then picked up a pen and threw it across the room.

"You bastard, you lied," she screeched.

She stretched the picture gently, bringing it closer for inspection. There was no doubt. Chandler was sitting having lunch with Patrick Silverman.

CHAPTER 32
11.30pm
Tottenham

THE CALL CAME as Chief Inspector Pitcher was about to turn in for the night. It was PC Day.

"I've had a tip – my source. Something might be kicking off tonight."

"Where are you?"

"Old Compton Street. Good butcher's round. Everything looks normal. Restaurants full, crowds of tourists. It'll be thinning out soon."

"OK," Pitcher was thinking.

"One thing," Day continued. "Maybe something, maybe nothing. Walked through Chinatown. Two groups of ugly-looking Chinese youths. One in the Golden Pagoda..."

"Chang's place?"

"That's right."

"The other in the Hong Kong Noodle Company."

"What were they doing?"

"Eating."

"Just eating?"

"Eating. Got a bad feeling..."

"Keep those coming. They'll save your life one day. I'll send a couple of patrol cars, and an armed response van – just in case. Low profile. Butcher on and shout at the first sign of trouble."

Pitcher switched the television back on. *No point trying to sleep,* he thought, fancying a glass of something strong. Instead, he went into the kitchen and brewed dark, bitter coffee.

Match of the Day was rerunning the Arsenal versus Spurs match. Dull the first time, it badly needed a goal. He watched on, keen for a diversion as his mind raced – watched on until 10 minutes into extra time. Then he could take it no more – put on a jacket, headed for the door, and set off in his car for Soho.

It was gone 1am when he pulled into Cambridge Circus, alongside the armed unit – his phone ringing. It was PC Day.

"They're on the move. I'll follow at a distance. They seem to be heading for Soho Square."

Pitcher banged on the side of the response van. "We're off," he said. "Soho Square."

Three officers leapt out the van and advanced with Pitcher down a deserted Greek Street. There was no sign of Day. Pitcher's heart pumped louder with each step. He knew what he would find when he reached the square. He'd seen it dozens of times before. Gangs facing each other off, knives twitching for blood.

Please God let's get there before the slashing starts.

Then a nerve-shattering scream fractured the night air.

Jesus Christ, where's Day? Pitcher broke into a run, his armed officers in the lead.

When he entered the Square, his blood froze at the gleam of a deadly blade. A vicious thug – inhuman and unrecognisable thanks to the hideous web of tattoos covering his face and razored head – was about to crack a machete down on PC Day, who stood guarding a fallen body.

"Jesus Christ, No." Pitcher roared in horror as the killer tool started to plunge towards the young PC.

The tattoo monster braked instantly, startled by the loud noise – arm suspended mid-air.

"Put down your weapons," one of Pitcher's officers spoke calmly through a loud speaker. "You're surrounded."

Sirens announced the arrival of more police, racing down Frith Street, Carlisle and Soho Street – an ambulance tailgating.

Suddenly it was over. Tattoo-face dropped his arm and ran. The gangs vanished into thin air.

Patrols gave chase. Pitcher ran towards Day.

"You OK?" he asked, placing an unusually affectionate hand on his officer's arm.

"I am, thanks...for a moment I thought...I was trying to stop them killing this guy."

Pitcher knelt.

"He's still breathing. They'll take him to hospital. I'll get you home."

As they walked back to his car together, Pitcher thought how close he had come to losing one of his most valuable and promising officers.

This has to stop, he promised himself as the car pulled away.

CHAPTER 33
Friday August 20

HOW COULD I'VE BEEN so naive? Julia asked herself over and again as she tossed through the night. Silverman lied to her consistently about not seeing Chandler and not knowing where he was. Not just to her, but to everyone. To Rebecca, who deserved better. The police presumably. But why? It didn't make any sense.

I've been such a fool.

Flashbacks of the trip to Cornwall kept crashing her thoughts. He seemed so genuine. *But he was strange in that cave*, she remembered. *Like someone transformed. What was that all about? Was he scared? What was his role in Lee's death and Chandler's disappearance? Did he mastermind it all?*

She remembered, as she drove away from the castle, a chilling sense someone was watching from the shadows. Could Chandler have been on the island all the time? Was he being held against his will?

Julia left early to catch the Heathrow Express for her flight to Hong Kong. She grabbed her morning edition of the Square Mile and thrust it into her bag, as she struggled to get her suitcase out the door.

Not until the Express was whizzing its way out West, did she unravel her copy and look at the front page headline.

Empty vaults at the Bank of England – Britain's gold reserve sold to China.

More lies lies lies, she put her head in her hands. Sitting up she read the article slowly and in full. *This would never have happened if Ludgate were here. He'll have a fit,* she thought.

Fake news could bankrupt a newspaper.

Always a silver lining, she flicked to the next page. *Silverman might lose his shirt.*

Despite this potentially catastrophic cock-up, Julia couldn't resist a surge of excitement, as she climbed the aircraft's steps.

Is it the lure of the East? she wondered. *Or relief at running away?*

The cabin was full so the view to her seat was blocked. As she neared, the file of people began to clear. Her heart nearly stopped when she saw a familiar figure. Yes, he was sitting in the aisle seat, beside her window seat - 22A.

I can't believe this, she thought. It was Ziggy, the Ambassador's nephew.

"What a wonderful happenstance," he greeted her. "Of all the people travelling to Hong Kong this week, what chance should we not only be on the same plane – but sitting side by side?"

No chance at all, Julia thought.

She removed her jacket, folded it, and stretched up to stow it away in her overhead locker. Ziggy stood to allow her to reach her seat. She sat, tightened her seat belt, and took the newspaper out of her bag.

"Interesting story on your front page," Ziggy's face lit with a mischievous grin.

Julia raised her eyebrows but didn't speak. The plane started to taxi.

"I take it, the story's true? It must be to secure so prestigious a slot on such an august publication?"

"Time will tell," Julia replied without expression. Their eyes met briefly. Ziggy burst into giggles and despite herself, Julia joined in.

"Disinformation should be a crime," Ziggy was still beaming. "Not that it happens in China naturally. Nor in London I hope."

Julia's snigger subsided – replaced by a stab of fury at Hopkins for turning the Square Mile into a laughing stock.

"Going to Hong Kong for business?" she changed the subject.

"Partly business, partly to catch up with friends and family. You?"

The pilot went full throttle and the plane blasted upwards.

Julia seized both arms of her seat. "Sorry, I'm not good with takeoff."

She tipped forward feeling the full force of a kick to her stomach, straightening again as the speed of ascension eased slightly.

"Always like this," she apologised, closing her eyes.

What's he doing here? she wondered. *Is it honestly a coincidence? Or has he been told to mind me? If so, by whom? The Embassy, the Hong Kong authorities, the Chinese People's Republic? How will I get through nearly twelve hours sitting next to him?*

222

She opened her eyes. "Look, I'm sorry – not feeling great. Mind if I watch a film and then sleep? Don't want to seem rude."

"Of course not. Can I make a suggestion before you rest? Whatever your purpose for this trip – I'm guessing research. If you need a friend, you can always call on me - someone you can trust."

He placed a warm palm on the back of Julia's hand. Her heart froze.

No, not the tiniest corner of me would ever trust you.

She managed to squeeze out a smile and say "Thanks," before snuggling down in her blanket and dimming the light overhead.

SHE SLEPT for several hours, and was woken by the clatter of dishes. Cabin lights turned up bright, stewards were serving a meal.

"Good morning Julia," Ziggy grinned. "Breakfast's on its way."

"Morning. Sleep well?" Julia screwed her eyes sleepily.

"Not at all. I've been reading. Kim."

"Kipling?"

"A child has to decide between East and West."

"It's a spy story, I seem to recall."

"Is it? It's a very complicated story."

The breakfast trolley reached their seat. The steward offered noodles or rice. Julia picked noodles and Ziggy rice.

"Where are you heading when we land?" Ziggy asked. "A car's picking me up. I can drop you somewhere if you like."

Julia hesitated. A lift would be helpful, but she wanted to keep her distance from Ziggy.

"I'm staying close to the Foreign Correspondents' Club at the Pottinger Hotel."

"Good choice. Very central, but pricey. Square Mile paying? It's one of the oldest streets in the city. Named after the first British Governor Sir Henry Eldred Curwen Pottinger."

"Curwen. That's a new one on me. I'll be surrounded by history will I?"

"You know Hong Kong. Brash modernity side by side with British colonialism and oriental gentility. In the past, this district was the centre of trade, with warehouses, labourers plying their wares, fisherman, porters, dockers and ship captains."

"All human life eh? Like our docklands?"

"Similar, in some ways – very different in others."

"You make it sound exciting."

"It was, and still is. Every bit as exciting as you want it to be."

As I want it to be, Julia wondered. *Is that a promise or a threat?*

224

CHAPTER 34

Friday August 20
Scotland Yard

PITCHER LOOKED up as the Duty Sergeant entered his office.

"And?" he raised questioning eyes.

"Nothing Sir."

"Nothing?" he bellowed.

"They disappeared. The lads gave chase – difficult terrain. Scum bags disappeared into cellars, attics and sewers around Soho. We assume it was some sort of gang fight. We know they were Chinese."

"Part of a war?"

"Maybe. Goes with the territory in those parts. Descend, kill or maim, then disappear as quickly. Injured individual's in intensive care. Unconscious. When he comes round, maybe..."

"ID?"

"Not yet, but it's not all bad news. We've got a possible ID on the body out at Epping," he said, stooping to pick up some papers discarded on the floor. "Name Walter Halamanning keeps coming up. Desk's taken several calls after the appeal in the local press. Lives in Wanstead and works in the City. Shall I pass it on to the City of London Police?"

"Tempting," Pitcher scratched his jaw. "He was found on our patch, and lives in Wanstead. Strictly speaking, he's ours. Let's get an ID confirmed then maybe let the City boys know. Anything else?"

"I printed off a biog I found on the internet. Respected City figure, or so it says. Does a lot of charity work apparently – list of places he advised. Why would he be found hacked to death in Epping? Doesn't add up."

"When does it ever add up? Great work, thanks. Get family liaison round to talk to the family. See what they can find out."

The Duty Sergeant left. Pitcher scanned the article. One name leapt out. The Whittingdale Trust.

"So you had a finger in the fund that's now missing a million," he said aloud. "Maybe we've found Cody's missing Treasurer."

Why was he left at the Guide Camp? He's certainly upset someone.

"Damn, why isn't Julia here? This is her area," he said aloud, tapping his desk three times. Then he stood, put on his jacket, left the office, and drove to Bermondsey Street, parking outside Julia's office.

"You can't park there," said Mr Bardetti, who was standing at the door of his Deli.

Pitcher climbed out his car, nose twitching at the wonderful Mediterranean aromas emanating from the Deli. He bent and reached back inside, placing a police hazard light on the roof, with a flourish of his arm.

226

"I think you'll find I can," he said, smiling broadly at Mr Bardetti. "God, you get my juices going. Skipped breakfast, what do you suggest?"

"No, problem, come inside. I'll fix you a wrap. Now what do you fancy? Dried tomatoes, ham, salami, mozzarella cheese, lettuce, red pepper, red onions and artichoke?"

"With some olives on the side. Heaven." Pitcher licked his lips. "And Julia would want you to put it on her tab."

"She's not here you know," he gave the Chief Inspector a sideways glance as he assembled the wrap.

Pitcher nodded. "I know."

"You're here an awful lot," the barista drizzled dressing over the ingredients.

"Don't worry Mr Bardetti. I'm not going to steal her away from you. We help each other out."

"That's not what I worry about. You need to take better care of her. She puts a lot of noses out of joint. You and me both know, angry people can be dangerous."

"I do tell her. Right now she's on the other side of the world, so there's not much I can do."

"When she gets back, you take care of her," Bardetti repeated. A broad smile lit up his face as he handed over the wrap. "Enjoy Chief Inspector."

"Ciao," Pitcher waved as he made his way to Julia's office entrance. He turned back, thinking about Bardetti's words. "Great you're here, too," he said.

He took the stairs to Julia's office two at a time.

"What can I do for you Chief Inspector?" Cody asked looking up from a desk awash with papers.

227

"I need your help," the detective sat opposite him. "But first I need to taste this delicious creation," he bit into the wrap.

"Cool," the young reporter said, watching its contents ooze all over Pitcher's face. He handed him a tissue.

"We've got an unconfirmed ID on the body at the Guide Camp," Pitcher said, when he finished wiping his mouth and fingers. "We think it could be your missing Treasurer from the Whittingdale Trust. Can you run through with me again all you know about this trust, and what exactly you think's missing?"

Cody recounted how an anonymous envelope had arrived the morning after Adam Lee was murdered, and Julia asked him to look at the contents. With the help of the librarian at the Guildhall library, he discovered the papers were accounts relating to the Whittingdale Trust.

"How d'you manage that?"

"There were loads of clues, names of directors, offices, so forth. But I couldn't work out what the story was, so Julia put me in contact with her friendly forensic accountant."

"And he said there was a million missing?"

"At least, he couldn't be sure. But yes money was gone. I contacted the Chairman of the Trust, James Montague, and he told me to speak to the Treasurer – only he was nowhere to be found."

"Until now," Pitcher said.

"Not sipping Martinis in Panama after all – " Cody threw the debris from Pitcher's wrap in the bin.

"We can't be sure but possibly not. Who would want him dead?"

"And why take the money in the first place? Maybe someone was blackmailing him?"

"Why?"

"Or he had an accomplice – and they fell out?"

"The orchid. It can't be a coincidence."

"I'm sorry, Inspector, I'm not quite following you."

"Adam Lee had an orchid in his top pocket. So did Halamanning. It has to be a sign of something. They both worked in finance. There has to be a connection."

"Well, maybe there was," he slid a wad of papers across the desk.

"If you look at last year's list of Trustees, you'll see a name you might recognise. Julia certainly would. Jonathan Silverman – Patrick Silverman's father."

Pitcher scratched his head. "No, you've lost me there."

"Golden Boys, I think they called them. Adam Lee, Stephen Chandler and Patrick Silverman, all worked together at Peak Bank for a while."

"What! Adam Lee, Stephen Chandler and Patrick Silverman all knew each other. Why wasn't I told this before now? And Silverman's father was involved in this trust, where a million pounds is missing. Adam Lee's dead and Halamanning murdered. Chandler's disappeared."

"Silverman's the last man standing. What d'we do next?"

Pitcher belched. "Well, I know what Julia would say."

"That would be?"

"She would say, write it, for tomorrow's edition. The deadline should be looming – it always seems to be for her. She would say – what're you waiting for Cody? You can do this."

229

"I've never written anything this big," the young reporter said tentatively.

"Come off it, there's nothing to it. The fuss these journalists make. If I can confirm the ID in a couple of hours, which I'm hoping, you're ready to roll."

PITCHER DID CONFIRM and Cody's story rocked the charitable sector. A major London charity – a £1 million black hole in the accounts – the Treasurer found dead. The other Trustees resigned on mass. The next day the Chairman, Sir James Montague, was admitted to London Bridge hospital with a heart attack.

Cody was downcast.

"Don't waste your pity on him," Pitcher said, when he called to compliment him on the piece. "He's swanned round the City for decades picking up lucrative board positions, way beyond his capability."

"It doesn't get us any nearer to discovering what happened to the money, and why Halamanning was murdered."

"Nor what the orchid means."

"Inspector," Cody began, hesitating, "You do know that orchids are sometimes a calling card of the Triads."

CHAPTER 35
7am Saturday August 21
Hong Kong

ZIGGY DROPPED Julia at the Foreign Correspondents' Club. *Good riddance to him,* she thought, stepping inside. The woman at Reception recognised her and waved her through. *Just as well, as my temporary membership card has expired. Must apply for full membership and pay fee as soon as.*

She drank deep the atmosphere of the bar. *How wonderful to be back. Like coming home. How I love this place.* The wood, the fans, the cartoons, the award-winning editorials – each held a special welcome for her.

She ordered a coffee to ward off jet lag, found a quiet table, and dialled Kathy's number.

"I'm back in Hong Kong. Any chance of meeting up?"

"Sure," Kathy seemed eager. "Same place – Botanical Gardens, King George statue. I can be there for 9 o'clock."

She was enjoying her coffee when her mobile buzzed. It was a text from London. *Must've been delayed on the flight,* she thought, quickly scrawling through the message. It was from the gynae clinic, informing her the annual test had shown some abnormalities and letting her know more tests were being conducted.

Huckleberry Finn, w*hat's that about? There's no cancer in our family.* She shrugged off a worrying niggle, setting off for the uphill climb through the gardens. It was even hotter than Julia remembered. Though still early, the sun burnt down overhead. She was tired and dehydrated from the flight.

I can hardly breathe in this tropical climate. Sweat slithered between her shoulder blades.

She paused to catch her breath, the sweet smell of exotic blooms wafting through the air. The sound of crazy laughter crackled from the direction of the De Brazza's monkeys. He Len's ugly features loomed before her, and she shuddered.

Poor monkeys, she thought. *It's not their fault the bad guys stole their name.*

Kathy was waiting for her by the statue. She waved when she saw Julia.

How elegant and serene she looks, Julia thought.

"Good to see you again," Kathy clasped her hand in friendship.

"Good to be back…I think."

"You look hot and tired, shall we go down to the fountain? It'll be cooler there."

Julia nodded. When they reached the fountain, she stood for a few minutes under the deliciously-cool jet spray.

"So refreshing," she said, sitting beside Kathy on a bench. "How are you keeping? Well?"

"Well enough. What brings you back so soon?"

"Work, and curiosity. Hear any more about Laura?"

Kathy bit her lip. "No, and news of bird flu is harder to come by than ever. We suspect the Government is not honest

232

about the numbers dying. I fear any news, when it comes, can only be bad."

"I'm thinking of going into mainland China to see if I can find her. It would be an interesting trip for me. People in London want her found. They fear she might be in danger."

"For sure, she's in danger. That's what we're all worried about." Kathy's face darkened. "Avian flu is deadly and she's in the front line. The official Chinese statistics are a pack of lies. According to our medical back-channels it's spreading virulently. It breaks my heart to say this," Kathy's chin trembled. "If Laura were alive, I'm sure she would have got news through by now."

"Then help me make the trip," Julia pleaded. "If I hit dead ends, I'll give up and go home. At least I'll have tried."

They sat staring into the fountain, listening to the whooshing sound of its reviving jets. Kathy pulled a bag onto her lap, opened it, and took out some papers.

"I know she intended to head for Guangzhou. I've a friend in the International Hospital, a British doctor. He confirms she arrived there, but was sent to one of the specialist viral units. You can catch a high-speed train direct. Hardly an hour. I'll call my friend, Dr James Lippert. He'll be a good place to start."

"Thank you. That's what the West used to call Canton, isn't it? I'll book a ticket to go tomorrow. I need to sleep first."

"Tomorrow is Sunday."

"Is that a problem? Won't the trains run?"

"Yes, they run every day of the year. I need to check Dr Lippert will be at the hospital. If you want to stay a few days, James will help you find accommodation."

233

"That would be helpful. I'm not sure how long I'll need to stay."

Kathy's tone changed – her smile replaced by a worried frown. "I must warn you Julia. The virus is spreading. It's dangerous. If you're determined to go, you must minimise your time in the infected area. Leave as soon as you can. This is a killer disease."

"I will. I promise."

"Don't forget, you must also get in and out before the authorities are on to what you're up to. Is there someone who could go with you? I would come, but I can't leave the hospital."

"Of course, you've done enough."

They said goodbye. Kathy walked away, leaving Julia to enjoy the cool breeze of the fountain for a few moments more. She wondered about calling the gynae clinic but dismissed the thought.

It'll be fine and I need to get myself in gear.

She opened a map and worked out a route to the hotel. Thankfully her path was down hill, and she reached the Pottinger, in the heart of the central district, in about twenty minutes. It occupied a prime position in an ancient cobbled street at the crossroads between the new and old city. For all its luxurious glamour, it retained a hint of past mysteries. Her luggage was waiting in Reception.

"All part of the service," the bellboy said. Surges of tiredness closed her eyes as she queued to register.

Come on, wake up, no time for jet lag.

Her room was chic but compact. "This is what I need," Julia mumbled as she set the coffee machine in motion. She took the cup to the table near the window, fired up her laptop and reserved a seat on the following morning's train heading for Guangzhou.

Her next move was to call Richard.

"You're back," he greeted her. "Didn't think you'd miss us quite this much."

"Haha, very funny. Yes, I'm back, for good or ill. But I need to ask you a huge favour."

"Shoot."

"Not now. Can we get together later? Could you come to the Foreign Correspondents' Club?"

"Sure. What about an early supper – say 6pm?"

"Cool, see you there."

Julia hung up and turned to check her Inbox. There was an email from Ludgate. Short and concise. She read it aloud.

"I have today accepted the resignation of Matthew Hopkins."

Nothing more. No eloquent thanks for service, or praise for the extraordinary talents of the demised member of staff – customary even when someone is sacked. No attempt to save anyone's face or reputation. The message was clear – dismissed in disgrace.

"I did try and warn him," she said to her screen. "And you Andrew. Neither of you would listen."

She lay down on the bed and closed her eyes for a few moments. Jet lag knocked her out for the count. She sank into a heavy slumber, and woke with a shock.

235

"Damn – it's 5.15pm already," she cursed, walking briskly to the bathroom, for a quick shower, before heading out to meet Richard.

SHE ARRIVED first, ordered a couple of drinks, found a table and killed a few minutes browsing an English language business magazine. She gasped then burst out laughing when she saw a glossy advert for a Power Business Breakfast the day after tomorrow – tickets US$1,500. Keynote speaker was none other than Warwick Mantel.

Croissants must be solid gold at that price, she thought.

Her phone buzzed as a text from Kathy landed. *James Lippert in hospital next few days. Looks forward to seeing you.*

Richard walked in, grinning, broadly. "You must be overjoyed," he said sitting opposite, swigging thirstily from his drink. He, too, had crossed swords with Matthew Hopkins. "Nothing more satisfying than watching a treacherous back-stabber bite the dust. Gloating isn't the word."

Julia couldn't resist a wry smile, but she quickly straightened her expression.

"You're wrong about gloating."

Richard threw her a sceptical look.

"OK. Once, you would've been right. I would've danced on Hopkins' grave. But I've bigger fish to fry. My world's been revolving non-stop since I saw you last."

"I saw your analysis of the crash. Mind-boggling – but sound. Where'd it come from?"

Julia laughed. "Come on, you know better than that. Deep source. Remind me to tell you one day – in about a decade."

"We followed it up," Richard nodded warmly. "Hard to believe, but definitely struck a nerve of truth. Are we eating?"

"I'm so jet-lagged I hardly know what time it is, let alone what meal."

"Then you should eat," Richard picked up the menu. "You'll feel better on a full stomach." He went to the bar, ordered some food and returned with two more glasses.

"So what else?" he put a white wine in front of her.

"No you first. What impact did the collapse of First State have here?"

Richard shook his head. "No contagion so far. Some kickback. Street attacks on low-level bank staff. People are angry."

"Punishment beatings? Senior directors?"

"Gone, we still don't know where. Anyone locked up at home yet, for presiding over the most catastrophic banking crash for a century?"

"Not so far. We can live in hope. Everything's in chaos."

"What about Square Mile? You've a new owner I see. Perfect time to swoop. Share price of most newspapers in low pence – those still standing that is."

"Indeed, which brings me to the favour. I need to go to Guangzhou tomorrow. I've booked a seat."

"Tomorrow? Sunday?"

"I think it'll work. The trains run as normal, my interviewee is free to see me."

Julia stopped as food arrived. She had doubted she could eat, but at the sight of crunchy vegetables, and steaming beef noodles she realised her stomach was empty.

"Still looking for the mysterious Laura?" Richard asked, as he poked chow mein into his mouth.

"Yes, but this time on the orders of the management. No longer lone-ranger."

"That's good to hear. How can I help?"

Julia put down her chop sticks.

"Will you come with me? I'm going to struggle without any language or any idea how to deal with Chinese bureaucracy. Even coping with the transport. You know your way round. I might only be gone a day or so – not a long trip. Surely you can make some excuse about need for research to get time out of the office?"

Richard stopped eating but, using his chop sticks, he slowly moved his food around in the sauce.

"Please Richard," Julia pleaded. "It would be such a help. I'll pay you. Cover your expenses. I could pay a freelance fee. I've got money."

He flexed his jaw and sighed.

"Julia, I can't come with you. The authorities know me, a bit too well. The minute I stepped on that train, they'd be watching. We'd probably be turned back at the border. You've a much better chance of slipping through on your own. I'm so sorry. You have to do this alone."

Julia's stomach tightened. She was gutted – even though deep down she knew Richard was right. This was one journey she had to make alone

238

CHAPTER 36
Sunday August 22

JULIA CHECKED email first thing, and opened one from Cody, which she read with widening eyes.

Pitcher says the body hanging in the wood at Chigwell is the missing Treasurer of the Whittingdale fund. See Story attached.

She clicked on the file. "Huckleberry Finn, the shocks just keep coming," she said aloud, before adding, "Good boy, Cody – not a bad job and heaps of initiative."

Her return email said: *Fantastically well done. Gold stars all round. Keep going. Drill deep into Halamanning. Listen carefully to Pitcher. You won't get anything from the Charity Commission or the Fraud Squad. Keep digging, and stay in touch. I'll be back as soon as I can.*

Julia slammed her laptop shut, quickly showered, packed her bag, and headed down to reception, where she checked out, leaving her luggage in safe-keeping. She carried a few overnight things in a small shoulder bag in case she couldn't get back. She took a taxi to Kowloon's giant railway depot. It was vast and crowded. Julia decided to follow the crowds and hope for the best.

The strategy worked. Soon she was passing through various airport-style security and immigration desks. Railway staff seemed to pity her sense of drift, and tried to help, shouting at her hurriedly in incomprehensible Chinese – always with a smile. They steered her through with much patience and compassion, until she found herself in a giant lounge more like an airport than a railway waiting room, with destination boards on every wall. She sat near the gate for Guangzhou – one word she could read. She guessed her train was called when other passengers nearby her stood in panic, and massed for an exit. More checks and she was finally allowed aboard.

How to find my seat? Helpful stewardesses were on hand every few yards. One directed her to a carriage, pointed to the number on her ticket, then showed her where it would appear above her seat. The carriage was packed, so she had to queue to find her place. When the queue cleared she stumbled with astonishment. Swallowing hard, she rubbed her eyes in disbelief. Sitting in the aisle seat next to hers was a grinning Ziggy, waving an enthusiastic hello.

"I don't believe this," she exploded. "Are you following me?" She leant across him and slammed her bag on her seat.

"Following you? Why would I follow you? I saw you're going to Guangzhou today. I've a meeting myself at the university. I thought it would be hospitable to make your journey as pleasant and memorable as possible," he paused, pointing to her bag. "I think you'll be more comfortable if you place this in the luggage compartment."

She grabbed it with a jerk. "How d'you know about my travel plans?"

Ziggy smiled. "Julia, this is China. I'm the British Ambassador's nephew. You're British. Why d'you think I wouldn't know? You must stop thinking like a Brit and more like a Chinese citizen if you want to go into the PRC and come back again under your own steam."

"That sounds like a threat."

"Don't be ridiculous. You're staying as a guest in my country. I care everything should go as smoothly as possible. Surely you must welcome some company when travelling so far from home in a country whose language you can neither read nor speak, of whose customs you've no understanding?"

"No, I don't want your help or your company," Julia struggled with the overhead locker. "I'll be perfectly OK on my own. I've got this far haven't I?"

Ziggy stood, took the bag from her, and put it effortlessly in the luggage store. She noticed a faint tattoo on the inside of his arm. It looked like a magpie. He signalled for her to move into her own seat, and waited a diplomatic amount of time before sitting beside her.

"Why d'you keep pestering me?" she hissed in whisper, so other passengers would not hear.

Ziggy took a deep breath and spoke softly. "Julia I ask you again sincerely to reconsider your position. You're a clever girl. Can't you see the folly of your stubbornness? In London, we're friends. In China, we're friends. I can get you in and out of the People's Republic. Without me, you won't make it past the border. It's your decision."

Julia rubbed her lip. *He's right,* she thought. *I'll never manage this trip alone.*

"If you're determined to go alone…" he stood, reached for his jacket, and turned to leave. "Enjoy your trip."

Julia panicked and stretched out a hand. "No. Stay."

He sat with a sigh. "I wish you'd trust me."

"Trusting isn't what we journalists go in for much," she said, attempting a smile.

The train pulled away, and they rolled on together for about twenty minutes.

"What's the plan for your trip?" Ziggy eventually spoke.

Julia explained she hoped to visit a friend of a friend, and she would begin with an interview with a British doctor, James Lippert at the International Hospital.

"He's expecting me," she said.

"Good. If it's convenient, you can share my taxi. We'll be there before too long. I suggest we sit back and relax."

No one bothered them at the border. The train chundered on through largely flat valleys – hills a distant shadow.

Such a vast country, she thought. *But where are the people?*

"Ten minutes until we pull in," Ziggy said. "One more thing, I should warn you Julia. There's a virus on the loose. It's dangerous to visit Guangzhou at all, particularly if we're going to a hospital. We have to take great care. I've some facemasks. It makes sense to use them. Without wishing to sound too dramatic, our lives from hereon in are in danger every step of the way."

CHAPTER 37

THEY JOINED THE CRUSH of passengers pouring out of the train and jostled along the platform with the fast-moving mob. No sign it was Sunday – no church bells ringing as they emerged from the station.

Where to now? Julia wondered.

Ziggy walked ahead, slightly tense, as if looking for someone or something. Then he relaxed and waved at a man holding a board with Chinese writing that Julia could not read.

"I arranged a car and driver," he said. "It's the only practical way to get around our cities."

They followed the driver to a comfortable-looking VW Santana. Ziggy opened the door for her to climb in the back. He got in beside her, and leaned forward to speak to the driver in Chinese.

As the car pulled away, Julia turned to Ziggy. "Remind me again why you came to Guangzhou?"

"To visit a colleague at the university. We run an exchange programme together. He sends me about 1,000 students a year and I place them in campuses around Britain. So you see – it's all worked out most conveniently."

It sounded plausible, but Julia still didn't trust him. Her eye caught the tattoo on his arm. Didn't magpies mean bad luck?

Guangzhou followed the pattern of other Asian cities. Vast, modern, high-rise conceptions knitted through with multi-carriage highways, looping round, up and down like runaway balls of wool.

"I thought Canton was an ancient city?" Julia said as she stared out the car window.

"It is – goes all the way back to pre-history. Prominent destination on the maritime silk route. During China's long isolation, Canton was the only port allowed to trade with the outside world. Shamian Island still boasts splendid Portuguese architecture. Maybe later, we can take a tour."

After twenty minutes, the car swung into the broad drive of the modern International Hospital, and came to a halt at the entrance to Reception.

The driver got out and opened Julia's door. Ziggy didn't move.

"This is where you wanted to visit, isn't it? Dr Lippert's expecting you, I understand. I'm off to the University and will return in an hour. Is that enough time for you? See you back here then."

Julia laughed. "Are there no secrets in this country?"

Ziggy shook his head, a wry smile on his lips. "Julia, this is China. We are nothing, if not a land of secrets. Now go!"

THE HOSPITAL was vast, ultra modern – a magnificent institution worthy of the best from Dallas to Dubai, Tokyo to Sydney.

"Can I help you?" a woman at Reception asked in perfect English – unencumbered by the mask she was wearing.

"I'm here to see Dr Lippert."

"His office is on the twenty-third floor. The lift is through there," she pointed left.

The lift swished rapidly skywards – doors opening in a blink. Julia found herself standing at another Reception desk, where she asked for Dr Lippert – again.

JAMES LIPPERT was a feast for the eye. The very sight of him cheered her. Entering his office was like a warm homecoming – easy on senses and nerves. He was young, engaging and super-bright.

"It's Julia, isn't it? Can I call you Julia? You can take off your mask while you're here. I'm virus free – natural antibodies, I'm glad to say."

She took off her mask and held out a hand.

"It's wonderful to see a friendly face. China's such an..." she hesitated, "interesting country, isn't it?"

"Absolutely! That's what brought me here."

"And you're enjoying your time?"

"Couldn't ask for more. The research opportunities are world class. Plus it's an international hospital. I fancied a stint abroad and this hospital is a United Nations – staff from all over the globe. So much to learn, but enough of me. How can I help you?"

Julia cleared her throat and took in the room. Like James, it was bright and airy.

"I'm looking for a Hong Kong doctor, Laura Wan Sun. Some colleagues in the Duchess of Kent Children's Hospital said they thought she might've come here to work on the Avian flu virus."

"From Sandy Bay?" he nodded. "Laura did come here, but we're not an epidemiology hospital so she was quickly reassigned to a viral unit across town."

Julia relaxed, an enormous weight lifting from her shoulders.

"That's brilliant. Can I visit her?"

"I can't see why not. I'll tell you how to get there."

"That's very kind. I have a car and driver. If you could write the address down. That'd be great."

James chuckled as he scribbled.

"Smart move. Get instructions in writing. Here," he slid a card across the table.

"Just a warning," his face darkened slightly. "Don't expect this place to be like here, or hospitals you're used to. It's not. It's a Government hospital, struggling to cope with many very sick patients. There may be some initial suspicion or hostility. If she's there, they should be able to find her."

"That's fantastic, I can't thank you enough." Dr James' beeper sounded. I'd better let you get back to work. Where did you train?"

"St Thomas's."

"Westminster Bridge Road," she said, thinking of Cody.

"Indeed, and where I'll be going back."

ZIGGY WAS leaning on the car, arms folded across his chest, when she emerged from the hospital. His face lit up when he saw her.

"How'd it go?" he asked.

She shook her head. "Laura's not here, but I've a new lead." She handed him the card. "This is where we think she's working. Is it possible..."

"Pretty name Laura," Ziggy nodded. They got in the car. The driver took the card and ranted loudly in unfathomable Chinese. Whatever it meant, the car was soon moving.

Ziggy sat back and secured his seat belt. "It's the other side of town, that's all. Traffic's heavy in the middle of the day, even on Sunday. It'll take time."

They sat in silence watching modern China slip by as it went about its business.

"How was your meeting?" Julia asked after a while.

A veil descended. "Fine, thank you, it was fine," Ziggy fixed his eyes firmly on the view out the window.

Who did you really go to see? Julia wondered.

The journey was slow, the view dreary. Thousands of vehicles barely moving on mass highways, winding through suburbs stacked with endless rows of gargantuan tower blocks.

"Not the prettiest part of town, I guess," Julia broke the silence.

"No, but a miracle. Housing for ten million people built in just a few years."

"Oh shut, up," she laughed, trying to lift his mood. "You sound like a People's Republic broadcast. China undoubtedly suffered a difficult century in the 1900s, mainly at the hands of foreign powers and should be proud of its great achievements in overcoming adversity. There. Happy now."

"Very happy," he smiled, his gloom lifting.

They crawled through the traffic for another half-an-hour.

"Julia, you haven't told me why you're so keen to find Dr Laura."

"I also didn't tell you she was a doctor. It's complicated."

"Confucius says life is really simple but we insist..."

"On making it complicated," Julia finished. "Yes, I know."

The driver accelerated sharply and sped off at an exit. They were heading into the country, leaving the City behind. The landscape changed as they raced along rural roads, the driver moving fast now, eating up the miles. Wide dry-looking plains stretched as far as the eye could see, with dark, austere hills rising steeply in the distance. So vast and so isolated, Julia thought, mesmerised, drifting away into a half-dream.

She came back to earth with a bump, when the car slowed and then stopped sharply. A police roadblock was spanning the carriageway.

"Let me deal with this," Ziggy said, putting his mask on. "I've got a feeling this is as far as we're going."

Julia stayed in the car and watched as Ziggy spoke to the officers in charge. His face was largely concealed by the mask, but his body language exuded charm and reasonableness. She noticed signs at the side of the road in Chinese.

Damn – if only I could understand them, she cursed.

The policeman pulled a phone from his pocket and seemed to be speaking to someone. Ziggy waited patiently. Conversation over, they exchange a few more words. It all seemed to be going well. Ziggy bowed his thanks and walked back to the vehicle. He climbed back beside her, leaned forward and spoke to the driver, who began manoeuvring the car around.

"What?" Julia raised her palms questioningly as they set off back down the road, retracing their steps.

Ziggy removed his mask. "We're in a quarantined area. That's as far as we can go. They were not unhelpful. They called the staff office and confirmed that Laura was here until about six months ago when she was sent to another viral unit in the Conghua district. It's about an hour away. If we get moving we can get there and back before dark."

"Are you sure they aren't deliberately sending us on a wild goose chase?" Julia rapped her thighs in frustration.

"No, I'm not sure at all," Ziggy replied. "D'you have a better plan?"

What option do I have? Julia clicked her tongue and stared out the window. They drove steadily on empty flat roads, leaving the built up city far behind. The landscape was dust-dry and deserted. As they left mile upon mile behind, the terrain threw off its barren cloak. Scrubland gave way to verdant streams and twisting rivers, gnarled shrubs to fertile pastels and blossom. As the land became bountiful, so people returned.

"It's beautiful," Julia said softly.

"Technically, we're still in the city of Guangzhou – or rather Canton as you Brits used to call it – at least its urban region. Yes, it's beautiful," his voice faded, as if he too were hypnotised.

Julia started to slip away. Their dawn muster and the rhythm of the car rocked her into a sleepy no man's land. Her eyelids became heavy, and she could no longer fight tiredness surging in waves. She surrendered, closed her eyes, and dozed.

"Julia, wake up," she heard Ziggy calling through her dreams and woke with a start. The car had stopped at a gated complex, which looked like a high security prison.

As before, Ziggy put on his mask, got out the car, and walked towards security on the gate. He spoke to them politely, judging by his body language. The response he got looked anything but courteous. From where she was sitting Julia could see Ziggy's shoulders tighten.

Something's wrong, she sensed, sitting upright and straining to hear.

Suddenly Ziggy was shouting and gesticulating with his arms. A car engine roared behind the taxi, approaching at high speed and braking hard to a sharp halt. Her door swung open, and two vicious thugs in police uniform grabbed her and wrenched her out, sending her crashing on the tarmac. She screamed, as she landed badly twisting an ankle.

In an instance, Ziggy was at her side, screeching violently at the police, waving his arms authoritatively and in fury. Stunned, they backed off briefly, but soon resumed their shouting.

Ziggy would not be bettered. He grabbed Julia by the arm and thrust her back in the car. Ziggy's violent verbal tirade showed no sign of abating. He turned and hurled what seemed like some final abuse, and jumped in his side of the car, yelling at the driver to get out of there as fast as the hell he could. Julia didn't need Chinese to understand that.

250

They were all breathing heavily as they sped down the road in reverse gear, before turning and retracing their route the way they came. Julia turned to see if the heavies were following.

"Don't look back," Ziggy ordered, his face flushed with anger.

Julia sank back in her seat, rubbing her ankle. She watched Ziggy take a bottle of water out of his bag, rip off his mask and begin to sip. Slowly he regained control.

His voice was calm when he spoke again.

"I'm sorry Julia. Our adventure is over. Those goons are from police HQ. They've given you four hours to leave the province. We must catch the next train back to Hong Kong."

"What about Laura, we're so close?"

Ziggy took another swig of water and shook his head. "Laura isn't there. They say no one of that name ever arrived at that viral unit. They say we're mistaken."

"No, Ziggy. No. Someone's lying."

"Whether someone's lying or not, we're out of options. If we don't leave now they'll throw you into jail. This is not the English Home Counties. I won't be able to protect you. We have to go."

Julia slammed her back into her seat.

"Fuck," she said. "D'you think they're lying? Is Laura there, but they didn't want us to find her? Or did she really never make it there?"

Ziggy slumped back in his seat and closed his eyes.

"I don't know and I'm tired. Let's go back to Hong Kong. I've contacts. I'll get my uncle to pull a few strings. See if we

251

can get to the bottom of what's happened to her. I'll do what I can to help."

Julia's heart ran cold.

Maybe you've done enough already, Julia thought, gently massaging her swelling ankle.

What really went on out there? If only I could speak Chinese.

CHAPTER 38

BACK AT GUANGZHOU station, Ziggy forged ahead to the ticket office to reserve seats on the next train. Julia texted Richard.

Please meet me at Kowloon. Train arrives at 8pm.

I'll be there. His reply came through after a short delay.

Julia shuddered as Ziggy emerged from the ticket office.

I have to shake him off at the first opportunity, she thought. *The very sight of him makes me feel ill.*

They walked in silence to the train. She needn't have dreaded sitting beside him for the long journey back to Hong Kong. He didn't speak a word as the train rumbled South – his face set hard in an unfathomable expression. Julia's panic turned slowly to bewilderment.

Who is this man? she puzzled – not for the first time. *Who's he working for?*

HER SPIRITS LIGHTENED when she saw Richard waiting at Kowloon station. She said a cold goodbye to Ziggy. He bowed, the inscrutable Chinese gentleman.

"I'll be in touch," he said, without smiling.

"So you had a travel companion after all?" Richard smirked. "Though from the vibes I take it the journey didn't go so well."

"No, it didn't go well. He's someone I know from London. He was in the seat beside me on the plane over. Then he was sitting next to me on the train."

"Ah!"

"Yes Ah! He's the London Ambassador's nephew and teaches at the School of Oriental and African Studies."

"Come on, we can walk to the flat from here. Have you eaten? Maybe pick something up on the way."

"That would be great. I'll have to get back to the hotel though – a lot to think about and resolve."

"You're limping, are you hurt?"

"Yes I am hurt. But it's not the ankle causing me most pain."

"Lean on me," Richard said, taking her arm. "I'll look after you."

JULIA DIDN'T STAY long at Richard's, just long enough to put some ice on her ankle, devour supper and outline the strange events of the day.

Richard scratched his head with a chopstick. "So, you reckon James Lippert's genuine?"

"Absolutely!"

"That means either Laura never set off from that first viral unit, and is still there. Or she did set off and was intercepted and redirected elsewhere. Or she did make it to the second unit, but they didn't want you to know that."

"It's a puzzle. Worse, a dead end," Julia sighed heavily.

Richard grinned. "Sleep on it. Things always look different in the morning. The pieces of the jigsaw fall into place in your dreams, I find. Don't worry, you'll get your mojo back. How's the ankle?"

"Much better. Swelling's going down."

He placed the chopstick in a perfect vertical line, and stared with intense concentration.

"The thing that puzzles me is where those other police came from?"

"They appeared from nowhere."

Richard nodded. "They don't seem connected to the viral unit. Someone doesn't want a foreign journalist sniffing round. I get that. This is China – always paranoid and secretive."

"How did they know about me? Is that what you're getting at? How did they know who I was or what I was up to?"

"Unless someone tipped them off?"

"Who?" A look of fury flashed across her face. "Ziggy. It has to be Ziggy."

"You said he had a fight with them?"

"More a very aggressive argument. If only I could understand some Chinese. I've no idea what the fight was about."

Richard stood. "More puzzles. Come on, I'll take you back to the Metro. You're only a few stops from your hotel. You'll have to get used to it if you're staying. It's cheap and simple, once you get the knack."

RICHARD WAS RIGHT. Navigating the Metro was easy and Julia reached the Pottinger without mishap. She was glad to pick up her luggage and unlock her room – the same she had vacated that morning. She unpacked her case, changed into a

255

nightshirt and was about to go into the bathroom to clean her teeth when her phone rang. It was Cody.

"Good time Julia?"

"I can't tell you how great it is to hear your voice," she said with a slight catch in her own.

"Things not going well your end?"

"You could say that. How about you? Where are you? What time is it?"

"I'm in the office. It's afternoon here, err… 4.10pm," she visualised him stretching across his desk to check the time on his computer. Suddenly she badly missed home, her office, her flat.

"I'm just getting ready for bed."

"OK, I won't keep you long. I've been checking out Halamanning. Found a connection you might be interested in. Had to plough through hundreds of documents to find it, but very glad I did."

"Go on."

"Years ago, he too worked in Hong Kong. For the old Hemmings, before it went bust. Finance director. Come down in the world since, I'd say. Guess who worked for him?"

Why do I feel I know what you're going to say next, Julia thought.

"A young Warwick Mantel," Cody burst out. "Looks like he gave him his first big break."

"That's certainly one hell of a connection."

"There's another. Jonathan Silverman…"

"Patrick's father?"

"Was a trustee of the Whittingdale Trust until just before he died."

"Huckleberry Finn! Surely they can't all be up to their eyes in this together." Her mind started to race. "What're we saying here? That Mantel or Silverman might have been behind the missing million at Whittingdale? It's too mad to think about at this time of night."

"I really don't know. I'm meeting your friend Pitcher tonight, although he's busy chasing Triads across London as far as I can see."

"No, a few crooked bankers wouldn't excite him. He'd see that as business as usual – or rather a job for the City boys. Why did Halamanning leave Hemmings?"

"He was sacked, some dishonesty. Still trying to find out what. No charges as far as I can see."

"Great – keep digging."

"I'll let you know how I get on."

"Yes, meanwhile I'll try to get in to see Mantel in the morning. I know just where to find him. Who knows? It might be my lucky day? It's time I had a break."

257

CHAPTER 39

Monday August 23
Hong Kong

JULIA ROSE AT 5.30AM, washed, dressed quickly, and dashed out the hotel, stopping only to ask the doorman to call a cab to take her to Upper House Hotel in Admiralty. Ten minutes later she entered the glitzy venue, and crossed Reception looking like she knew precisely where she was heading – which she did. Directions to the Power Business Breakfast on the 49th floor pointed to a lift, which whizzed her to the Sky Lounge.

She recognised Mantel immediately; perma-tanned, sharp-suited and with dark good looks. He wore an orchid in his top pocket. Scofield Crisp stood nearby with his back to her, drinking in the glimmering view across the water to the mountains.

Power Breakfast indeed! If it's dynamism he seeks, I can shock it to him.

Julia weaved a determined path through the tables set for guests, and advanced towards the podium at the top of the room where Mantel sat, sorting out papers. Crisp turned as he heard footsteps.

"Julia, fancy seeing you again so soon. What brings you here?" he said, slightly disarmed. "Are you joining us for breakfast?"

Mantel raised his eyes from the table.

"Warwick, this is Julia Lighthorn," Crisp continued. "Remember, the London journalist who came to Hong Kong to write about Peak about a week ago wasn't it? I thought you'd gone home."

"I did. I'm back, and no – I'm not here for your sycophantic breakfast. I've come to talk about Walter Halamanning, Mr Mantel. My time's short. I want answers."

Mantel stretched a fake grin across his thin lips, and laughed artificially.

"Are you always this aggressive, my dear? Hardly the best way to win friends and influence people."

"I'm not here to win friends. But I'm happy to embarrass you in front of your little gathering."

"Warwick," Crisp seized the initiative. "We're both free at 11am. Why don't we see Julia back at the office?"

Warwick said nothing.

"After all, we like to be helpful to visiting analysts and journalists, and our guests will start arriving any minute."

Mantel cleared his voice. "OK, 11am in our offices," he looked over Julia's head, to make her feel small.

"Please leave the Rottweiler at home. We'll all get on much better."

MANTEL'S CHARM offensive was up full volume, when she entered his office on the dot of 11am.

259

"I'm so sorry, my dear, we seem to get off on the wrong foot this morning. If it was my fault, I humbly apologise. Perhaps you're tired. I'm guessing your trip to Guangzhou didn't quite work out as you might've liked?"

How did they know about my trip? Julia wondered, instantly on a back foot.

Mantel gestured for Julia to sit.

"Small town – everyone knows everything in Hong Kong. No secrets."

"Really? Here's me thinking Hong Kong did secrets like no one else. And thank you I'll stand."

"You didn't find Laura Wan Sun, I take it?" he continued. "Lovely girl. My cleverest protégée ever. A big disappointment when she gave it all up. Sorry you had a wasted trip."

Crisp leant forward and softened his voice. "I'm genuinely sorry to hear Laura is over the border. We're all very fond of her. With this virus, she would be safer back in Hong Kong. Will you try again d' you think?"

Am I hearing genuine concern in his voice? Julia wondered.

"I'm not sure. Maybe."

"We can put out some feelers, if that would help." Mantel spoke next. "Why are you so determined to find her?"

"London wants to speak to her about Adam Lee's murder. Friends fear she could be in danger."

A menacing laugh gurgled deep in his throat.

"That's ludicrous. I'm afraid sweet Laura is most definitely in danger from this killer virus the longer she stays in China. To suggest a role she played as a junior banker a decade ago has any implications in a serious crime today is absurd."

"Absurd is it Mr Mantel?" Julia lurched towards him, deliberately getting up close. "Economies around the world have gone into meltdown. People are watching fortunes wiped out. Adam Lee dead. If there are no secrets in Hong Kong, please tell me what all this is about?"

"I admire your imagination, truly I do," he replied, edging back slightly. "Trust me – there's no connection between any of this, or with us."

"Walter Halamanning?" Julia eyeballed Mantel. He didn't flinch. She sensed Crisp was studying his boss closely too.

Mantel shrugged. "I worked with Walter thirty years ago at the start of my career. He was financial director of Hemmings. I was new to the game. He appointed me his personal assistant. Fast-tracked me up the bank. They were good times. But..."

"He was sacked wasn't he?" Julia interrupted. "For dishonesty."

"There were some discrepancies in a couple of accounts. This is ancient history. Nothing ever came to court."

"It would've done in London or New York."

"Maybe. We weren't in London or New York. We're talking decades ago. He went back to London and picked up his career."

Julia narrowed her eyes slightly. "He was found axed to death in a forest in Epping. Local police see hallmarks of a Triad killing. They think the same about Lee. Connections, connections. Both men lead back to you Mr Mantel."

Didn't even blink, Julia thought. This hadn't come as news to Mantel.

261

Julia watched Crisp from the corner of her vision. Blood drained from his face.

"I'm glad I'm not a former associate of yours Mr Mantel," Julia spoke softly. "It seems a dangerous occupation."

This time he lashed out. "I resent that. It's time for you to go. Repeat slander against me and I'll set my lawyers on you. Then you'll find out just how dangerous it can be to..."

"Julia, let me show you out," Crisp's voice was calm and courteous, but she could see he was shaken.

Julia wasn't ready to call a truce. "Are you connected to any Triads?" Julia shouted at Mantel. "First State bankrolled a number of so-called secret organisations. How heavily is Peak involved?"

"I assure you Peak is not involved in any criminal activities," Crisp said, steering her towards the door.

She heard Mantel erupt into a roar of sinister laughter. "Good luck with your hunt for Laura," he bellowed. "You'll need luck chasing the shadow of a dead woman."

EXHAUSTED BY the early start and adrenaline drain of the morning, Julia decided to go straight back to the hotel. Washed up, she had no idea what to do next.

Maybe it's time to take a break. Have a night off, and relax over a quiet supper with Richard and his pals at the Foreign Correspondents' Club, she thought, unlocking her hotel door.

She made coffee, and collapsed on the bed, hugging her knees close for comfort, when her phone buzzed. Another text from the gynae clinic.

We need to see you. Please call to make an appointment as soon as possible.

She deleted it with one quick stroke. *One thing that will have to wait.*

She hadn't been back long when the phone rang. It was Ziggy.

"Look Julia, I'm sorry about yesterday. It didn't turn out how either of us wanted. D'you fancy another go? I've picked up a fresh lead. There's a chance Laura may be in a camp in Guangxi – in the mountains. We could go tomorrow on the train."

Julia threw back her head and laughed. "You must be mad if you think I'd go anywhere with you again."

"My informant tells me they're going to start evacuating the camp in a few days. If you want to find Laura we must go now."

"Are you deaf?"

"I know you're disappointed. Look, I'm going – with or without you. She has dual British-Chinese citizenship. I've booked tickets for us both for the 9.30am train to Guilin in the morning. I'll wait for you at Kowloon station at 8.30am. If you want to make the trip, be there."

Julia slammed down the phone, and stood with her back to the wall, thinking hard. *I don't trust Ziggy*, she thought, *I've no idea who he's working for, or what his agenda is. Is there even a viral unit there?*

She felt worn out and completely alone. Suddenly a light bulb switched on, she grasped her phone and dialled a number.

"Julia, how did you get on in Guangzhou?" Dr Kathy said at the other end.

"Hi Dr Kathy. We followed Laura's trail, as you suggested, but..."

"It fizzled out. That's China for you. Events always moving faster than you can keep up."

"At least we confirmed she started at the International Hospital and transferred to the viral unit."

"It's something I guess. The big question is where's she working now?"

"I may have a new lead. There's a chance she may be in the Guangxi mountains. Is that possible?"

"Very possible. Some years ago there were rumours of a mystery illness in the mountains. It's possible it was an early outbreak of bird flu, and it's resurfaced."

"I have the chance to go there tomorrow. I'm going to sleep on it."

"That must be your decision Julia. It will be dangerous. If you decide to go, take my very best luck with you."

Julia spent the night tossing and turning, trying to talk herself out of catching the train. When she woke at 6.30am, she sat bolt upright.

"I don't like him, I don't trust him...but I don't have any other choice."

CHAPTER 40
8.30am Tuesday August 24
Kowloon station

TO DESCRIBE AS MIXED her emotions at the sight of Ziggy had to be the understatement of the century. *I must be out of my mind*, Julia thought, as he waved at her. She couldn't even summon up a fake smile, but advanced towards him with a heavy heart.

"Nil desperandum, as you Brits like to say," he greeted her, with a smile. "We'll have better luck today. I feel it in my bones."

She followed him into the station, walking a few paces behind as they headed for the train.

"I'll pick up our tickets at the machine. Then just endless hurdles of security to leapfrog," he said, with a smile. "Can I get you a coffee to go? Price of coffee on the train is criminal."

Julia gritted her teeth, aware how hard he was trying to break the ice. She sighed. I can't spend the entire day without speaking to him. We'll need to communicate on some level, to stop the trip ending in yet another disaster.

"Thank you, yes," she smiled a truce. "Let's get coffee and pastry. I didn't have any breakfast. Why don't I get these, while you sort out the tickets?"

She went to a Western-looking bakery and, with a bit of pointing and nodding, emerged with their breakfast, just as Ziggy hit the front of the ticket queue. They proceeded towards departure, where long lines waited to validate tickets.

Julia half-expected police to arrive, out of nowhere, and haul them off, but they were waved through with nothing more than normal hostile efficiency.

Once in their seats, Julia handed coffee and a pastry to her travelling companion.

"I'll pay you for the ticket when we get back," she said.

"If you wish. I wouldn't want to compromise your impartiality..."

"Exactly. Will we have problems at the border, though, if we're now on police radar?" she asked, sipping her tepid drink.

"Technically we've just gone through the border. That's what all those checks were about."

"Yes but..." she began.

"Relax Julia. People do get fished off the train and sent back to Hong Kong. I know that as well as you. No point worrying. If it happens, it happens. You're a British citizen. They won't line you up against a wall and shoot you," he paused. "Tempting though that may be."

He laughed, eyes dancing mischievously.

I don't know what it is about you, she thought, anger melting. Despite her near-certainty that Ziggy was a double-crossing, treacherous, probable agent of the communist regime, there was a side to him she couldn't resist. But then, she could never resist anyone with a good sense of humour.

Their new light mood didn't last long – or rather it lasted another forty minutes. As the train approached the Shenzhen border, the crossing into the People's Republic, Julia spotted two uniformed police, one man, one woman, enter the carriage and walk in their direction.

She looked at Ziggy, who winked at her.

The male officer had bad scarring down his face. It reminded her of Wo Chang at the Golden Pagoda.

Once level with their seats the officers started an animated conversation with Ziggy, who answered politely, shaking his head calmly and repeatedly. Intermittently the woman officer pointed aggressively at Julia, but Ziggy refused to be provoked or budge. Finally, the male officer exploded with something that sounded like an official warning, turned on clipped heels and marched away. The woman followed him.

"What's all that about?"

"D'you really want to know?"

"Hadn't I better?"

Ziggy took a deep breath.

"You won't like it," he swallowed. "They want to turf us out and send us back to Hong Kong."

"And?"

"I serenely explained we are entitled to travel, have legitimate tickets and our paperwork is in order."

"I see."

"Then I explained it again and again and again, until they departed."

"They now know we're on the train and where we're going."

Ziggy's eyes crinkled in amusement. "My dear Julia, they always did."

The high-speed train weaved its path through flat dry plains, gobbling up mile after mile of drab landscape, before breaking into lush fertile valleys, edged by distant mountains. Before long, they were pulling into Guilin station. They got their masks out and prepared to leave the train. Passengers poured off on mass and Julia found herself squeezed up against Ziggy, trapped in the crowd swarming down the platform. Sun burned down on them – the heat unbearable. I can't breathe, Julia thought, fearing a migraine as dazzling rays flickered through her Polaroids. Ziggy smiled encouragingly.

They emerged from the station into a blistering sun. *Huckleberry Finn, I'd no idea sun could be this hot.* Julia watched as other passengers quickly shot up umbrellas to protect themselves from the burning rays. The air was thin, breathing further constrained by the masks.

"I've ordered a car. The driver should be here somewhere," Ziggy said, looking around.

A man in his early 30s walked up to them and spoke to Ziggy. He led them to a silver VW Jetta and opened a door for Julia.

"I left the air-con running," he said in faultless English. "It should be cool. My name's Hill. Welcome to Guilin."

He got into the car, put it into gear and pulled calmly out the car park.

"I'm Economics graduate. Sometimes I teach class – sometimes I drive taxi. We have many tourists to this region.

English drivers are in great demand. I earn more driving taxi than teaching class."

"Thank you, Hill," Ziggy said in English. "My companion doesn't speak any Chinese."

"We should teach her," Hill smiled. "First she choose which language. We speak Mandarin, or Cantonese. In the rural areas, the people of the villages speak different dialects. My wife comes from one of the Yao villages in the mountains, where I think you want to visit. Many different dialects again. I can understand my in-laws just about – but with speaking I'm not so good."

"Probably best when it comes to in-laws," Julia said. They sniggered. She gazed out the window at the bustling City going about its business – so different from the soulless metropolis of Guangzhou.

Young people on bikes streamed along boulevards lined with Chinese Banyan trees.

"Angel tears," Julia gasped as she pointed to the weeping aerial roots. "Or maybe witches' locks. It's so beautiful. Reminds me of big French cities. Commercial yet elegant."

"The key thing to remember if you want to understand our region is we are not part of China," Hill spoke over his shoulder.

"Excuse me?"

"No, life is much more relaxed here because we are part of the autonomous region of Guangxi Zhuang. The city is industrial, just like in the West, pharmaceuticals, IT, machine tools and so on. But also very beautiful with two rivers, many lakes, mountains and forests. Our name means Forest of Sweet Osmanthus."

"Because you have so many fragrant Osmanthus trees?" Ziggy said.

"Indeed."

"How long will it take us to get to the Yao people?" Julia asked.

"Four or five hours if we're lucky."

"So we can get there before dark?"

"No, no, we leave very early in the morning. Must get there before the heat of the day or too tiring for you."

"I need to go straight there," Julia repeated.

"No, Julia," Ziggy intervened. "It's out of the question. The journey's too difficult. I've booked a hotel. We can rest – maybe leave at say 5am or 6am in the morning."

"No, no, no!" Julia banged her armrest in frustration. "You said we were going straight there."

"Come on, it's after lunch. We're both tired. It's not practical to set off today. It gets dark here early."

"Your friend's right," Hill said. "The road is dangerous. I can't drive you there and back before dark. Anyway, I must spend time with my family this evening. My wife's parents have come to the City for a visit and are having dinner with us. It's more than my life's worth not to be there."

Ziggy laughed enjoying the joke, but Julia set her mouth in a grim line.

Why do I always feel the joke's on me?

"Frustrating, I know, but what choice do we have Julia?" Ziggy leaned towards her. "We can't drive ourselves along such a treacherous route."

Bet we could if you wanted to, Julia thought, but held her tongue. Finding Laura was the only thing that mattered. *I guess one more night won't be the end of the world.*

The car pulled up in front of a hotel. Hill got out. They followed to the Reception. Ziggy went to the desk to check them both in.

While they waited Hill said to Julia, "This is called the Elephant Trunk Hill Hotel – best views in the City. You can see water, mountains and most important, you almost close enough to touch famous Elephant Trunk Hill.

Ziggy joined them with two electronic keys, one of which he handed to Julia.

He shook hands with Hill. "We'll say goodbye and see you at 5am tomorrow morning for an early start."

"I'll be waiting outside. I'll bring plenty of cold water. We'll need it."

They watched him leave.

Ziggy turned to Julia, "Let's go to our rooms, freshen up. Then maybe take a walk and come back for some early dinner here. The top-floor terrace restaurant is famous."

Julia was all out of choices, so she followed him to the lift. They parted when the doors opened, Ziggy turning left and Julia following the signs pointing right.

Wonder if he asked for rooms apart to be tactful, she thought, even though she was past caring.

271

An icy blast hit her as she stepped inside one of the most luxurious rooms she had ever stayed in.

Huckleberry Finn, this is huge. More a suite than a room, she thought as she inspected the accommodation. Two double beds, two settees, a dressing room and writing table. The bathroom was enormous, with vast walk-in shower and marble bath.

Julia threw herself on the bed to see how soft it was. It was so exquisitely comfortable she lay there for half-an-hour, relaxing her aching body. Her mind, though, kept running through troubled thoughts. How did the police know they were on that train? How had Ziggy managed to persuade them to leave them alone? Why must their journey to the mountains be postponed yet again?

She relaxed a little when she finally hauled herself off the bed and stepped into the shower. *Can't deny, it's rather pleasant to enjoy some comfort and pampering for a change*, she thought, wallowing under the cool power shower, before wrapping a thick, baby soft towel around her head, and stepping into a silk dressing gown.

An hour later Ziggy called. She agreed to meet him in Reception in 15 minutes. It was already getting dark.

"They lose the light so early," he said. "Hill was right. Impossible to start tonight. Let's take a walk, see a few sights then go back and eat."

Guilin lit up after dark, with gardens, trees, boulevards and lakes an ever changing rainbow of colour. Julia associated light shows with cheap tourist traps, but these were different. The Guilin illuminations were magical – spellbinding.

The streets were crowded with tourists, but none had Western features – as if she were the only European in the heaving City that night.

"It's busy because it's festival time, and a popular destination for holidays," Ziggy said.

"Everyone's Chinese," Julia realised how stupid that sounded even before the words left her lips.

"Not exactly. China's an enormous continent comprising many different ethnic groups and nationalities. You should join the Communist Party if you want to pretend all Chinese are the same and all one race. Particularly in a place like this, you would be very far from the truth. And don't forget," he pointed to his right. "Vietnam is just over there."

She started looking more closely at the faces of the people she passed and saw he was right. They displayed a wide variety of ethnic features, although which region of the vast Chinese empire they came from she could not say. She saw the wide features and high bone structure reminiscent of films about Genghis Khan and the Moguls. *I guess their past lies in Mongolia.* Many had the broad cheeks and smooth skins she knew were associated with the Han dynasty, and the dominant features of the Chinese. *They're no different from us, with our mix of English, Irish, Scottish, French, Anglo Saxon and Viking*, she thought. *The whole world's a melting pot.*

"I feel conspicuous and very far from home," she said to Ziggy.

"There you'd be right. Unlikely you'll find any other Brits in the city tonight. Sometimes a few Europeans visit. The

French like this area. If it's company of your own kind you hunger for, I'm the closest you'll find."

"Hardly," she laughed.

They walked round the tree-lined lake and admired the illuminated twin pagodas in the middle – dazzling shrines. Crowds of beautifully dressed families mobbed the lake, taking snaps.

"Are they dressed in their holiday clothes? The ladies look lovely," Julia asked, admiring the pretty chiffon and silk dresses and casual Western clothes of the men.

"You mean they don't all look like oppressed communists?"

Julia giggled at the joke on her. "Am I really that bad?"

Ziggy shook his head with good humour. They meandered away from the lake to the main street of what looked like the old town. Julia found herself confronted by an unremittingly Chinese scene – shops selling food and clothes of all kind. Many were piled high with fruit and vegetables, some of which she nearly recognised – others she could not guess at. Similarly the fish stalls. She couldn't recognise the various ocean animals, but was bewitched by their grotesque beauty. Colours vivid and strange – blacks, greens and brilliant reds. Many tanks held live crustaceans, fish and snakes.

Julia saw animals moving in cages outside a couple of shops - mainly poultry.

"What's that?" she asked pointing to a cage of scaly creatures.

"Pangolins. They shouldn't be here. The Chinese use them in medicines. Not good."

274

"Are they?" Julia said, passing more cages.

"Bats yes. Come on, let's go back to the hotel."

"No, just a bit further, there's a market down here. I'd like to see what they're selling."

They meandered by medicine shops aplenty, rice and noodle stalls, and signs for restaurants, down a street bustling with happy Chinese families enjoying the warm evening. When they reached the market, Julia took a sharp intake of breath.

"Epic," she said to Ziggy, sucking up the patterns of reds, golds, and greens, decorating the stalls. *I couldn't be anywhere but China,* she thought.

Yet when she looked closely at the merchandise, the clothes, bags and other market fare, she felt crestfallen. *I can buy all or any of this in a market at home.*

"Disappointed?" Ziggy asked, watching her puzzled expression.

"Why should I be? Everything we buy's made in China. Why would things be different here?"

He smiled, "Come on, I'm hungry, let's go back."

They caught the lift straight to the roof-top terrace restaurant overlooking the spectacular Elephant Trunk Hill, lit by waves of ever-changing colours – first green then blue, then yellow, crimson, red and scarlet.

"You haven't asked why it's called Elephant Trunk Hill," Ziggy said, as a waitress came to the table. "Shall I order a bottle of white?"

Julia nodded. "It's fabulous. The view – absolutely breathtaking. And the mountains in the distance. They're...what can I say? Thank you for bringing me here. I mean that Ziggy. Thank you."

"The one right in front of you –" he pointed to the nearest peak.

"Yes I know – shaped like an elephant trunk. The whole thing's magical, like a fairyland. I could stay here forever."

"Well, you can't."

"Tomorrow we head into the mountains."

"Tonight we can enjoy," Ziggy said. "The food is good. There's a Chinese buffet or we can go a la carte?"

Julia looked at the menu, then closed it, laying it flat on the table. "Can't understand a word."

"No worries, I'll order a selection."

He did, and it was delicious. Julia sat charmed as the light melted from colour to colour. Hypnotic.

Everything about Guilin was hypnotic.

CHAPTER 41
Wednesday August 25

ZIGGY AND JULIA emerged from the hotel at 5am the following morning. Hill waited for them as promised. Bleary-eyed, they exchanged minimal courtesies. Ziggy sat in the front. Julia was happy to put distance between them, so climbed in behind the driver. The streets were deserted, the hum and bustle of the previous evening spent. Progress was swift and they were soon leaving a sleepy Guilin behind.

Hill's steady speed swallowed mile after mile through low plains and fields as they headed for the mountains. The rising sun unleashed a blazing tongue across the landscape, like a slow dragon roar, gradually filling the dawn with light.

It was going to be a long day, so Julia closed her eyes and dozed lightly. She came to, when the car began to climb. Her spirits lifted as they navigated a path through the mountains.

Is it possible, this time we'll find Laura? So near and yet so far. Will this be our lucky break?

To this point, finding Laura was Julia's exclusive goal. Now that hope had a prospect of becoming reality, a chill ran through her.

What will I say to her and what next?

Julia opened the window a crack, closed it and opened it again. Then she flicked her phone open and closed repeatedly.

I can see it now, she thought. *London journalist in madcap rescue of courageous doctor risking her life in a treacherous part of the world. She'll think I'm mad!*

"You OK in the back?" Ziggy asked, distracted by her jittering.

"Yes thanks, how much further Hill?" Julia looked out the window at the spectacular backdrop. They were climbing fast. Her ears popped.

"We've made good time. Maybe another half-hour. Would you like me to adjust the air-con?"

"No it's fine," Julia closed the window again.

Ziggy spoke next. "We're looking for a doctor. Any thoughts where to begin?"

"There's a sanatorium a little way from the Yao village. If she's not there, they may know where she is."

The landscape was dotted with isolated, wooden houses, balanced on stilts, tiny against the gigantic peaks.

"Reminds me of Switzerland – wooden houses built into the mountains – or maybe Austria," Julia said, looking back down the sharp assent.

"It's the traditional way to build houses since before anyone can remember. The ground floor is storage, with families living on the first and second floors in case of flooding. Take a look over there," Hill pointed into the distance. "These modern brick developments are built by the People's Republic of China. They want to move ethnic people from their homes, make them like everyone else."

"What do the Yao think?"

278

"It's difficult. Life's not easy, and many, like my wife, move away. The Yao are happy people. Their outlook is simple. They have a deep-rooted faith in Daoism. They value harmony, balance and the power of nature."

"Doing nothing is better than being busy doing nothing," Ziggy nodded with a smile.

"So my wife is always telling me. As for the Yao. They are heavily-incentivised to go to the new developments. Some go, some stay."

The road turned sharply upwards. Hill climbed steeply and they entered a small town, bursting with colour and vitality, like a carnival. Long four-storey, red wood buildings ran along both sides of the dirt track. *Like medieval coaching inns –* Julia thought, *with airy galleries running along the front of each floor.* She knew the George Inn in Borough well.

Here in the mountains, wooden shutters flapped open. No glass anywhere. Life a free-for-all conducted on the broad verandas, like main streets, running along the full length. Men with flat faces sat at tables with a drink in front of them. Women wrestled with household chores, laughing raucously together, as they beat carpets, washed laundry in tubs, weaved and baked rice in outdoor stoves – hair piled high on their heads. Children in ethnic dress ran out to see who was passing.

"We'll keep going to the sanatorium. Perhaps we can return here for lunch." Hill rammed through the gears to get some extra kick for the last stretch of the steep climb.

"The people look different – not Chinese at all," Julia said from the back.

Hill seemed irritated. "How many times must I tell you. There is no such people as Chinese, any more than there is such a race as European."

Ouch! Mustn't make that mistake again. "Sorry you're right," she apologised, as the car swung before what looked like a modern clinic.

Hill parked in front of the building and switched off the engine. He pointed ahead and said, largely to Ziggy, "There's the Reception. They should be able to help you. Manage on your own?"

"Sure," Ziggy got out the car, and waited for Julia so they could walk in together. Julia's stomach muscles tightened. Her palms started to sweat, even though it was cooler here in the mountains. They entered the hospital, both masked, and headed for Reception. Ziggy addressed a woman in a mask, his eyes crinkling into a smile. She picked up the telephone.

Julia swallowed hard. *Could this be it? Had they found her?*

The Receptionist replaced the handset, and spoke to Ziggy. He replied in Chinese then turned to Julia beaming.

"She's here," he translated. "She'll see us. Fate favours us at last. She has a gap now, so we must be quick."

The Receptionist moved from her post, signalling for them to follow her down a corridor on the left.

Julia raised a hand. "No Ziggy. You stay here. This is my interview and my quest."

"But Julia," he tried to protest.

"My way or no way."

"Do as you must," Ziggy clenched his jaw as anger flashed across his eyes.

280

The journalist followed the Receptionist, who stopped at a door with a nameplate in Chinese – knocked, then stood aside for Julia to enter.

Laura was sitting at her desk, framed by a large window looking out across to the mountains. The petite, dark-haired, almost childlike figure peered up and smiled. She looked frail, as though she had been ill.

In that instance, Julia knew why Patrick Silverman loved her, why Rebecca loved her. Why Hugo, Crisp, Kathy, why everyone she asked about Laura at one level or another loved her. Julia recognised it immediately.

She has that special something. Saint – Angel. That spark, that magical moon dust, we none of us understand, yet never fails to bewitch.

"My name's Julia Lighthorn," Julia said, standing at the door. "I've come a long way to meet you."

"Well, I hope you'll think it's worth it," she smiled a gentle welcome. "Feel free to take your mask off. I had the virus many months ago, so am now immune. Sit here, you can still keep your distance, for safety's sake. Now tell me, how can I help you?"

"It's been such a long journey," her voice trembled. Suddenly she felt crushed by the strain of it all. "I hardly know where to begin."

"Well, you're here now. I can see how tired you are. We have plenty of time. Catch your breath. Genuinely, there's no rush."

Julia's bottom lip quivered. She dug her thumbnail into the palm of her hand, exhausted, overwhelmed.

"I'm a journalist," she began. "A financial journalist. I write about things like the financial crash, analyse what caused it."

It all seemed so inconsequential so far away.

"The Golden Boys," Laura seemed to read her mind.

Julia nodded. "That's where it started. Then Adam Lee was murdered in Soho. Stephen Chandler disappeared."

"Good God, I had no idea," she turned her gaze away and stared out the window, as if scrolling her thoughts back in time.

"What did we do?" She shook her head. "I tried to warn them that fateful weekend. We were young – "

Julia smiled. "I'm not here to judge."

"Oh judge away. I think of that evening sometimes, when it's hot and still here in the mountains – the storm raging and waves lashing below that granite castle, imprisoned by the sea. The Golden Boys high in spirits. Thunder...lightning. It all comes back in vivid colours. Skeletons dancing in the stained glass - the devil with his wheel of torment. I knew that night we'd created a monster – the havoc it could cause. I should have stopped them."

"Could you've stopped them?"

Laura placed her hands in her lap, and said softly. "I could've tried."

"Warwick Mantel?"

"Oh yes. Warwick Mantel. He'd never have agreed to put the genie back in the bottle. Sometimes he comes to me in dreams, as Warwick Mammon – one of the seven Princes of Hell."

Julia raised her eyebrows.

"Obsessed with money," Laura continued. "His greed knew no limits. He exploited us. And this is where it's landed us. A busted global economy, and a mini pandemic in the making."

"Not strictly connected?" Julia said quietly.

"Don't be so sure. That's what global means. Money-go-round, greed-go-round, sloppy-go-round, sickness-go-round. Mistakes that could once have been contained locally, like financial contamination, rage out of control. Shadow banks detonating every day in our major cities and shadow clinics hiding among the mountains."

"Is that what you're doing? Hiding?"

"No. I was brought here."

"By force?"

She nodded. "Initially yes. But I've come to love it here. I was making too much noise in Guangzhou. They wanted me out the way. The virus raged for many months."

"But you're OK now?" Julia asked, noticing how lined her face looked.

"I arrived amid chaos and despair. I was ill for a while myself. Very ill. Thanks to control and hygiene measures we contained it. Not before we made some impressive discoveries. I've been studying my patients closely. Those who get very ill, those who recover quickly."

"Then you must come back with me." Julia drew in a deep breath. "That's why I'm here. I believe you know Patrick Silverman."

"Of course," her voice softened. "A good man. He just doesn't know it."

283

Julia furrowed her brow. *Not quite how I would have put it.*

"Well," she continued. "Patrick thinks you could be in danger. He thinks, I believe, that someone is coming for all the Golden Boys. Lee and Chandler have been dealt with. He feels threatened himself, but is well protected. He's worried about you."

"This is nonsense, isn't it? Who would go around bumping off bank staff who worked together a decade ago?"

"Really, I don't know." It did sound far-fetched, now Laura put it into words. "Someone who lost a fortune in the crash maybe? Someone who invested a lot of money with Adam Lee?"

"First State banked the Triads," Laura said with a matter-of-fact shrug.

"So I understand," Julia narrowed her eyes. "Silverman sent me here to bring you back to safety."

"Is he paying you?"

Julia hesitated. "Indirectly I guess. His fund's taken over the title I write most for."

"I see. It's kind of you to come, but there's no question of my returning to London. My work's here among the Yao. Time is so short. I've no interest in travelling the world at the beck of rich men."

"Ouch," Julia flinched as if kicked.

"No, no, I didn't mean to be unkind – but you must understand my patients and my work come first."

"You said you've made some impressive discoveries. What you've learnt here might help stave off a wider pandemic. Come back and test your theories. Kathy said originally you came to

284

study the illness because you couldn't trust the Chinese data. That hasn't changed has it?"

"Ah Kathy – "

"Come home. Publish your research on a global stage. That could help save more lives than living here in the mountains."

Laura looked down at her hands.

"There's something else," Julia continued, pulling out her trump card. "Silverman has promised to pay £10 million into a children's charity if I manage to bring you back. Just like you, children mean a great deal to me. I lost a baby some years ago."

Julia thought she saw a sympathetic glimmer in Laura's eyes.

Laura's gaze wandered again out to the distant mountains. "I had thought – " she began, but drifted away.

For a brief second Julia thought she was about to say, "I had thought to stay here for the rest of my life."

No that can't be right. It would mean staying here for decades, locked away in the mountains. Why would she do that?

They were interrupted by a knock at the door. It was Ziggy.

"I'm sorry to interrupt, but Hill says there's a mist coming down the mountain. We need to set off soon."

"I'm not finished here," Julia threw him a furious look.

"I'm sorry, Julia, I think we are." Laura paused, reflecting. "Honestly, I'm not sure they would let me leave."

"Are you being watched?"

"Not so much now. It might be possible."

285

Ziggy cleared his throat. "You have joint Chinese-British citizenship don't you? I realise the border might be tricky but I have contacts. I'm sure I could get you out."

Laura sighed – a dark shadow clouding her eyes.

"Perhaps it's meant to be. Perhaps I'm meant to go back to..." She looked up at Julia and Ziggy.

"Can you return tomorrow? If I can tie things up here tonight, I'll return with you tomorrow."

"Is that a promise?"

"I want to be helpful. You can achieve great things with £10 million. If I can get permission from the hospital and the rural medical authority for a short absence..."

"Is there anywhere here we can stay tonight, so we could all go back together in the morning?" Ziggy asked.

"Not really. I'm sorry, you'd better return to Guilin."

"It's a long way to come back."

"Then don't," she shrugged. "We're all free to choose."

"If we do come back, will you come with us?" Julia searched Laura's face for a definite answer.

Laura stood to show them out the door. "Give me a night to get used to the idea."

JULIA AND ZIGGY returned to the car park – not much more than dirt ground. Hill was waiting.

"Are you busy tomorrow?" Ziggy asked him.

"Not particularly."

"Could we come back here in the morning?"

"Sure."

"Then how would you feel about driving us back to the border?"

"Shenzhen border? Long drive," Hill said.

Ziggy waited.

"I'll do it. I can't come further with you."

"I know," Ziggy smiled.

THEY NEVER drove to the border. When they arrived at the clinic the next day, Laura had disappeared.

"Some men arrived and she went with them," the Receptionist said.

Try as they did, neither Ziggy nor Julia could get any more information. Hill tried but added little. "They are afraid. They said some men came and took the good doctor. They think they came from the new development."

"How did they know we were here?"

"Eyes and ears everywhere. Government officials control the new estate – with the help of Triads. Not the village people."

"Let's go down there and find her."

Ziggy shook his head. "Dear, dear Julia, she will be long gone. China covers nearly 10 million square kilometres, much of it remote and dangerous. She could be anywhere. No, we have to go. Will you take us straight to the station Hill?"

They set off down the mountain. Julia looked across at Ziggy and bit her lip so hard she drew blood. Someone had betrayed her and Laura every inch of the way. All doubt was now removed. The traitor was sitting right in front of her…

287

CHAPTER 42

Thursday August 26

JULIA STRANGLED HER FURY until they were standing on the platform at Guilin waiting for the train – when she finally exploded.

"You bastard! You lying treacherous bastard! You've been spying on me ever since I left London. Tipping off the authorities every step of the way."

"Don't be ridiculous. I've been trying to help speed things up."

"Speed things up? How does blowing up my investigation – and more importantly putting Laura's life in danger – speed things up? Many more lives too. With her goes all her discoveries. Just who are you working for?"

He choked out a short laugh. "I'm not working for anyone – just like you."

The train came. They climbed aboard. With the train in motion, Julia lowered her voice and began again.

"Every step of the way they've been waiting for us."

"I'm not sure who you mean by 'they'."

"The police, the authorities. Your bogeymen."

Ziggy smacked his lips. "Certainly not mine, but I agree with you. Someone has been feeding information about our movements to..." he lifted his palms in apparent frustration.

"It has to be you," she spat. "No one else had details of our movements. You made all the arrangements, with your "oh so helpful" drivers. This investigation has been derailed from Day One – by you."

"Not by me. Take a look in your own mirror. You confided in people about where you were going."

"No way! Absolutely no way!" Even as the words left her lips, Richard's face floated into mind.

"You see me as the enemy Julia. You always have. I'm sorry about that. It's unfair. Poor judgment isn't something I associate with top journalists. In your case, selective blindness is little short of tragic."

"How dare you patronise me. Laura's disappearance is tragic. Your treachery is tragic. I am anything but tragic."

"As we have nothing useful to say to each other, can I suggest silence," he reached for his bag, took out his copy of Kipling's Kim, and started to read.

Selective blindness – me! How dare he! Award-winning journalist, lauded for my acute powers of perception. I haven't told anyone where we were going or what we were doing. Only Richard. And no, it couldn't be Richard, it absolutely couldn't.

AT KOWLOON STATION, they parted with the briefest of nods.

"Good riddance, you creep," Julia thought heading for the Metro and the return trip to the Pottinger. Back in her room, she threw her coat and bag on the bed, and sat for a moment, still stunned. She looked at her watch. Lunchtime in London.

"Pitcher," she said, dialling his number.

He answered at the third ring. "It's Lois Lane alive and well. Here's me worrying you might have been mauled by tigers."

"I feel as though I have been," she let emotion rush ahead of her, at the welcome sound of his voice.

"Oh dear. Things not going smoothly your end?"

"Smoothly? When did things ever run smoothly?"

"Well, we're doing much better here. Young Cody's a find. Clever lad – just wish he would stop saying "cool" all the time. You'll be interested to hear Silverman's agreed to an interview this afternoon. With his lawyers present, of course."

"You've arrested him?"

"No, no. He's not a suspect. Goodness me, your antennae's knocked off course. Get your compass back girl. But I'd bet my pension he knows more about Adam Lee and Chandler than he's let on. It's time he came clean. Any progress on Halamanning?"

"Not really. Warwick Mantel admitted they worked together many years ago. Claims not to have seen him for years. I haven't finished with Mantel."

"My sources tell me Halamanning was a regular at a gambling den run by one of the Triads in Limehouse. We're working on a theory he may have run up big debts."

"Didn't pay – so was dispatched as a warning to others?"

"Not sure. Bit too dramatic. Broken legs usually suffice. Met any nice gangsters yourself?"

"I'm told the Triads run everything here. First State banked a number of wealthy Triads. Plenty are angry at losing money in the crash. Baying for blood. Staff have been attacked in the street. Maybe Adam Lee was a proverbial sacrificial lamb."

"Neat, I suppose. On the other hand, maybe his murder has nothing to do with the crash. How's the hunt for the missing doctor going?"

"Don't ask. Found her in a remote outpost in the Guangxi mountains."

"Clever girl – well done."

"I talked her into coming home."

"Even better. She'll tie up our loose ends."

"No she won't. She disappeared."

"Disappeared!" his voice boomed. "Tut, tut, careless, Julia, careless."

"No, I wasn't careless. I was betrayed. Sabotaged. One minute she pretty much agrees to come with me. The next morning she's gone. Some men came and took her. Everywhere I go, the bogeymen get there first."

"Bogeymen? Get a grip, Littlehorn. Whatever's come over you?"

"Remember Ziggy?"

"The Ambassador's nephew? Yes, Cody told me, he travelled out with you on the plane."

"I can't get rid of him. He follows me everywhere. Or rather pre-empts me everywhere. He's always one step ahead."

She heard him chuckling at the other end of the line. "Probably fancies you."

"I'm sure he's working for someone. Probably the Chinese Government, or if not a Triad – or a Triad in cahoots with the Government."

291

"Julia, Julia. What've you always told me? If something looks obvious then you're almost certainly barking up the wrong tree."

"In this case, there's no one else."

His voice turned dark. "There's always someone else. How many times have you warned me – never trust a journalist. Look at your friend Hopkins. Have you confided in any colleagues? Could anyone else be cheating on you?"

Julia said nothing.

"You're tired. Get some rest. I'll call tomorrow and let you know how we get on with Silverman. Anything you want me to ask him?"

London seemed so far away, Julia felt sick with a sad longing.

"Ask him where Chandler went after their lunch in the British Museum," she said. "And you're right. I'll feel better in the morning."

JULIA WAS CLIMBING into bed when her phone rang. It was Warwick Mantel.

"How was your trip to Guangxi? It's a beautiful country. Hope it proved fruitful."

"It's late and I'm tired. What d'you want Warwick?"

"I've some news for you. Can we meet up?"

"I'll come to the office in the morning."

"Tonight is better."

Julia checked the time. "It's 11pm."

"The evening's hardly begun. Have you visited our famous night markets yet? They'll just be lighting up."

"Temple Street, right? I'm not crossing over to Kowloon at this time of night."

"I'll send a car. You can be here in 15 minutes. Shall we say I'll see you at Midnight. I won't keep you long. The driver knows where to find me."

"I'm not sure about this."

"You won't regret it."

CHAPTER 43
Midnight
The Night Markets, Kowloon

JESUS THIS IS MY WORST NIGHTMARE, Julia thought breathing deeply as she followed the driver through the Paifang gates at the opening to the Temple Street Night Market. They had abandoned the car a few streets from the entrance.

Narrow alleyways rammed with stalls piled high with food, butted so close there was barely room to pass. More oriental dishes – noodles, rice, beans and bamboo shoots – spilled out of restaurants at both sides. A rat ran along the top of a line of stalls, jumping from canvas to canvas. Everywhere Chinese lanterns flickered their half-light.

Julia swallowed, a putrid taste rising in her mouth. They walked through the cloying gourmet delights until they came to the tourist market proper. Here more stalls crammed with cheap fakes of designer brands – seedy, shabby and squalid.

Still they walked on, Julia fighting to keep claustrophobia at bay. It was hot, even at this late hour, the air thin. She struggled to breath. Sweat dripped down her neck. Lights, noise, crowds – everything seemed loud and intense. At any moment her vision could go, and she might collapse with a vicious migraine.

When they emerged from the tourist alley, the scenes became weirder still – part circus, part nightclub in the open air. Close to the temple, where Buddhists queued to pray, were fortune tellers, alongside opera singers in traditional Cantonese garb, their painted faces, ugly. Others wore devil masks. Prostitutes lurked in the shadows, near stalls selling sex toys, dildos, vibrators, blow-up dolls and other adult paraphernalia.

Julia was not sorry to move on to yet another food section, this time authentic. Queues, many hours long, snaked at serving hatches. Not for the locals the glitzy fast food reserved for tourists. Here they had to wait patiently. Groups of men sat eating noodles or rice, playing cards, drinking beer, at basic dirty tables straddling the walkway.

Bands of brothers, plotting, she thought, noticing gold teeth flashing in the darkness. *Will some of these be Triads*, Julia wondered. *Is this where it all begins?*

She peered down unlit side-alleys piled high with black rubbish bags, food spilling out. A black shadow flashed behind one. More vermin.

Finally, the driver stopped.

"Down there," he said, pointing into the dark. She hesitated.

"Go, go," he repeated, giving her a shove. "He is waiting."

She started to walk gingerly forward. She shivered as though a spider crawled over her skin. Ahead, nothing but darkness. She tried to switch on her mobile phone. It was dead. Damn.

Hairs on the back of her neck quivered. Was someone skulking up behind her? She turned sharply. But no – no one was there. Or rather she couldn't see anyone in the shadows. She moved forward again. One step at a time. She thought she heard a footstep grazing the uneven loose dust track, followed by a shimmering sound. She remembered the opera singers in their masks, their silk costumes and synthetic beard – the prostitutes and addicts in similar garb.

It's only my mind playing tricks, she thought. *Just keep going, this must lead somewhere. Mantel can't be far. He's waiting for me down this alley.*

But the further she walked the darker it became until she could see nothing in the pitch black. So she stretched out a hand, to feel her way forward. But rather than a way out to a brighter path, her hand hit a wall. There was no escape.

Fuck, it's a dead end, I'm trapped.

At that moment, she sensed a weak light behind her. She turned to see dim Chinese lanterns swaying at the opening to the alley. Screwing up her eyes she detected the silhouette of a weird pageant coming towards her. As the lanterns approached, the dark lifted, and she could make out five giant figures in devil masks and crown, with long vivid beards – orange, purple and yellow. She couldn't tell if they had come from the circus, the opera or the brothel, but they were terrifying. Sinister eyes gleamed from the masks and painted faces. There was no mistaking the menace in their advance. They held their lanterns with arm stretched out, throwing hideous shadows across their ugliness. One held a knife.

So this is how my story ends, Julia thought. *Lying dead in a pool of blood down a Hong Kong back-street.*

Something clicked deep inside.

No. Not without a fight. She started to run like a wild thing into the line of assassins, ramming fingers into the eyes of the first one she reached, the one with the knife, and kicking out viciously at another. The first one dropped the knife, and squatted to pick it up. She shoved him, pushing another in his direction. The first collapsed, sprawling to the ground, while the other tumbled down over him.

That'll teach you to wear a dress for a fight.

The other three came at her now. One punched her in the shoulder. She scratched his face with the spite of a cat – kicking his friend in the groin. She stamped on their feet and kicked their shins.

But it was hopeless. She couldn't win.

Amid the grunts, groans and squawks of their struggle, Julia heard the creak of a door opening.

"That's enough," a voice boomed in the darkness. The goons froze. She looked up from their pincer hold to see Warwick Mantel, his features lit by a torch like a mask in the dark.

"Well done for finding your way here," he clapped his hands. "You men can go."

"You bastard. You fucking treacherous monster of a man," she spat at him, shaking her arms free.

"Calm down dear. I'm nothing of the sort. The night markets can disturb the imagination. It's a wild world out there. Wilder than you're used to. But you misjudge me. I'm

297

here to help. You trouble me, a young innocent abroad, thrashing around helplessly in a place like China – understanding nothing of its history, practices and intricate web of relationships which must be maintained. It moves me... really it does."

"You sent those thugs to hurt me."

"I wanted you to see how much you need my protection. I have contacts. Not always ones I choose, but relationships bring duties and cares as well as rewards. A society of Chinese gentlemen..."

"Triads," Julia interrupted.

"My dear, you've been watching too many cheap American B movies, but if it makes you happy, yes, we can call them a Triad. Whatever you call them, they asked me to pass some news on to you. News is your business, or so you're always telling me?"

"Fuck you."

"No my dear, you're not my type. But thanks for the offer. These gentlemen have a much more interesting proposition. They have a certain doctor in their possession."

"Laura?"

"They're prepared to trade her."

"Trade her for what?"

"For $10 million. Personally, I think they're letting her go too cheaply. Then, unlike me, they've never seen the way Patrick Silverman looks at her. Oh, and they want it in diamonds."

"You want me to act as middleman in a hostage trade?"

"We're all middlemen one way or the other my dear. Isn't that what working in the media is all about. Newspapers – the man in the middle of the world's big events. We're all free agents. You can pick and choose your stories and your crusades. You can decide whether Laura lives or dies. Have a think and let me know. I'm sure you'll need to call London. I must get going. Busy day tomorrow. When you have an answer get back to me."

Julia felt sick.

"Ah," Mantel pointed behind her in the dark. "Your ride's here."

Julia turned to see the driver waiting in the shadows of the torrid side-street. "Sweet dreams my dear, and call when you have an answer."

Mantel switched off his torch. His heels clicked in the dark. She heard a door creak open. With trembling legs, Julia picked a path back up the alley, and returned to the ghoulish night markets – sickening and macabre.

CHAPTER 44
12.45pm
Scotland Yard

"WHO IS ADAM LEE?" Pitcher rapped his chin with broad knuckles, leaning back from his desk. For sure, Lee fitted the role of top villain, running a bank for criminal Triad organisations. Many lost fortunes in the crash. Julia said they wanted revenge, a scapegoat. So which was Adam Lee? Bad guy or fall guy.

Pitcher looked at his watch. 12.45pm. Lunchtime.

"No," he shook his head. *It doesn't ring true. He's too much comic super-baddy. I'm sure that's not what this is about.*

He stood to get some lunch when his desk phone rang.

"Bugger," his stomach was rumbling. He was hungry. He sat down again and reached for the receiver.

"Chief Inspector Pitcher," his voice was brusque.

"Amy Denys here. I'm acting on behalf of Patrick Silverman."

Pitcher grimaced, prospects for lunch fading.

The lawyer cleared her throat. "About the meeting this afternoon. My client agrees to talk to you voluntarily. He has no obligation to attend."

If she thinks I'm going to respond to that, she can think again, Pitcher tapped the desk with his forefinger.

'So in acknowledgement of his co-operation, my client would like to ask for some flexibility on the venue for the interview."

300

"He doesn't want to come to the police station?"

"Correct. He has an alternative suggestion. He would like to see the location of the scene of Halamanning's murder."

"Excuse me?"

"He feels it's pertinent to your interview. He's a free man, under no obligation to provide information. We feel it's a reasonable request."

"Do we? To me it sounds highly unorthodox." Pitcher was silent for a few moments, weighing the pros and cons.

"OK. 4pm, we said? I'll be there."

CHIEF INSPECTOR PITCHER pulled up outside Julia's office at 3pm. Cody was waiting for him. He waved as he opened the passenger door.

"Big meeting, thanks for asking me along. Let's hope it all goes smoothly," Cody grinned as he tightened his seat belt.

"That would be a first," Pitcher winked back. "Who knows? Today may be our lucky day."

With that, their conversation stopped. Neither exchanged a word, as Pitcher weaved his way skillfully through the London traffic. Soon they were careering towards Chigwell and the Girls' Camp.

"You're a much quieter companion than your boss," said Pitcher, as he turned into the campsite drive.

"Better for that?"

Pitcher laughed. "Sometimes she drives me nearly insane, but I'm fond of Julia."

As they got out the car, Mrs Cadbury emerged from her reception hut.

"Chief Inspector Pitcher," she held out her hand.

"Mrs Cadbury, sorry to trouble you again."

"We're here to serve. D'you want to head down to the scene of the crime?" she mouthed the last four words for emphasis, and then giggled.

Pitcher and Cody exchanged a look.

"I thought we were waiting for the others?" Pitcher said.

"No no, the lawyer was absolutely clear. They want to meet you down where the dastardly deed was done," again mouthing the last few words for emphasis. "I'll wait for them here."

Pitcher nodded, setting off with Cody down the path past the St Pancras hut, through the field towards the copse.

"I think she's been at the sherry," Cody said.

"Going all Agatha Christie. Probably already writing her first murder mystery. Murder Round The Camp Fire."

"Camp's the right word for it." They walked on.

"Seems a long while since we were here with Julia."

"Not so long. Less than a week. Get your facts right."

"You're right, I should. If Julia were here she'd say, journalism lesson ten. First get your facts right."

"Then distort them. Isn't that what you journos say?"

"You spend too much time with the gutter press, Chief Inspector."

Pitcher laughed. But the mood darkened when they reached the thicket of trees.

"Must've been terrifying for those girls," Cody shuddered, at the thought of the body hanging in the dark, blood dripping.

He looked up at the thick green curtain blocking the sun, damp musty smells rising in his nostrils.

"Let's walk down to the river," Pitcher picked his way through the trees, pausing to pick up a fallen branch to beat back nearly six feet high thistles, nettles and brambles. Cody trailing behind.

"I can't imagine how they found their way through here in the dark. There's no path as such," he said lashing at the weeds.

"It was full moon, wasn't it?"

"Yes, and a few weeks ago the weeds wouldn't have been so tall. Even so."

They emerged into the light, and onto the bank of a narrow rippling stream. Pitcher stared into the dark clear water swirling over stones.

"I guess this little stream ends up in the Thames at some stage...via the Ching," he said as he stared. "In the end everything's connected. The Thames flows into the sea, and the sea into the ocean. The oceans all flow into each other. The water here could one day be part of the South China Sea."

"From Ching to China. Bit philosophical for you Chief Inspector?"

"I like a bit of philosophy," Pitcher cleared his throat and started to walk back through the forest to the clearing. "Small trickles powering big waves."

"Came out this way on a Geography school trip. If I remember right, the Ching flows into the River Lee and then on to the Thames."

"The River Lee eh? See what I mean. Everything's connected."

They fought their way back through the forest. Cody burst into violent sneezes as the pine and woodland smells triggered his allergies. Finally they emerged back into the clearing.

"Look, they're coming," Cody raised his arm to point at the figures trampling down the field. "Four of them, with Mrs Cadbury."

"Well, I'll be damned," Pitcher squinted into the distance, a hand over his eyes to block the sun. Then he threw back his head and roared a booming laugh, clapping his hands together.

"I can't wait to see Julia's face when I tell her."

They stood side by side and watched the figures approach. Three of them swaggered in a line, marching robustly down the sloping field, heads held high. Mrs Cadbury followed behind. Silverman broke ranks first, waving at Pitcher. A few more steps and they arrived.

Pitcher didn't wait to be introduced but held out his hand.

"Stephen Chandler, I take it?"

"Pleased to finally meet you Chief Inspector."

"Not as pleased as I am. Not every day I shake hands with one of my unsolved crimes. You're going to have a lot of explaining to do when you see your wife again."

Pitcher extended a hand to Silverman. "Good to meet you Mr Silverman. This is Cody. Works for Julia Lighthorn."

My imagination? Or did Silverman's eyes flicker at Julia's name? Pitcher thought.

"He's made himself very useful," he continued .

"Good to hear," Silverman said. "And good work, on your recent scoop."

"I guess indirectly, I work for you too. You bought the paper didn't you?"

"Sleeping partner. I shouldn't worry about that. This is my lawyer. Amy Denys."

"We've spoken, Chief Inspector," she said exchanging a cursory handshake. "I'm here to observe."

"Observe what? I'm not sure what we're all doing here," Pitcher lifted questioning palms.

"My client wishes to see for himself what happened that night."

Pitcher talked them through the layout of the field, and where the girls' tents stood. He rehashed the story of the midnight feast, the girl feeling ill, the two pals leaving the tent, escaping for fresh air, then making their way down to the little stream where they previously washed their dishes. He held out an arm pointing the way through the copse, down to the stream. They picked their way through the gloomy trees, emerging at the rivulet.

"The girls played here for a short while before deciding to go back to their tent. I believe they raced back Mrs Cadbury?" he added.

"So they were out in this wood in the middle of the night alone?" the lawyer tut-tutted, as they returned to the dense trees.

"I'm afraid that's correct," Mrs Cadbury blushed, biting her lip nervously at the thought of a negligence claim. "And yes Inspector, they raced back through the trees, before Grace slipped on a pool of blood and little Lily arrived to see..." she stopped by a large oak and looked up.

A flock of birds weaved a path through the branches, shaking the treetops. An owl hooted. "Creepy," Cody muttered, and started to sneeze again at the dispersing tree pollen.

"This is where he was found hanging, his back slashed to ribbons. A machete rammed between his blades," Pitcher said. They all looked up.

"Why here? It's so weird – so vicious," Stephen Chandler said.

"Not weird at all, if you want to send a message."

"To little girls?"

Pitcher decided not to answer that one.

"Gentlemen, now we've found Mr Chandler, I'm left investigating two murders. Both stink of money, Triads and Hong Kong. If you have any information you're not telling me, it's time."

Chandler cleared his throat, "As you say Chief Inspector, it's time."

Silverman nodded, and the six of them strolled back up through the field. They said goodbye to Mrs Cadbury. After a short exchange between Silverman and Pitcher, they left their cars and walked to the Two Brewers. The bar was deserted. Lunch clients had gone, the evening crowd not yet arrived. Pitcher, Silverman, Chandler and the lawyer sat at a table in the far corner.

"Get some drinks in Cody," Pitcher said.

He took an order, then left the others to talk.

CHAPTER 45

Thursday August 26

"I GUESS IT ALL STARTED with the call," Stephen Chandler began.

"The call?" Pitcher quizzed.

"I took a call from Adam Lee on the evening of July 26. Can you believe that, with all that's happened? Only a month ago. Completely out of the blue. Hadn't spoken to him for years. He was in London and wanted to meet up."

"Just like that?" Pitcher folded his arms, leaned back in his chair and stared hard at the speaker.

"Yeah, just like that. I wasn't keen. I was busy. Prices were yo-yoing. I'd never liked the guy. Looking back he always gave me the creeps. On top of that, he reminded me..."

"Of a time you'd rather forget?" Pitcher said. Cody returned to the table, placed a glass before each of them and sat down.

"Maybe. He said it was a matter of life or death, which I confess didn't make the idea of meeting up any more attractive."

"But you agreed?"

"I did Chief Inspector. I said I ran early, and usually ended up at a health club in Holborn where I showered before going

307

into the office. He suggested coffee in the British Museum. Discreet. Not to tell anyone, not even my wife."

"But you did." Pitcher drummed his middle finger impatiently on the table.

Patrick Silverman leant forward. "Stephen called me. He didn't trust Lee. I was in London. We agreed, for the time being, he wouldn't tell Rebecca."

Stephen Chandler looked away, embarrassed.

"What did he want?" the Inspector asked.

"I was shocked when I saw him. He looked gaunt. Couldn't keep his eyes still, constantly flicking around, as if looking for someone. His hands trembled when he lifted the coffee cup."

"He was worried?"

"Spooked, I'd say Chief Inspector. He said his life was in danger and so was mine, and it all went back to Mantel and Hong Kong."

"Where you all met?"

"Not entirely," Silverman intervened. "Stephen and I were both at Cambridge – different colleges. Laura I met through friends of Dad's"

"But we only became close..." Stephen continued.

"At Peak?"

"Actually no. At Cornwall. That strange weekend, where we made a pact with the devil."

"Bit strong there Stevie," Silverman laughed.

"I'm not ashamed of what we did, Patrick. We were young, so full of ideas. We wanted to change the world for the better. It could've worked. It did for a while. But we didn't account for greedy bastards like Mantel."

"Stick to the facts," Silverman touched Chandler's arm gently.

"OK. Essentially Lee had gone back to Hong Kong and worked for Mantel for some years. Top job at First State came up and somehow Lee was shoe-horned in. Not long behind the desk before even he realised he was a puppet. To Mantel, First State was a golden goose, ripe for hatching."

"Wasn't he rich enough already?" Cody couldn't resist.

"For some men, greed is a hunger they can never satisfy. Julia taught me that," Pitcher said.

"Exactly. Peak served the legitimate economy, but Mantel knew Hong Kong's black economy was vast. He used Lee as a front to grow a massive Triad banking empire. Money laundering, tax evasion, crooked accounting. Nothing too hot to handle. Garbage in – garbage out. They were drowning in cash, investing heavily in all kinds of dodgy junk."

"And then the markets crashed."

"They did," Chandler nodded grimly at the Chief Inspector. "Many of these investments were worthless. The Triads wanted their money back. The Dragon Masters didn't understand market volatility. If someone lost their money, they'd stolen it – just like gamblers who didn't pay their debts. Lee was at a meeting with some goons who turned ugly. They threatened Mantel. It was a question of face. To lose face was shame. They wanted revenge."

"So he needed a fall guy?"

"Mantel gave them three names to get them off his back – me, Patrick and Laura. They wanted names and Mantel gave them to them."

"Names for what?" Cody asked.

"To punish. The Chinese have always been big on punishment. Lec came to warn us the Triads would be coming for us."

"Just because you came up with some kind of get-rich-quick scheme a decade ago? That's preposterous." Cody picked up a beer mat and rolled it across the table.

"That's what we thought – a huge joke. Honestly, I thought Lee must be losing his mind. He acted so weird. It all sounded crazy. So I called Patrick and asked him if he could spare some time to chat."

"Stevie and I met after Lee left. I was heading back to Cornwall that afternoon, and asked Stephen if he and Rebecca wanted to come for a few days until things settled. He said maybe."

"The meeting with Lee had been so bizarre, I craved normality." Chandler took up the tale again. "I suggested we take an hour off and escape among the Egyptians. For old time's sake. We were just leaving, when news of Lee's murder appeared on a news wire. What a shock. Suddenly it didn't seem so funny. It seemed real and terrifying."

"You'd never knowingly accepted Triad money into your funds?" Pitcher asked.

"Of course not. We had accepted investments from Hong Kong via Peak. There was no reason to think they weren't legitimate. Our money laundering checks are scrupulous."

"Scrupulous enough?"

"Lee hinted some of the money which came via Peak might have been Triad. Of the three of us, I was the number one target."

Silverman bit his lip. "I'd never taken Mantel or Lee's money. Never trusted them."

"The easiest thing for me to do was disappear," Chandler continued. "I didn't tell Rebecca, to protect her. Simpler to disappear without her. Lee was dead, the first to pay the price. Who would be next? That's right isn't it?"

"Maybe right but for the wrong reason," Pitcher interrupted. "I'll explain in a minute. What interests me is why would he care? Why bother to warn you? You weren't friends. Hadn't seen each other for years."

"That's what I couldn't get," Silverman creased his brow.

"I wondered at first, too," Chandler sighed. "And I still don't know, but shall I tell you what I think? In a strange way, I think he did care."

Pitcher and Cody exchange looks.

"Compassionate to a fault," Silverman leaned back, his lazy eye blinking.

"Think about it, Pat," Chandler turned to his friend. "Adam Lee drew a lot of short straws in life. His family may have been powerful, but they traded in violence and double dealing. He spent his whole life looking over his shoulder. He was scared."

"Why come running to you?"

"I realise this will sound crazy Chief Inspector, but that weekend, locked away in a castle, the storm raging outside. We

311

all gelled. Team bonding, that's what it was supposed to be about."

"A new family?" Pitcher raised an eyebrow.

"You bought the place," Cody added, looking at Silverman with a touch of irony. "It must've meant something to you?"

"You don't think he was killed in revenge?" Silverman stretched a questioning hand towards Pitcher.

"No I don't. This is all very interesting, and it would make a great detective story, but Lee was in London for a very different reason. We now know that one of Mantel's biggest Triad customers here is threatened by a new rival from Hong Kong. They needed guns, and Lee was the bag carrier, sent across with cash to fund the haul."

"So the crash has nothing to do with it?"

"I wouldn't say nothing. People are angry. They've lost money. Tempers are tested. Rivalries become more bitter. Everything's connected in the end. I'm sure he believed the warning he gave you was for real."

"And this new gang works for?" Silverman asked.

"Like them all, works for itself and its community. Britain's full of legitimate Chinese businesses. Even legitimate businesses like to have friendly accountants who can handle tax and VAT fraud, not to mention lose small fortunes if they need to hide it away."

"Do dodgy accountants hack people to death?" Silverman couldn't resist.

"Gambling, prostitution, trafficking, drugs and benefit fraud. Intimidation means power. Messages – short, sharp and not particularly sweet. You finance guys talk about empires.

These are the mega empires of the 21st century. And they have armies and arsenals to protect their interests."

"There's a war coming?" Silverman asked.

"We're not sure how far he got to sealing the deal. He didn't have the money with him when he was found. We believe we found the weapons. Which were never collected."

"The weapons were abandoned?" Cody scratched his head.

"Not abandoned. Triads work in silos. Information costs lives. Something broke down somewhere, with Lee's murder. The first part of the deal, the delivery, was honoured, but this information never reached the customer."

They were quiet for a few moments.

"Which brings me on to Halamanning," Pitcher began again. "Did Lee mention him too?"

"Yes he did," Stephen leant forward. "Said he owed it to Patrick's father to stop them."

"Patrick's father?" Cody sounded astounded.

"Yet again, it all goes back to Hong Kong," Silverman said. "Dad did various stints working on the island. When Adam was very small, maybe six, he was caught carrying a parcel of heroin by the police. It was still a British colony, Dad was a magistrate. He came up before Dad. Could've been serious, even for a small child. He let him off and was very kind to him. Not only that but he got him a place at St Paul's. A scholarship. His way out."

"What did he have to say about Halamanning?"

"He gave Mantel his first job," Chandler took over. "He'd helped him get on fast – rocket to the top at Hemmings. There was some scandal, all hushed up. Halamanning went back to London."

"For God's sake Stevie spit it out. The man had a gambling problem. Then and now."

"Not so much now," Pitcher couldn't resist.

"OK," Chandler agreed. "Anyway, according to Lee, Halamanning was again in hock, big, to the Triads – gambling debts. He was a regular at the Limehouse casino. He'd already taken £1 million lose change from the Whittingdale Trust. He was getting desperate, so called Mantel and asked for another loan – for old times' sake. Mantel being Mantel saw an opportunity. He offered several millions on condition together they mortgage property held by the trust."

"Think about it," Silverman said. "The plan was First State would make massive advances of cash on the back of this property. They were selling London. Mantel and Halamanning would take the cash and disappear never to be seen again. Triad problem solved."

"While they lived out their days on some remote exotic island," Pitcher tapped his empty glass.

"Steal from a trust dating back to Shakespeare? Rob millions of Londoners of what was rightly theirs?" Cody sounded shocked, as he stood to return to the bar.

"Yes, Cody, that was the plan. But it didn't happen. I had some powers of attorney from when Dad was ill. I froze all transactions, and removed all the deeds I could find to safe-keeping, after Lee tipped us off. In a strange way Lee was repaying my father by protecting his legacy."

"Halamanning never got his money?" Pitcher said. "And the Triads didn't get their gambling debts paid."

"You can't raise mortgages without deeds," Silverman's face was grim.

"They murdered him, because that's what happens if you cross the Triads," Pitcher took a fresh full glass from the tray Cody was carrying back to the table.

"And they did it in the Girl Guide camp, because that was owned by the trust of which he was Treasurer. They wanted to ram home the point they didn't care who they hurt, no matter how young and vulnerable."

THEY WERE GETTING ready to leave when Pitcher's phone rang.

"It's Julia," he mouthed. All eyes were on him as he listened.

"What time is it there?" he looked at his watch. 6pm London time.

"One in the morning. OK, I see, I see, go on," he said calmly. "OK. Go straight back to your hotel room, and make sure the door's locked. Wait till you hear from me."

He looked at the faces turned towards him round the table.

"A Triad gang has kidnapped Laura and is demanding a $10 million ransom. Julia's their messenger. And they want the ransom in diamonds."

"I'll pay it," said Silverman without a blink of an eye. "But we can't leave this to Julia. It's too dangerous. She's out there on her own."

"At least there, I do have some good news," Pitcher smiled. "She is not alone."

CHAPTER 46
1am Friday August 27
Hong Kong

JULIA CLICKED her phone shut at the end of the conversation with Pitcher. Her first move on returning to the car had been to reach for the charger. As soon as she saw life, she dialled the Inspector. It was over to him. She couldn't think straight any more, but slumped back in her seat, watching the cheap mean streets glide by. A sharp pain stabbed her ribs, where one of her attackers had kicked her. Her shin ached, and she felt a bruise coming up on her face. But it was not the first time she had been attacked in the line of duty and it wouldn't be her last. It disgusted and terrified her, but she pushed these thoughts aside, as the midnight lights of Hong Kong flashed past the car driving her back to the hotel.

I must be strong, she dug a nail into her palm hard enough to draw blood. *Laura's in danger. What if they kill her?*

Anxious thoughts blitzed her brain. Events were descending into a tawdry nightmare. Out-manoeuvred, played for a fool and above all, betrayed. She looked down at her nails, and saw they were still caked with the thick grease paint of her attackers. She scraped out the odious filth, spotted with blood, where Julia had dug her nails into her assailants' flesh.

How did I ever get so way out of my depth? she thought.

ONCE BACK INSIDE her hotel room, door bolted, her heart-rate gradually slowed. She took a calming tea sachet from the welcome box, and made a cup. Adrenaline slipped away, as she sipped slowly. She stopped shaking.

She ran a bath to soothe her bruises, and scrubbed and scrubbed to remove the last traces of that night's defilement. She dressed her cuts, then rubbed foundation over her facial wound.

I don't need constant reminders of the dangers ahead, she thought, brushing on some powder. *Pitcher will sort this. I need to stay strong and focussed.*

She turned on the television and flicked between channels in search of distraction, to help her wind down to sleep. Some half-an-hour later, her blood froze at a knock at the door.

My God, who's this, at this time?

The knock came again.

"Are you there Julia?"

She recognised Richard's voice.

"Julia, are you there?" he repeated. "Can I come in?"

She hesitated. Could she trust him? Had Ziggy been right? Could Richard have betrayed her?

Don't be ridiculous, Julia answered her own question. *There's only one traitor round here*, Ziggy's face drifted before her. *Richard's as honest as the day is long.* She unbolted the door.

"It's late, why you here?" she asked, stepping back to allow him to enter.

"Had a call from a policeman in London. Big shot friend of yours."

"Chief Inspector Pitcher?"

Richard nodded handing her a bottle of wine. He threw off his jacket and hurled it across the bed.

"Said you needed a friend. This gun's for hire."

Laughing, he did a hammy impression of a gunslinger. Despite herself, she laughed. But tears soon welled in her eyes. She bit her lip.

"I'm in big trouble Richard." She recounted the events of that evening, the terror in the alley, the devil masks coming for her, the violence.

Richard eyed her wounds with compassion.

"I don't want you to tell anyone about this, especially not the Chief Inspector."

"Are you crazy? This changes everything. You should be in hospital."

"I'm fine, stop fussing."

"Julia, be sensible, it's far too dangerous."

"Maybe, maybe not. Only you and I know what happened here tonight. As long as Pitcher doesn't find out, this could still end well. The bigger problem is how can I rustle up a cool fortune in diamonds by tomorrow night? I mean what does $10 million in diamonds even look like? How much does it weigh? Can I carry it? This is a nightmare without end."

"Calm down Julia. That end of the business is sorted. Silverman will foot the ransom. Apparently he didn't even blink at the thought. Got security contacts. They'll deliver the rocks here tomorrow."

"How does he know anything about this?"

"He was with Pitcher when you called. With Stephen Chandler apparently."

319

"What?"

"We don't need to get into that now. He'll make arrangements for the diamond drop tomorrow. You need to let Mantel know, and find out where the trade will take place."

"I can't bear the thought. What if something goes wrong? She'll be a dead duck. It'll all be my fault."

"You'll feel better in the morning. Wait until then. Think of it as a job Julia. A trade. Information like any other."

"You sound just like Mantel."

"Never. But hand over the ransom and free Laura Wan Sun. Finding Laura and bringing her home is what you've wanted all along."

PITCHER CALLED as Julia was sipping her first coffee of the day. She slept deeply, and woke refreshed. The Chief Inspector confirmed what Richard told her the previous night. Silverman was arranging for a packet of diamonds to be delivered to her hotel room later that afternoon.

"Are you up for this Julia?" he asked. "Meeting Mantel again at some kind of secret rendezvous?"

"No. I'm terrified," she managed a laugh, but said nothing about the previous night's attack. "Honestly, Pitch, what option do I have?"

"If I thought you were in danger, I wouldn't let you take the risk. You know that don't you?"

She smiled. *If only he knew.*

"There's no one else," he continued, "if we want to find Laura. I can't get there fast enough to be sure it wouldn't be too late. Hand over the diamonds and get out of there as fast as you can."

"Trust me, I can't wait to get home, smell the river and taste the smog."

"So you'll call Mantel this morning and tell him the trade's on."

Julia bit her lip. "I will."

SHE WAITED until 11 o'clock before making the call. Her hand shook as she punched the number into her mobile. Butterflies clawed her stomach.

Mantel picked up immediately. "Glad you're seeing sense, my dear. As I said yesterday, neither of us has skin in this game. We are middlemen. Nothing to win or lose."

Can't believe for a minute you won't be lining your pockets, Julia thought.

"I just want to get Laura safely home."

"She may not want to go home as you call it."

"She has a right to decide for herself."

"Have you been able to arrange the diamonds? Not a huge sum at today's prices."

"Yes."

"Silverman, I presume? He's in love with her, you know?"

"I can bring them to you later tonight," she said, ignoring his comment. "I'll hand them over after you discharge Laura into my keeping."

"Is that supposed to frighten me? Julia you must give up these negative thoughts. Think of us as partners rather than adversaries."

"Partners, huh?" Julia laughed. "Forgive me if that's an invitation I can refuse. Look, don't let's make this more painful than it is. Where can we make the switch?"

"I've thought about this. We need privacy, and solitude. We don't want to be interrupted. All difficult in this frenetic city."

"I'm sure you have a suggestion."

"I do. How does Victoria Peak sound? Yes it's a big tourist attraction. But it closes at 11pm. After that it's a ghost town. No tourists, no trams, no buses. If we meet at, say, 2am at the Lion Pavilion, we can guarantee to be quite alone."

"How will I get there?"

"I'll send a car. The whole site will be locked up, but our driver knows paths up through the jungle. Make sure you come alone. Can you be ready at say half-past midnight? It's a long difficult drive to the top."

Julia said nothing.

"And never forget my dear, you're a long way from home. No friendly police or politicians in your pocket. So no tricks. This is Hong Kong. We do things differently."

"Send the car," Julia said.

Richard rang at noon.

"Spoken to Mantel?"

"He wants to make the switch in the early hours of tomorrow morning. At Victoria Peak."

"You'll be isolated up there. Want me to come?"

"Thanks Richard but no. He said to come alone. I started this journey alone and that's how I'll finish it."

Julia stayed in her room for the rest of the day, flicking across romantic comedies on the networks. She needed to keep her mood light. She ordered a substantial lunch from room service, chicken, vegetables and noodles, plus a sandwich for later.

At 5pm a bellboy knocked at her door. Beside him stood a man in black leathers wearing a motorcycle helmet. He handed her a package.

She closed the door behind him and locked it again. She sat on the bed, holding the brown parcel for a few moments, before stripping off the sellotape and paper. Like an onion, inside was a gold box, tied with a silver ribbon.

She opened it gingerly to find a black velvet purse, the contents of which she emptied into her palm.

They were so small, yet brilliant, sparkling in the light, edged with thousands of tiny cuts.

Nothing left now, but to wait.

She placed the diamonds casually on her dressing table, and returned to her film.

CHAPTER 47

THE EVENING CREPT by at an agonising pace, as if a power surge slowed all the clocks, and silenced the telephone. Tick Tock. Julia measured out the waiting hours in commercial breaks. She stretched, she sang. She checked out numerous online maps, and committed every corner of Victoria Peak to memory. She drew a dozen diagrams of the Lion Pavilion and the terrain below. She massaged her bruises from her street fight. They looked uglier with the passing hours, but the pain was easing.

She drank coffee after coffee to keep the terror of the night at bay.

At midnight – it was time. She had a quick wash, placed the velvet purse in her inside jacket pocket and zipped the zipper tightly. As she pulled it up, her mind turned bizarrely to the Mary Quant zipper-dress in the Fashion and Textile Museum. She thought of Rebecca, where for her the story had begun.

Sweaty night heat blasted as she emerged from the hotel. Her skin was clammy when Mantel's car arrived. She got in and sank back in the air-conditioned leather as the driver pulled away, crossing a handful of streets, before swinging up a winding back road to Victoria Peak. Julia gulped a sharp intake of breath as he accelerated fiercely up the steep climb. *If he keeps this up, I'll be sick.* She closed her eyes to block out lights flashing by. *Keep calm,* she exhaled slowly. *Look down and the flickering will fade.*

Still the car wound higher, the streets becoming more deserted – traffic and buildings left far behind. Julia took the velvet purse from her pocket and held it in her lap with an iron grip, nervously twisting one of her fingers round the cord.

What did Mantel call it? A business deal. A simple trade. No different from the trades in shares and commodities made in their billions every day. Here she was trading people's lives. Laura's life. Potentially the lives of thousands who could be saved with her epidemiological findings.

No, this is too much, an inner voice groaned from somewhere deep inside, gripping her stomach, clawing up from her very bowels. The second brain they call it.

Stop! Go back! Abort! What am I doing here? This is not my story. Wrong person, wrong place, wrong time.

Her first brain overruled. Julia stayed put.

The driver pushed down harder through the gears, throwing the car at high speed round bend after bend as he raced up the near vertical final lap of the ascent, high above the jungle. Julia moved her tongue round her drying mouth.

Finally, they reached the top. The car swung sharply into a parking bay, braked hard and stopped. The driver pointed straight in front of him, and said something in Cantonese, indicating she should get out and walk.

No thanks for the ride, she thought, standing upright. She knew where she was going. She had rehearsed the route so many times in her imagination. Cord still tightly wound round her finger, she shoved the purse up her elasticated sleeve, and headed towards the Lion Pavilion, a populous tourist site during the day – now deserted. As she drew near, she heard the low hum of voices. Then she saw him in the half-light. Mantel with his ubiquitous orchid in his pocket. Four men stood with him. They withdrew slightly as she approached.

Not exactly the sort you would want to meet on a dark night, in a lonely spot, Julia thought. *Problem is that's me, dark night – lonely spot.*

There was no sign of Laura.

"Why always an orchid?" she asked nearing Mantel, who stood under the single spotlight shining in the Pavilion.

"National flower of Hong Kong. Each orchid has meaning. Tonight I wear a white orchid – the symbol of elegance." He removed the flower from its pin and held it out.

"Here, you have it. To show how glad I am you've come."

She took it, looked at it closely as if examining it, then crushed the petals letting them fall to the floor.

A flicker of anger flashed across Mantel's controlled expression.

Good, at last I'm breaking through his Teflon coating.

"Where's Laura?"

"Do you have the diamonds?"

"Where's Laura?" she repeated.

"All in good time my dear. The way this works, you give me the diamonds, and Laura will be returned to you in due course."

"Are you mad?" she raised her voice in defiance.

Mantel let out a cruel laugh. "Shout away. No one will hear you up here. We're completely alone. The tram closed hours ago. Save your energy. You may need it later."

He moved towards the parapet. "Before we conclude our business, let's take a moment to look down on this fabulous city and the wealth it has created. Look at it. Those sparkling lights, like diamonds glimmering in the dark. How much of that wealth was earned honestly do you think? Either by the British, the Portuguese or the Japanese. People like your friend Mr Silverman. He created a scheme to squeeze the system that weekend, which made him very rich. How's he different from the drugs pushers and racketeers? That's what everyone's after – a way to squeeze the system. This way he gets to repay a bit."

"They were kids. You were their puppet master. You should've stopped them. Put in controls."

"And wipe out the biggest boom the world economy has ever enjoyed – a chance for so many to become rich? Why would I do that?"

"You're nothing but a two-bit crook."

"Maybe. For the record, I had nothing to do with Adam Lee's death. I was fond of Adam."

"Where's Laura?" she asked again.

Mantel turned to one of his henchmen.

"Get the girl," he said.

Julia moved to the viewing platform overhanging a sharp descent. She stared out across the city lights, as she waited; breathing calmly, waves of subdued relief gently stirred. Soon

327

Laura would be here. She could hand over the diamonds and they could escape. She would be free to go home, salvage some stories from this mess and everything could go back to normal. She looked out again into the black night, lights glistening like shards of glass. Tall skyscrapers with lanterns blazing, a city built from a jungle – beacons to the pinnacle of human achievement.

Hard not to be moved, Julia thought. *Then again, am I looking at the pinnacle of man's endeavour – or man's greed.*

She heard footsteps. A smile warmed her lips. At last she would see Laura again. She turned determined to savour the moment.

But her blood froze as her eyes focused in the dark. Her heart pounded so loudly she thought her ears would burst.

Stay calm and think, a voice inside warned. *Don't let them see your shock and fear.*

Two men dragged an exhausted Dr Kathy before her. She was badly beaten. One eye was closed shut, the other red raw. Both had taken a hammering. Her pretty hands hung lifeless and crushed. Her usually serene features were swollen and distorted, stained with bloody gashes. They released their grasp a few yards from Julia, and threw her like a broken doll to the ground.

Her sight, her hands, Julia thought as she reached towards her. *What have they done to your beautiful eyes?*

"Leave her," Mantel's voice boomed ugly through the night. Gone the sophisticated charmer.

"You monsters," Julia said softly. *Keep control,* her inner voice repeated.

328

"Did you wonder on your Odyssey, how the authorities were always ahead of you? Here's the answer. Your beloved Dr Kathy betrayed you every step of the way. And betrayed her good friend Laura."

"Kathy?" Julia whispered.

"For what? For money pure and simple. Once you came sniffing round, my Triad friends saw potential for profit. They knew what Laura was worth and they wanted her. Everyone can be bought. Everyone has a price."

"Where is Laura?"

Mantel threw his head back again and laughed that dark sinister laugh.

"Here's the really funny thing. We don't know. Absolutely no idea where she is. We stole her. Then someone stole her back. No honour among thieves. You've had a wasted journey. Not quite. We must decide what to do with the diamonds. Obviously you're going to give them to me. The question is, what's your price? One million enough?"

Julia hesitated.

"Alright then, you can have two. How many gems are in the purse? Ten, twenty? We can split them easily. The car's waiting. You can disappear into the night."

"For what? To be like you? Like Adam Lee? A life always looking over my shoulder?"

"One way or another, you will give me the diamonds. Your friend here, Kathy, took this beating so you would be clear what would happen to you if you didn't co-operate. Last night we were playing with you. Tonight the game is over. What would your life be like without your sight – with your hands crushed to useless? Where would your precious sword of truth and journalism be then?"

"I don't care," Julia shouted running to the very edge, freeing the black pouch from her sleeve and loosening the tie. She leaned over the parapet, dangling the diamonds into the dark unknown.

"You're not having these. Come one step closer I'll spray these diamonds into the jungle. Look as long as you like, you'll never find them. Maybe a child might one day stumble across one buried in the undergrowth. Or a granny ten years later. They'll be lost to you."

Mantel took out a gun.

"I count to three and then I shoot," he pointed the weapon directly at her face.

"And then I drop," Julia shouted back.

They stared deadlocked – each daring the other to move first.

Time stood still as they faced each other in a life or death standoff.

It was Mantel who blinked first. Suddenly distracted by a rumble to his right, he turned away at the sound of an engine humming. The Peak tram had restarted and was climbing fast. Julia saw fear flash across his face.

He wasn't the only one. *Who's this?* her chest tightened. *Rival gangsters after the gems? Shit, where does this leave me?*

Time unwinds as the scene unfolds. Julia watches as if in slow motion. Tram doors open. Men spill out wielding weapons, a private army. Gun fire pierces the air. Flares, blue, pink, red and yellow break the night. The battery divides and advances, ordered but chaotic. Noise blisters her ears, a commotion of shouting and shooting, orders and threats. Gradually, the cloud of flares clears.

Julia focuses on the man leading them. She gasps. *Ziggy. They're led by Ziggy.* Her knees weaken. She all but collapses against the wall. The gunshots fall to silence.

My God he's got his own private army. Ziggy – he's a rival Triad boss.

She struggles to grasp this new reality, when behind him, she sees Michael Chen, Chief Fraud Investigator. To his right, another figure she can't quite see in the darkness.

Ziggy shouts something in Chinese. Mantel puts up his hands in surrender.

Michael Chen walks up to Mantel. "I'm arresting you for conspiracy to fraud."

"At least we can start with that," Ziggy bars his teeth at the fallen banker. Without looking at her, he shouts across to Julia, "You OK?"

She opens her mouth and tries to answer, suddenly aware that one arm is still dangling the diamonds over the wall.

A figure, the one she couldn't quite see, is walking towards her. She feels a soft touch on her arm.

"Give me the bag Julia, you need to rest now. I need to look after you. And we both need to look after Kathy."

Julia pulls back from the precipice and hands the diamonds to Laura.

CHAPTER 48
Early Hours Saturday August 28

AN EXPLOSION of flashing lights and sirens brought police and ambulances racing to the scene. Michael Chen took command, yelling orders, choreographing men and movements. Dr Kathy was placed on a stretcher and carried away. A knife twisted in Julia's heart.

To think I trusted her more than anyone on this island.

Ziggy touched her arm. "We're leaving now. None of us is safe on the island any more. We have a yacht in the harbour. Casting off as soon as we get there. Want to come?"

She hesitated, her mind numb.

"I think you should come, Julia," Ziggy repeated. "We must hurry."

I can't think, I can't think, her mind panicked with indecision, like a cat caught in headlights. *What else can I do? Who'll protect me now?*

"OK, I'll come."

They flew down the Peak in the high speed tram. A fleet of cars were waiting. These whisked them through the night to the harbour.

"Prepare yourself for a couple of surprises," Ziggy whispered to Julia, as he led the way along the dock. She climbed aboard, when the first bolt hit from the blue. Patrick Silverman stood on the deck.

"Huckleberry Finn, you're the last person I expected to see."

"I've only just arrived. Sorry I couldn't get here sooner. Flight only landed half an hour ago."

The shocks kept coming when Silverman took Julia's hands in his own, and stared deep into her eyes.

"I can never thank you enough for bringing my sister back to me," he said.

"Your what?" exhausted though she was, Julia still had strength to be astounded. "Why didn't you tell me?"

"I don't know. I thought maybe if it got out, her life would be in even greater danger."

Suddenly she was angry.

"From the start, I've had nothing but lies from you."

"Ah! You're right. What can I say? I know..."

He held up both hands with first and middle finger crossed.

"Oh no you don't. Don't try that fainites stunt on me again. This is serious."

Ziggy was coiling up lines ready to get moving. Julia realised she owed him an apology.

"I don't know what to say," she said.

He smiled. "Least said, I reckon. We need to get this boat out the harbour. These diamonds make us sitting ducks."

He wasn't alone in that thought. Silverman shouted an instruction and Julia heard the engines throb into life.

"We'll get as far out into the ocean as we can. The plane's ready," Silverman said, coming over to them.

"There's a seaplane aboard," Ziggy explained. "Plan is to fly to Singapore, then take a private jet back to London."

"This must be costing a fortune," Julia said, before tapping her palm on her forehead. "Oh no! Don't tell me. You own the company."

"My personal investments are top secret, so I'm afraid you'll have to keep guessing," he smiled. "You've saved me $10 million. This is small change. We need to get those diamonds back to London."

He turned to join Laura who sat at a table sipping tea. Julia noticed he didn't sit close beside her, but kept his distance.

"They've a lot to catch up on," Ziggy grinned.

"I think we've got a lot to catch up on, but right now my head is spinning."

"I tried to tell you from the start I was on your side."

"Next time, try shouting louder." She placed a gentle hand on his arm, her eyes drawn to his tattoo.

"My lucky charm. Magpies are a sign of happiness and good fortune in China," he said smiling.

"So not a bad omen like at home. Who are you, Ziggy? That's what I haven't been able to work out. Who're you working for? And who were those men with you?"

"Why I'm the Chinese Ambassador's nephew, and I work at the School of Oriental and African studies. How many more times must I tell you?"

She stared at him squarely in the eyes. He pulled a face and they both burst out, laughing.

"Have it your way," she said, turning to join Patrick Silverman and Laura.

"No Julia, it's best if you sit on the other side of Patrick."

"No worries," she said, although her brow wrinkled, puzzled.

Patrick handed her a plate of sandwiches and poured coffee from a piping hot jug.

"That's the most terrifying thing I've ever been through," Julia said, sipping the reviving black liquid. "If Ziggy and his henchmen hadn't appeared, I'd probably be dead by now."

"Thank God for MI6," Patrick said.

"What?" Julia choked on her coffee, as yet another curved ball bounced off her chest.

"Ziggy works with MI6. He's been looking after you all the while, reporting back to your friend Chief Inspector Pitcher. Thank God he has. His henchmen, as you call them, yes — are Triads. Not all Triads are criminals. There are good Triads who fight crime. Some work with the British Government to protect our interests in South East Asia. They got wind of where Laura was hidden and staged a raid of their own."

"Face saved, pride and prestige restored," Laura said.

"Order renewed. But Ziggy's the Chinese Ambassador's nephew. He can't be MI6."

"It's a murky world."

"My head's spinning, spinning, spinning," Julia spun her coffee saucer.

Laura laughed. "Now it's my turn to say thank you. You were so brave Julia. They were going to kill me once they got their hands on the diamonds. Mantel convinced his criminal customers we were the cause of their losing so much money on the markets. Killing me would show the world Patrick and Stephen had been punished."

Patrick turned to Laura love brimming out of his eyes.

"All these years, I didn't know I had a sister, but I knew there was something special about Laura."

"I thought she was your sweetheart."

"No, Julia, never that. But someone I was inexplicably drawn towards."

"Thicker than water. Sometimes I think we have some kind of atavistic knowledge, buried deep in our genes, we can't explain."

Patrick nodded. "Maybe. It was only reading Dad's will that I discovered the truth. He was engaged to mum when he was sent out to Hong Kong. He had an accident and broke his arm. Laura's mother, Clare, was the doctor at A&E. They fell in love. Clare was engaged to another doctor. They were both racked with guilt. In those days a promise was a promise. You didn't break your pledge. When she discovered she was expecting, her fiancé agreed to bring the baby up as his own. They all thought it best if Dad returned to the UK and married my mum, as planned."

"I don't remember much about her," Laura said. "Mum died when I was very young. Dad a few years later in a car accident. My grandparents brought me up."

"Something else we have in common," Patrick winked his nervous wink. "And this is the bit you don't yet know big sis. Dad left his entire fortune to you. I guess he thought you would put it to better use than I would. I couldn't be happier."

336

Laura nodded in her calm thoughtful manner.

"Oh yes. I've plenty of ideas how to improve healthcare among poor communities. Our father's money will be well spent."

THE SEAPLANE linked up with the private jet in a secluded disused army runway, deep in the Singapore jungle. Julia talked more to Ziggy about her journey of misunderstanding and misconceptions. She spoke to Laura about Dr Kathy, who when the chips were down, betrayed them both for money.

"I'm fairly sure, she thought I was dead. They offered her money. It was tempting. She never thought to see me alive again."

"But we did," Julia said.

"Did you really, Julia? Did you honestly expect to find me?"

Julia nodded. "Part of my training. You always believe in your story, until you have irrefutable proof you're on the wrong track. My hunch all along was we would find you and bring you back."

Next she questioned Patrick about hiding Stephen and keeping it a secret.

"You could've trusted me. Why didn't you?" He screwed his eyes into a barbed expression. "It wasn't your secret to share?"

"Something like that," he grinned, sheepishly.

A doubt niggled at the back of her mind.

"Why did Mantel order the murder of Adam Lee if he was his main sidekick? He told me he was fond of Lee."

"Ah," said Ziggy, stepping down the aircraft steps behind her at Heathrow Airport. "I think your Chief Inspector's working on that. The trail to Lee's killing leads all the way back to London and..."

"The Triad war," Julia finished for him.

"Poor Adam," Laura's voice was full of compassion, as she walked gingerly down the steps. "I knew him as a boy. We were at the same school. St Paul's. Very difficult childhood. Left him damaged."

"He was driven and not in a good way," said Silverman. "He was always going to self-destruct."

"He turned good in the end, Patrick. Never forget that," Laura said. "He warned us all. Without his tip-off, who knows what might have happened to any of us."

CHAPTER 49
Thursday September 2
Bermondsey

STORIES flew fast and furious from Julia's fingers following her return to the office. Day after day she released a new exposé of major crime syndicates in Hong Kong and their paymasters at two corrupt international banks.

"And health has a major exclusive for tomorrow's front on the pandemic threat from China," Andrew Ludgate said, when he called to congratulate her. "Met the chairman of the Wincott Awards at lunch yesterday. Tipped the wink you could be up for a prestigious prize. Great work, all round."

"Let's hope Laura's research will help universities and hospitals."

Safely out of China, Laura was happy to go public with her experience and findings of the Avian flu trajectory.

"Indeed. We must have lunch sometime soon, so you can tell me all the sordid details. Sounds quite an adventure."

Julia laughed. "That's one way of putting it. Honestly, Andrew. Trust me, you'd rather not know. Or let me put it another way, the insurers would have a fit. Just be happy I got back safely with the story."

"However you did it, congratulations. Much feedback?"

"Not so far. A few congratulatory emails. Banks are quiet. Good to see Warwick Mantel behind bars."

"Only a committal hearing, isn't it?"

"I know, but after everything – "

"Different system. Can't be sure of anything. By the way, your young lad Cody's a find. Great promise and talent."

"Cody? I know," Julia screwed up a piece of paper and threw it across the office, hitting her side-kick on the nose. "Don't go getting any ideas."

"No, you keep him for a bit. Keep knocking the rough edges off, then I'll take him."

"You'll be lucky to get him. He'll walk into the job of his choice when I'm finished with him."

"In his dreams. He did well, though, nailing that trust fraud, and finding the Treasurer."

She heard him moving his chair, and say, "hang on a moment." Someone had entered his office. He turned his attention back to her.

"I have to go. Remind me? Did we ever totally nail down who was responsible for the murders of Adam Lee and Halamanning?"

"Andrew, can I remind you, I'm your money reporter. These are stories for your crime team, or a title that has a proper crime team. I'd like to get back to writing boring stories about share price movements and interest rates."

"You didn't used to call them boring," Ludgate teased. "I have to go. Knock me off a boring piece on the stock market."

Julia put the phone down, and shouted across to Cody, "Big praise from boss man, Cody. You've made your mark. It'll be plain sailing all the way. I knew that first day you stood here," she pointed to the other side of the desk, "you had what it takes. You did brilliantly when I was away."

"Chief Inspector Pitcher was a great help."

"That I doubt."

Julia's phone vibrated as a text message landed from the gynaecological surgery.

You have missed four appointments with the clinic. Please attend this evening at 6pm. You require a further test urgently.

A slow chill ran through her. *This can't be happening. Not after all I've been through.*

The telephone rang.

"Ms Lighthorn?" the voice was abrupt.

"Yes?"

The voice softened. It was the clinic. "We need to see you urgently. I don't want to worry you, but your tests show abnormalities. We need to examine you further. Do you understand?"

Julia slid her tongue across the back of her front teeth.

"Ms Lighthorn?"

"Yes," she conceded.

"The consultant's staying late to see you at 6 o'clock. It's imperative you attend."

"Are you trying to tell me..."

"Your tests point to the need for further investigation. I'm sorry, but you must treat this matter seriously."

"Yes of course, thank you. I'll be there," her voice weakened to a simper. A steel band tightened round her rib cage.

She turned back to the story she was working on, despite a rising dread. *Don't think about it, focus on your work,* a voice inside tried to calm her.

So she banished dark thoughts, determined to look on the bright side.

Who'd have thought, the makers of My Little Pony would have been one of the best performers in the aftermath of the crash? she chuckled to herself.

She clicked to blow up a chart comparing the top climbers when her phone rang again. Pitcher's number flashed up.

"Glad you got back safely. Trust you didn't catch Kung Flu?"

"Very funny. What took you so long to call?"

"I've been busy, writing the Riot Act I'll be reading when I see you again. Which is why I'm calling. Drink tonight? We need to talk. By the way, have you upgraded your security? Judging by your columns, you don't seem to care how many enemies you make."

"If I'm not making enemies, I'm not doing my job properly."

"Is that so? Be careful Julia, this story isn't over. We haven't solved the murders of Adam Lee or Halamanning. We're on the brink of a gangland war in London. You may have covered yourself in glory my little Lightbulb, but we're a long way from faces in the dock."

"Lighthorn, my name's Lighthorn. Can you come to Casse Croute?"

"Opposite your place? OK, I'll see you at six."

"No not six. There's something I have to do. What about seven?"

Julia replaced the phone and sat staring blankly at her screen.

Surely, it can't be cancer. I've not had any symptoms.

With a heavy heart she googled cervical cancer, bile rising in her stomach.

No, nothing, she thought, reading through a list of symptoms, until she came to ones relating to sex and pain. *Can't comment there, bit of a desert since...*

Get back to work, a voice inside jogged her along. She returned to her piece, struggling to get it right. Cutting it, rewriting, and cutting again. Only when satisfied, did she hit send, checking the time as she did so.

She started clearing her desk.

"Cody, I need to leave early," she said, as another call came in.

It was Ziggy. She switched onto speaker phone.

"When I think how you lied and lied to me," she began, laughing.

"Julia, this isn't a social call. I have news."

Cody looked up.

"Mantel got bail, he's out."

"Bastard," Julia slammed her fist on her desk.

"What about all that protective custody and re-education the Chinese are supposed to go in for?"

"There's more. He's disappeared."

"What?" she looked over at Cody. "You mean the Chinese have him?"

343

"Not this time. He's gone."

"Gone where?"

"We've no idea."

"Did he get his money out?"

"What do you think?"

CHAPTER 50

"DON'T STAY too late," Julia said to Cody as she left. "Tomorrow could be a long day."

"I know, journalism will kill you if you let it," he grinned. "Still, nothing else will make you feel this alive."

Julia tried to smile but her spirits were reeling in the face of endless assault. She ached at the thought of Mantel escaping justice, and felt sick with dread at the appointment ahead.

A walk will do me good. Probably quicker in the rush hour, she thought, as she set off. Soon she was flying along the Embankment, across Southwark Bridge and down Fleet Street to the clinic.

"Ms Lighthorn?" the Receptionist said, kindness deep in her voice. "Straight through. He's waiting for you."

His door stood open. Julia paused outside, looking through into the surgery. She took a deep breath, a dead thump in her chest. *Surely this can't be happening?*

She knocked on the open door and stepped inside the surgery, stretching her face into a fake smile.

"You're here," her taxi thief turned to greet her, a kind expression warming his eyes. "I hear you've been on your travels. How was China?"

"Fine," she said, knowing he was trying to help her relax.

"Come and sit down."

She sat. He explained as clearly but gently as he could, that her last test had shown some abnormalities, which further examination had not resolved.

"Today, I need to look with a camera. It's a tiny thing. Not entirely comfortable for you, but it's quick and conclusive. Nurse is here to help you."

He stood, and the nurse approached, pulled a curtain dividing the room and signalled for her to get on the couch.

Julia swallowed hard then bent to undress.

WITHIN HALF AN HOUR, she was skipping back over London Bridge. "I am happy, oh so happy," she sung under a breath, jubilant at getting the all clear – an enormous weight lifted from her shoulders.

She bounced under a London Bridge railway arch and turned into Bermondsey Street. Further up the road, she saw Pitcher's car pull out of Tanner Lane, on his way to meet her. She started to think about the delicious dinner ahead, and what Pitcher would say about the latest Mantel news.

Her thoughts were shattered by a sudden crashing noise. Glass cascaded from a first floor window further down the road.

"Dear God, it's my office," she broke into a run.

Before she could get there, a gang spilled out the door and into the back of a van which tore away at breakneck speed.

Pitcher jumped out of his car, and stood in the road to block their escape.

"No," Julia screamed, as the vehicle raced towards him. He jumped aside at the very last moment, just as it brushed past him.

"Cody," Pitcher shouted, storming the stairs. She had never seen him move so fast. Julia's heart hammered in her ears as she leapt up behind him

"Fucking bastards," she cried seeing a scene of utter devastation. Desks upturned or smashed. One had a machete rammed into it – a menacing warning. A carpet of glass covered the floor. Telephones ripped from sockets lay liked beached seals on their sides.

"Oh my God, no, no," her gaze zoomed in on Cody lying crumpled on the floor. Pitcher was on the phone calling the emergency services.

She fought back tears as she knelt beside Cody, whose left eye was beginning to swell.

"I did my best. There were too many," he pushed his tongue to the side of his mouth. "I think they've cracked a tooth."

"That'll improve your smile," Julia said cheerily, though her chest felt ripe to burst. She watched Pitcher kneel beside Cody, and lift him gently into a sitting position, a supportive arm behind his back. Sirens rang in the distance, clamouring louder as they approached.

"You know what they say Cody," Pitcher said, "Never pick a fight with ugly people."

"They've nothing to lose, ouch," Cody smiled through his bruises, as paramedics raced through the door.

Pitcher and Julia stood back to make way for them. She felt an arm wrap round her shoulder.

"Don't worry, he'll be fine," Pitcher said.

Julia saw a dark shadow under his brow. Tears finally welled up in her eyes.

This is all my fault.

CHAPTER 51
Friday September 3

THEY WERE COMING for me. Julia pushed away pictures of Dr Kathy, her body smashed and shattered, of Adam Lee garroted and blinded and Halammaning slashed to ribbons hanging from a tree.

Pitcher insisted on driving her home.

"Something held them back, didn't it?" she said. "It wasn't him they were after. They were coming for me. I would've been there if I hadn't been called away. "

"I wouldn't go down any dark alleys," Pitcher replied, his face grim. "He'll be fine."

They both knew when Triads sought revenge, they seldom settled for less than a vicious murder.

The following morning dawned brighter. She called the hospital – yes, Cody was comfortable – then headed into the office. Mr Bardetti was waiting for her outside the deli. He wrapped both arms round her. They walked up the stairs together. Someone had already up-righted desks and chairs. Her money was on Pitcher and his team. Telephones plugged in, lines reconnected. A temporary screen fitted to the windows.

"I've been on to the insurers. Their emergency repairmen should be out later this morning. It'll all be as new."

"Or women," Julia couldn't resist.

"That's my girl," Aldo said. "Make yourself comfortable and I will fix coffee and breakfast."

She sat gingerly at her desk. The phone rang almost immediately. It was Patrick Silverman.

"Julia, I'm so sorry this had to happen. How are you?"

"Morning Patrick. I've been better. Poor Cody took a beating. I'm assured he'll be fine. Largely bruising and a cracked tooth. Gave us a bad fright."

"I'm sure it did. Can I suggest you lay low for a bit. Keep your by-line out of headlines – out of the press altogether."

"You sound like Chief Inspector Pitcher. I'm grateful for your concern, honestly I am, but I won't be bullied into silence. We can't let the bad guys win."

"These are dangerous people. Keep antagonising them and it may not end well. I heard there were six of them."

"So we think. Cody's a Tai Chi champion and swears he gave as good as he got."

Silverman didn't laugh. "It could've been much worse."

"I know. How're things your end?"

"That's partly why I'm calling." Silverman cleared his throat. "Laura's not well."

"The virus? I thought she'd had it."

"She's having a test today. It's possible it's something else."

"Send my best wishes, and keep me in the loop. Where are you?"

"We're all here in Cornwall."

"Stephen and Rebecca with you?"

"Yes."

350

"Some difficult conversations there."

"Rebecca loves Stephen, they'll be fine."

Ludgate called next with commiserations.

"Great stuff. You're rattling some very large cages. Keep doing what you're doing."

"Thanks for that, Andrew," Julia said after she replaced the receiver.

The insurers were as good as their word, and in no time her office was back to normal. At 5pm she called it a day and headed for St Thomas's to see Cody – down Tooley Street, past Southwark Cathedral, peeling off automatically along a medieval passageway at the side of Borough Market. She used this little known alleyway often, rarely meeting anyone. Few tourists took the rat runs.

Yet she found herself glancing repeatedly over her shoulder. Everything looked and felt different – confidence shaken. She sensed tiny hairs on the back of her neck tingle when she heard footsteps behind her. Her pulse quickened. *Don't get jittery,* she told herself, smiling when a nurse rushed past her on her way to her night shift, diving off left in the direction of the hospital.

Julia walked on alone again. *See, no Triads intent on murder,* she chuckled at her silly fears.

But the footsteps didn't stop when the nurse passed. Someone else was walking behind her. She slowed her stride, hoping whoever it was would overtake her. Her stomach flipped when the footsteps slowed and fell into step. With heart thumping, she started to run. She thought of the eyeless body of Adam Lee, Halamanning hacked to death.

She ran as fast as she could down the narrow, zigzagging lane, but her shadow ran faster.

He's gaining on me ...the lane opens onto the embankment soon. If I can just stay ahead.

Her lungs felt fit to burst.

Suddenly her hunter stopped. The clatter of running behind her faded away.

Instead a voice called out.

"Julia...Julia – for goodness' sake...stop!"

She could never mistake that voice. She turned and stared at the figure bent double, gasping for breath. The sight of him filled her first with disbelief, then fear and finally disgust.

"You monster. You disgusting monster."

"Not a kind way to welcome old friends."

"Friends! What're you doing here? The police are looking for you."

"We need to talk."

CHAPTER 52

JULIA DIDN'T get to the hospital. She sat in the Mudlarks pub by the arches of London Bridge, having a drink with a man she despised. As she stared into his repugnant face, it dawned on her he didn't frighten her any more. Sickened her, repulsed her – made her blood boil – for sure. But no longer frightened her.

Stay calm, her inner voice counselled.

"What is it you want?"

"I want to trade – or rather countertrade. Oh, I can hide away, live quietly somewhere under an assumed name. With money, it's not hard to disappear. Maybe I don't want to."

"What's this to do with me?"

"I need a middleman, and once more I find you best placed to help. Tell your Chief Inspector – yes I know all about him – I'll talk to him. Alone. Name names. He needs help stopping a vicious war on the streets of London. I'll hand him the Dragon Masters of the biggest Triads operating here."

"Why would you do that?"

"Questions, always questions. Why don't you let the Chief Inspector decide."

Julia tapped the table three times. She slipped her phone from her bag, and dialled Pitcher's number. Without looking at the man sitting across the table, she said, "Warwick Mantel's in London. He wants to cut a deal."

Silence at the other end. *First time he's ever been lost for words*, she couldn't help thinking.

"He's here with me now."

"Where?"

"Mudlarks. He wants to speak to you, but you have to come alone."

"He's not getting an amnesty from me."

"He has information."

"It's not the way I work."

"Your call."

Silence again. Then to Julia's surprise, he agreed to come.

While they waited, Mantel couldn't stop talking, droning on and on, like in a confessional.

"I've always been an alchemist, you see," he began. "Turning the basest of metal into precious commodities. It's true, Hemmings didn't work out so well. Did you never wonder why they were called the Golden Boys? With them I struck gold. We started the boom to end all booms."

"That's one way of putting it."

"They were just the beginning. My golden chances kept flowing. Putting Adam Lee into First State – pure genius. Good risks came to me at Peak, and the slightly shadier..."

"Slightly shadier? They were gangsters." Julia realised that like all narcissists the only audience he needed was himself. The longer he crowed on, the more convinced she became he was insane.

The Mudlarks doors swung open and Pitcher entered. He walked straight to the table.

"I should arrest you here and now," he choked the words, his face thundering.

"Sit down, Chief Inspector. Strictly speaking, I haven't committed any crime on your patch. Not one you could easily pin on me. Arrest me by all means, but as your colleagues in the Far East discovered, you'll be forced to release me again – a nuisance for us both."

"I'll sit when I feel like sitting," Pitcher pulled a chair across, placed his right foot astride, and towered over Mantel. "What d'you want?"

"An amnesty from the crimes various international jurisdictions might try to pin on me. And an escape route. Money I have."

Pitcher turned to Julia. "Drink?"

"Err..." she hesitated. "Why not?"

He returned from the bar with a pint for himself and glass for Julia. This time he sat, took a sip of his beer, then said, "That would include London?"

Mantel waved his hand carelessly as if swatting a gnat. "Try to think less like a policeman and more like a businessman. Like a trader. Deals are what keep the world turning. There's so much we could do to help each other."

Pitcher's eyes narrowed to tiny slits. "Corruption doesn't get far in the Met."

"Come, come Chief Inspector. Meeting me half-way might be the most important journey you ever make."

Pitcher pulled deep on his glass.

"Come down from your high horse, and I can hand you two of the most troublesome Dragon Masters operating on your patch. You're smart enough to know Triad crime in London is dominated by one particularly dangerous Overlord. Eluded you for years hasn't he? At a guess, I'd say you've no idea who he is."

Pitcher's face didn't flicker.

"You're asking a very high price," he said.

"Not really. Think of your satisfaction in coming face to face with your nemesis and putting this brutal war lord behind bars. The hours you've spent studying his vicious work. Torture. Mutilations. Death by a thousand cuts. Limbs and features slashed to ribbons, or like Halamanning, bled to death – slow and vengeful."

"Why don't you just tell me now?"

"Where would be the fun in that? There has to be some effort on your part. You know this empire is under threat from new Chinese organisations, with modern skills and ambitions. Fortunately for me, they both need the services of a reliable banker."

"That's what you are, is it?" Pitcher's lips curled in revulsion.

"They planned a war. You know that too. Adam Lee was dispatched to secure an arms deal for the older empire. The deal was made, paid for and delivered."

"Not quite a done deal. The arms were never collected."

"Quite possibly. Chinese walls. Triads work in silos. One side never knows who he's dealing with. That frees us to arrange many deals for all sides."

Julia curled her lip in disgust. "Middleman you call yourself, like that frees you from guilt. Your hands are stained with the same blood as those who wield the machete."

"Perhaps, my dear. But let's not digress. Events in Hong Kong, the new aggression by the police there, have made the societies think again. They want a temporary cessation. On Sunday, when London's quiet, they plan a summit, to discuss a truce. I'm their peace broker. The heads of the two Triads will be there, ripe for your picking."

"Armed?"

"They trust me. I arrange the security. Only I won't. The thugs I've lined up will be stood down. When our Triad friends talk, both sides leave their guns and machetes at the door. Even so, they don't need weapons. Their muscle can rip heads off with their bare hands."

"Where's this meeting?"

"My secret," he crossed his lips with an index finger. "Like all information, it's available for trade. You have to decide what it's worth. Imagine the police time and money it would save to clean up these streets. Like every other deal, it all comes down to a cost/benefit analysis. Do the sums, Chief Inspector."

"The other side of the balance sheet?" Pitcher leaned across the table.

"Look at it from my position. If I tell you they will kill me. I'll take you there on Sunday – before the meeting. You stake out an ambush. But first you hand me my amnesty and an escape ticket. From there I disappear."

Pitcher didn't flinch. "What time on Sunday?"

"Meet me here at half past one. You come too Julia, I'd like some witnesses."

Pitcher stared hard at Mantel for several minutes. He stood suddenly, gave a sharp nod of his head and walked out the pub.

CHAPTER 53
1.30pm Sunday September 5

THE STREETS were quiet but wet as Julia made her way to the rendezvous. Heavy torrents of rain washed away the hot sticky hours of the previous night when she had tossed and turned, wondering what would happen the following day. Would Pitcher make his arrests and finally expose the identity of the Dragon Masters? What would be the butcher's bill?

She cursed the downfall as her soaking intensified all along Borough High Street. Cars thundered by, spraying rain jets high from the gutters.

Typical, she thought, when she saw Pitcher emerge, bone-dry, from under the arches of London Bridge and walk towards the Mudlarks.

He waited for her in the porch.

"Don't worry about the rain. Works in our favour," he said, reaching for the door.

"Any idea who'll be there today, if they come?" Julia said, walking in.

"You know better than to ask me that."

Julia's jaw dropped when she saw Ziggy waiting inside, dressed in leathers, holding a motorcycle helmet. The bar was quiet, apart from a few diehard regulars providing a low-heat hum.

359

"No sign of Mantel yet," Ziggy said checking his watch.

"Do you think He Len is involved?" Julia said.

"Maybe, but he's still new on the scene," Ziggy checked his watch again. "Mantel should be here."

As if on cue, the next person through the door was the very man. He walked ramrod straight with an arrogant swagger.

"Drink gentlemen?" the cockney landlord shouted from the bar. "For you, whatever you want is on the house."

"Not today Jason," Pitcher replied, turning to Mantel. "Shall we get going?"

"Relax. We're less than ten minutes away. I take it you've wheels?"

Pitcher nodded.

"I've gone to a lot of trouble on your behalf," Mantel brushed a fleck of fluff off Pitcher's shoulder. Then he held out his hand, "Now your half of the bargain."

Pitcher pulled a brown envelope from his inside raincoat pocket.

Julia watched a slow malevolent grin spread over Mantel's face as he slit it open and unravelled a piece of type-written paper and a printout.

"My flights and our agreement. Very good."

"Now your half of the bargain," Pitcher swallowed.

"The meeting's at 2.30pm. Post code SE1 2BF."

"The print works in China Wharf?"

"Just so. First State is the tenant. How that information would have helped you, if you'd scratched deep enough. Only you never did. There are doors at the side and rear. I suggest you get going and get your men into place. It's all yours."

"Who'll be there?"

"Besides yourselves? I don't think you'll be disappointed Chief Inspector. You've waited a long time to meet your nemesis."

"How can we trust you?" Julia asked.

"More questions, my dear, and as ever, entirely the wrong ones. It's not you that needs to trust me. But me that needs to trust you."

He turned to Pitcher. "Fuck this up Chief Inspector and I'm a dead man."

With that he turned and left.

JULIA WATCHED him go, then followed Pitcher, out of the pub, under the bridge and across to London Bridge station. Ziggy at her side. The rain lashed down. They bypassed the new interchange, diving down a side street, into a disused railway siding. Four unmarked police cars waited, along with ten police vans with blacked out windows. Three helicopters whirred overhead.

Ziggy peeled off. "I'll see you there," he said pulling on his helmet, and walking towards the motorcycle parked close to the vans.

Pitcher got into the front of the first car. Julia slipped in behind.

"China Wharf," he said to the driver. The car eased down a series of side roads. Julia couldn't see much out the windows, as the torrent continued. The three, unmarked black police cars followed behind, but she couldn't see Ziggy.

A little more than five minutes later, the car pulled up on a piece of derelict scrubland near the sewage works by Bermondsey Wall. Julia could see the old print works where Pitcher had found the weapons stash. The helicopters shadowed them. The other cars kept their distance. No sign of Ziggy.

Julia's hands felt clammy. She sensed Pitcher swallowing hard over and again. *He's not as calm as he looks*, she thought. He cleared his throat repeatedly, then stretched to open the door. He got out.

Julia followed, her bowels pitching. *Dear God, what if we're walking into a trap. If Pitcher has gambled wrong, these trained murderers won't hesitate to kill.*

Ziggy appeared at her side. She smiled at him, as she watched some dozen men, dressed in jeans, black jumpers and stab vests, bounce from the back of the police vans and creep, bent double, down a dilapidated river path running along the side of the sewerage works. She spotted PC Day among them. They were followed by another team of six – this time in slightly different body armour, carrying semi-automatic weapons.

Bullet-proof, she thought. Other police were setting up roadblocks in the distance.

They filed into the abandoned print works from a side door. No one was there. Julia remembered her last visit. The wide open ground floor, abandoned presses at the rear. They crept up to the mezzanine floor of the old warehouse, and crouched waiting. They could see all the way down, but were concealed. Julia glanced out a side window and saw more police file into place down the side of the building – crack armed sharpshooters among them.

It all looks so slick. But what if Mantel has betrayed us?

She looked across at Pitcher. His face was unreadable.

Will today be the day you have wished for so long? Will today be the day you capture the man who has haunted you?

Through missing panes she could hear the powerful rhythm of the Thames crashing against stone river defences, as it breathed in the City's filth and dispelled it into a distant sea. The rain lashed on.

They waited. And waited and waited. An hour ticked slowly, painfully by. There was no sign of anyone – especially Mantel.

"He's tricked us," Julia whispered to Ziggy. "No one's coming."

"Be patient," he replied in a low voice. He looked across at Pitcher who nodded.

What do they know? Julia thought.

Then they started to arrive. From their elevated position, they watched a fleet of small boats pull up. One by one, Chinese men got out and dashed up the Night Rider waterman's stairs, dodging the downpour. Some wore waxed hats against the rain, while others covered their faces with scarves. A couple slipped on the treacherous steps, made more dangerous by the deluge. Intent only on avoiding a drenching, no one bothered to look around. So they kept coming, and slowly the warehouse below filled up. From her crouched position, Julia counted 40.

363

Two groups of men stood each side of a circle in the massive void in front of the delinquent presses. He Len at the head of one of the groups.

The two Triads, men bound by mutual hatred, who would tear each other's hearts out in the blink of an eye, stared across the circle. Faces taut and ugly.

These guys are more terrified of each other than the police, Julia thought.

They seemed to be waiting for someone important to arrive. *If He Len is one Dragon Master, where is the other.*

Still no sign of Mantel. She recognised another figure among the semi-circle opposite He Len, but couldn't place him at that moment. She thought back to the dinner at the Chinese Embassy. There had been so many faces.

Finally Mantel entered at the side of a small Chinese man, dressed in a silk imperial surcoat, embroidered with the outspread wings of a rising Phoenix.

At last the senior Dragon Master, Julia thought.

This new figure took up his place at the head of the circle, Mantel beside him. He stood with his back to them, so they couldn't see his face. The smell of sweet orchids wafted gently against the acrid damp of dereliction.

The figure in the dramatic Phoenix silk began to speak, and seemed to be delivering a long slow sermon. When he stopped He Len addressed the gathering. Then others joined in – all babbling over each other in Chinese.

"What're they talking about?" Julia mouthed to Ziggy. He placed a finger on his lips to silence her.

He Len had the floor again. His voice crescendoed – gesticulating wildly with flailing arms. His sudden movements spooked a pigeon which flew down from the roof, then soared up again, wings flapping wildly – towards the mezzanine floor. He Len stopped mid-sentence, turning his head sharply upwards. Others followed the bird's noisy trajectory.

Christ we've had it, Julia thought – and she was not alone.

Their covert operation exposed, Pitcher could wait no longer.

"Now," he shouted into a microphone in his lapel.

Police burst through doors on all sides, and the teams above chased down. Sirens whirred deafeningly from all directions. The three police helicopters whooped threateningly overhead.

Pitcher leapt down the stairs, followed by Ziggy – with Julia at the tail of officers. They spanned out on the ground floor – Pitcher stopping dead in the centre of the two half-circles, now ringed by armed officers. Julia came up behind him and stared at the Dragon Master cloaked in the Phoenix silk. She blinked several times to make sure she wasn't hallucinating.

Jesus Christ, it can't be?

But it was. This senior Dragon Master, who had terrorised London for decades, masterminding murder, torture and violence, was none other than an elderly Chinese gentleman, badly disfigured by an ugly scar on his face.

"Chief Inspector, how nice to see you," Wo Chang spoke as if greeting his favourite customer at his restaurant, the Golden Pagoda.

"Wo Chang. After all these years," Pitcher spoke softly.

He must be shaken to the core, Julia thought, yet all she detected was the slightest ripple of the muscle of his jaw. His body was braced like steel.

Julia looked at Mantel and saw he wore a yellow orchid. *Friendship and new beginnings.*

"You betrayed us," He Len screamed, lunging at the elderly restaurateur, his hand tightening around his throat, pushing at his neck with a force fit to snap it.

Police teams pounced in a flash, pulling him away. He Len was bundled out the building, shrieking curses.

"Dead men," he screeched, his red face bulging. "You're all dead men. We'll have revenge on you, your families, and anyone who's ever worked in or entered your restaurants or gambling houses."

Wo Chang threw his head back, and unleashed a roar of bitter laughter. "No revenge can hurt me. Save your breath for the court room."

He turned his gaze to Julia.

"I zee I have shocked you, Julia. How can a gentle, sweet old man like me be guilty of horror and depravity? It is so eazy. I feel nussing, you zee. I wish I could but I'm numb inside, dead. Oh yes, I can be charming. Charm iz the coat we wear when we pretend we are human."

"You need help," Pitcher said quietly.

"Help? Yes, there waz a time I needed help. But none waz offered. You never trusted the world, only for everyzing you love to be burned in flames before your eyes. I swore that day, when I lost everyzing, father, mother, family and friends,

366

nussing would ever hurt me again. Pain would become my friend, my only ally."

He pulled a blade from the folds of his magnificent surcoat, and raised the engraved sabre high above his head.

"Stand back officers. My experience wielding this knife is second to none. Come near and I will slash a dozen of you to pieces in seconds."

Then with one leap, he turned sharply, lunging at Mantel. He slit his throat as easily as slicing a ripe peach. Mantel fell to the ground, body twitching, blood pumping from the wound.

Before anyone could move, Wo Chang raised both arms high above his head, the blade glinting in the full light.

"My friend again," he shrieked, plunging the knife down violently into his chest.

"No!" screamed the man Julia thought she recognised and could now see more clearly.

Of course, Simon Chang, and that must be his brother Anthony beside him. The new generation of Dragon Masters waiting in the wings. Julia turned her head away.

After that everything moved like a film reeling slow. Gang members were taken into custody – mainly resigned to their fate. Scenes of crime officers attended the bodies.

Pitcher signalled to Ziggy, "Take her home. You shouldn't be here anyway. Take my car. She's seen enough. Take her home."

JULIA DIDN'T WANT to go home. When she got back in the car, she asked to be taken to her office.

"Sure?" Ziggy asked.

She nodded. "I need to file something tonight. I can make the final deadline."

The driver turned towards Bermondsey Street when her mobile rang. It was Patrick Silverman. Julia wrinkled tired eyebrows when she saw his number.

"Patrick," she answered, her voice exhausted.

"Can you come, Julia? Laura wants to see you," his speech was abrupt – words short and monosyllabic.

"Come where?"

"Cornwall."

Julia cleared her throat. "No, Patrick. It's out of the question. It's been a tough day – I'm spent. One more thing to do, then home to bed. I'll call tomorrow."

"Tomorrow may be too late."

A knife twisted in Julia's heart.

"Too late?"

"Laura isn't good."

"You said she was fine," a loud drum beat in her ears.

"She was, but she's sliding fast. She wants to talk to you. There's a flight from City to Exeter in about an hour. I can collect you from there."

The car pulled up at a red light. Julia knew in some strange way her fate and that of Laura's were bound together.

She made her decision, leaned forward and spoke to the driver, "Can you take me to City airport?"

"Sure," he changed lanes to make a sharp turn left.

"OK, I'll come," she said down the phone, before turning to Ziggy.

"D'you want to get out here? Laura's taken a turn for the worse."

"I'm sorry."

"She wants to see me. There's a flight to Exeter due."

"Would you like me to come?" he stretched a hand over hers.

"No. I'll be fine."

"Let me at least come to the airport with you."

SHE WAVED goodbye to Ziggy, ran across the forecourt, and raced up the escalator to the departure lounge. The flight was delayed half-an-hour, but Julia was glad. It gave her time to write a short piece about a police operation in a warehouse in Bermondsey thought to be connected to the murder of banker Adam Lee. She heard the final call for Exeter, hit the send button, and sprinted for last place in the boarding queue.

CHAPTER 54

Sunday 8pm

THE FLIGHT was short. Patrick was waiting for her, his car parked opposite the small terminal.

"You must know this road like the back of your hand," she said, as he pulled onto the A30.

"I do. Could find my way home with my eyes closed."

"How's Laura?"

He let out a sigh. Shaking his head, he changed gear to overtake a caravan.

She studied his sallow face, his eyes fixed on the darkening road ahead. *He looks dreadful*, Julia thought. *Please God, don't let her die.*

Conversation was thin for most of the journey. Visibility fell as the car ploughed its way through grey mist and dirty drizzle across the Bodmin moor. Windscreen wipers swished repetitively at high speed.

Julia's mind flicked restlessly over the showdown at China Wharf. How could Pitcher never have suspected Wo Chang? Then again, it seemed so unlikely.

Now he's dead, along with Mantel.

Her thoughts returned to Laura. *I travelled half-way across the world to keep her safe. After all we went through in Hong Kong, surely this can't be the end?*

What a journey it had been. Her imagination raced through memories like a home-movie on fast-forward. Fear of arrest in China, her terror in the night markets, the drama at Victoria Peak, Dr Kathy bruised and broken, Cody's beaten body, her wrecked office. Blood spouting from Mantel's throat, and Wo Chang's arms raised high ready for the ultimate act of violence.

She can't die. She mustn't. A shard of ice entered her heart.

Her mind flashed back to their first meeting in the clinic in the mountains. It's true, she seemed frail – weak. But then she smiled, and all Julia noticed after that were her bright eyes and gentle voice.

Now the kaleidoscope turned, presenting Julia with a different reality. She stared at the swishing windscreen wipers and saw anew the questions she should have asked, but failed to.

Why change her mind about returning? So unexpected – so welcome, they accepted it all at face value.

Silverman accelerated. Julia watched the speedometer touch 100 miles an hour. Her stomach lurched as they raced across the dark bleak moors.

"Perhaps it's time," Julia said softly. Those had been Laura's words, and suddenly their meaning was becoming clear. A new meaning. The way she puffed when they walked up the airport stairs. Her tiny appetite.

"It's not the virus is it?" she said softly.

"No. That we could deal with. It's cancer. Laura's known for months she had a short time to live."

"Her mother died young," Julia felt blood draining away.

"Yes. The virus weakened her and masked the early signs. By the time it was diagnosed, it was too late."

"Dear God," a sickening sadness overwhelmed her. "So that's why she was content to hide away in the mountains."

"She thought to die there, doing what she could to make a difference to the Yao people to the very end," Silverman said, staring grimly ahead.

It was pitch black when they reached the causeway. Not a soul stirred.

"We can drive across," Patrick said, moving down through the gears. The car rumbled over the cobbled ocean road. In the distance, Julia could hear a gentle lap of the water. The tide was going out.

She followed him up through rooms she remembered. The study, the banqueting hall, the chapel, and on to another suite. Silverman knocked at a door, and spoke to someone inside. Julia guessed a nurse.

He closed the door again. "She'd like to see you. Are you ready?"

Julia turned away, her lip trembling. *This is all happening too fast, we need to slow things down.*

The light was dim in the sick room. Laura looked tiny, as if she had shrunk since coming home. Julia noticed the rasping of her breath, the uneven rise and fall of her chest. The frail figure stretched her face into a wide warm smile when she saw Julia, but the effort hurt her. She screwed up her eyes until the pain passed.

"I'm so glad you came," she said, each word weightless like cotton fluff.

"Can I get you something?" Julia asked.

"Perhaps some water..." Julia poured a glass from the jug at her bedside, then leaned across helping her to sit. She held the glass to her mouth. Laura took a couple of sips then fell back against the pillow.

"I'm so glad you could come," she repeated, her voice painfully thin. "I've known my time was running out," Laura continued. "But I'm happy I came home to Patrick. I have you to thank for that. That's why I wanted to see you. To thank you and to set the record straight – to explain about that weekend all those years ago."

"It's not necessary, the story's over, you need to rest."

"It's why you came looking for me in the first place. You knew what had happened, but you couldn't understand why? What makes gifted, talented people chose one bend in the road rather than another."

"Tomorrow, Laura, we can talk about all this another time."

Laura shook her head. "My tomorrows are fading. You deserve an explanation."

"Not now..."

"We were too greedy," Laura raised a feeble hand to stop Julia interrupting. "All of us. We stole from the future. But we were little more than children – children led by a mad Svengali. That's no excuse. I knew that night in the castle, we'd conjured with the devil – in a way. I should have stayed – stayed and tried to prevent the turmoil which followed. But I walked away. I was a coward. That's why I admire you. You never give up, do you? You put me to shame."

"Don't be ridiculous, Laura, you're the bravest person I know. You devoted your life to helping others, and will do again."

A smile tickled her pale lips. "Yes I intend to, another reason I wanted to see you. Patrick's father left me a fortune. I'm setting up a trust to help underprivileged children. I want you to be on that trust, along with Patrick."

"Rest now. Everything will look differently in the morning..."

Laura stretched out a weak hand. "Dear Patrick. He has no one. Be a friend to him Julia. He needs a friend. Promise me you'll be his friend."

Laura closed her eyes, and Julia realised her energy was spent.

CHAPTER 55

LAURA DIED two days later. A small funeral was held in the Castle Chapel – the Chandlers, Silverman and Julia the only mourners. Patrick's face was gaunt as he fought back his grief. Julia was numb. She watched rivers of tears stream down Rebecca's distraught face.

Thick mist engulfed the bay, when they emerged from the service, wrapping the landscape in a dense moving fog. Julia could hear water lapping in the distance, but the sound was muffled and low. They walked slowly together behind the coffin, accompanying their friend on her final journey. Visibility was reduced to a few feet. Julia trailed Laura and Stephen's silhouettes blindly as they wound their way down the rocky path to the island churchyard. The air froze with an icy chill.

When they reached the grave plot, the vicar switched on a torch and bid the small party come closer. They encircled Laura for a last few prayers before her body was lowered into the ground. One by one, they threw sods onto the coffin. Julia waited last for her turn. As she moved away from the graveside, a strong beam of light broke through the clouds, and they were bathed in a warm shaft of sunshine. They stretched their necks to look up to the sky.

"Laura will always be with us," Rebecca said.

"She will," Stephen nodded.

"Thank God, she got out with her research," Rebecca added. "That'll be her legacy. Her good work and sacrifice will go on living long after this day."

The sun warmed their backs as they began the steep climb back up to the Castle. A simple lunch awaited them in the refectory. Julia was desperate to get back to London and normality, but felt obliged to stay a little while longer.

"It's so weird sitting here after all this time," said Stephen. "D'you remember that night Pat? The rain. The storm. Mantel's demonic smile."

He moved his chair, stood, and walked gingerly towards the stained glass windows. He bent from the waist, screwing up his eyes, scrutinising the figures on the medieval panels. "That skeleton racked by the devil. If only we'd heeded the warning."

"We made mistakes. Now it's our job try to put things right and prevent the same thing happening again." Silverman replied. "Will you help me with that work?"

"Poachers turned gamekeepers? Who better qualified?" Stephen nodded.

Julia turned to Rebecca. "Have you forgiven him?"

"Just about," she smiled in the direction of her husband.

"It was too dangerous. I couldn't risk involving you," Stephen said shame-faced, returning to the table.

"Patrick was as bad," Rebecca grimaced in his direction. "You owe Julia and me an apology."

If they wanted an apology, it didn't come. Patrick rubbed his palm over the old oak of the refectory table, then turned his head and gazed into the distance.

Rebecca took Julia's hand. "I'll never be able to thank you enough. In my darkest hour, you were the only person I could trust. Let's keep in touch when we're back in town."

"Which won't be any time soon," Stephen said. "I'm staying here and enjoying my life with my wife."

"Pull the other one," Rebecca laughed. "Tower Gate's opening on Monday. You'll be straight in there, sorting out that mess, and every other mess you and Patrick can find."

Lunch over, Julia stood to leave.

Patrick Silverman walked her back down to the causeway, where a car waited to take her to the station.

"I'm so sorry, Patrick. You wanted her in your life so much. We all did."

She looked up into his troubled blue eyes.

"You risked everything to find her. What kept you going Julia?"

"It's what I do."

He took both her hands in his. "Any chance we could start again? I'd so like us to be friends. I realise that may not be possible, but I'd do anything to make it possible."

"I'd like that too," she squeezed his hand.

THE END

Did you Enjoy This Book?

We hope so much that you did. Without satisfied readers no novel can thrive. You are our audience, and now hopefully our friend.

My ambition above all is to entertain. But I hope TAKE A THOUSAND CUTS also raised issues you may not previously have encountered, and planted thoughts which may linger.

For any author, the most important way of getting our books noticed, is to spread the word. This takes the help of a loyal bunch of readers.

Honest recommendations and reviews bring stories to the attention of new readers.

If you have enjoyed this novel I would be so grateful if you could spend just a couple of minutes leaving a review (as short as you like) on www.Amazon.co.uk or your favourite book store website.

I love making new friends and hearing from old ones. Please do visit my author page at www.TeresaHunter.uk. Or sign up to the Teresa Hunter Readers Club. There are no catches or costs and you will receive exclusive messages and stories. Your data will be secure and we won't spam you. Just send news now and again.

Thank you so much. You are fantastic.

With warmest wishes

Teresa

ABOUT THE AUTHOR

Teresa Hunter is an award-winning journalist, who has worked for the Guardian, Telegraph and Sunday Times – and also for the BBC in television.

She is married with three children and divides her time between her home in West Cornwall and London.

She has an MA in critical and creative writing.

DISCLAIMER

This is a work of fiction. Names, characters, businesses, and incidents are the product of the author's imagination. Any likeness to real life persons or events is accidental and unintentional. Timeframes may also differ from historic dates.

Printed in Great Britain
by Amazon